Win Me Over

Nicole Michaels

St. Martin's Paperbacks

Michaels,
Nicole

This is a work of fiction. All of the characters, organizations, and events portrayed in this novel are either products of the author's imagination or are used fictitiously.

WIN ME OVER

Copyright © 2015 by Nicole Michaels.
Excerpt from *Draw Me Close* copyright © 2016 by Nicole Michaels.

All rights reserved.

For information address St. Martin's Press, 175 Fifth Avenue, New York, NY 10010.

ISBN: 978-1-250-05816-4

Printed in the United States of America

St. Martin's Paperbacks edition / September 2015

St. Martin's Paperbacks are published by St. Martin's Press, 175 Fifth Avenue, New York, NY 10010.

10 9 8 7 6 5 4 3 2 1

Praise for the first novel in this charming new series by
Nicole Michaels

START ME UP

"Delightfully playful, Michaels's contemporary marks her as one to watch."   —*Publishers Weekly*

"Sexy and exciting . . . this is a book that makes falling in love even more fun."   —*RT Book Reviews*

"Cute and crafty! A delightful beginning to a new series that is sure to charm readers."
            —*New York Times* bestselling author Jill Shalvis

"Sometimes a book checks off all of your boxes and just hits the spot. *Start Me Up* did that for me. . . . a sweet contemporary romance that revolves around a single mom, her blog and a sexy, younger man. Oh, *Start Me Up*, you had me at hello!"   —*Romance at Random*

"Sexy, steamy with just the right amount of snark. Nicole Michaels makes falling in love fun."
        —*New York Times* bestselling author Christie Craig

Also by Nicole Michaels

Start Me Up

Blame It on the Mistletoe (e-original)

To Tracy, thank goodness our husbands brought us together.

Acknowledgments

There are always so many people to thank. First, Sarah Younger, my agent, and Lizzie Poteet, my editor, for their patience and guidance of a fledgling author. The wonderful marketing team at St. Martin's Press, SMP Romance, and Heroes and Heartbreakers. Gina Conkle, Shannon Richard, and Heather Heyford, for that night in NOLA and everything since. My unfailing support team Tracy and Jennifer. My family, children, and amazing husband. And of course, to the bloggers, reviewers, and readers. I thank you from the bottom of my heart!

One

Some people had skeletons in their closet; Callie Daniels had tiaras. Literally. Big, tacky, blinged-out tiaras. The kind that graced over-teased heads of little pageant girls, took an entire package of bobby pins to hold secure, and were so tall it was amazing they didn't tip children ass over teakettle. Something she knew from experience because once upon a time she'd been one of those little girls, and if beauty pageant life had taught Callie anything, it was how to put a fake smile on your face. A skill that came in handy when your mother unexpectedly walked through the front door of your bakery on a Thursday afternoon.

"Mom, what a surprise," Callie called over the display counter, hoping desperately that the tone of her words revealed more sincerity than dread. The light-turquoise walls of her beloved shop, Callie's Confections, clashed with her mother's unnatural shade of blond hair. Even still, the blond was better than the fire-engine red it had been a few months ago.

"Well, it seems the only way I can find out what's

going on in your life is to make a trip up here. That is, unless I want to hear it from Joan Jenkins while I get my nails done." There was no mistaking the hurt in her voice and instantly Callie's heart grew heavy with guilt. She vaguely remembered mentioning her new job to an old high school friend on Instagram. Word traveled fast. She should have known better.

"Oh, Mom, I'm so—"

"Do you want to know the worst part? I could tell that she loved telling me something I didn't know. You're my only daughter; I should know your gossip before anyone else in this world. Can you even imagine the embarrassment?"

Callie knew about embarrassment all too well, but she wouldn't list all the ways she could relate. It would break her mother's heart, and the truth was, Callie felt a little bad for not calling. But in her defense, her life was crazy at the moment. Today, for example, she'd spent the morning prepping cakes and cookies for the weekend orders. She'd been in the zone, the kind of baking Zen that almost made her want to spin around her ovens and sing like an animated movie princess. She was only missing the talking wildlife—and the Prince Charming. But that was no matter; she had no use or time for a man.

"I wasn't trying to keep secrets, Mom; I've just been busy," Callie said.

"Is that supposed to make me feel better? Of all the things . . . *dance coach*? You knew I'd be thrilled about that. I should have been the first person you'd want to tell that you've returned to performing."

"I'm the coach, Mom. I won't be performing."

Barbara shrugged. "Still you should have told me. I could help you."

Which was exactly why Callie hadn't been excited to share. Her mother, Barbara, had the tendency to over-step her bounds in the "help" department. And that was putting it mildly. Callie could only imagine all the ideas her mother would have had when she told her she'd been hired to be the new Pantherettes Dance Team coach at Preston High.

"You're right: I should have called. I'm sorry, but I promise I've got everything under control," Callie said, grabbing a to-go coffee cup and handing it across the counter. She hoped to move the conversation away from the dance team quickly. "Have some coffee."

"Oh no, I can't do coffee after lunch. It dehydrates my skin."

"Suit yourself." Callie walked around the counter toward the coffee station set up in the small dining area of her bakery.

"Callie Jo," her mother chided in a playful yet dead serious way. "Do you not care about your own skin? Maintaining your looks after thirty is a full-time job, might as well start now."

Facing the wall, Callie rolled her eyes as she added a liberal amount of half-and-half and sugar to her cup. Barbara meant well—in fact, these small reprimands were always delivered with love and concern—but she was a teeny bit obsessed with physical appearances. Always had been, always would be. She was, in fact, an attractive woman under all that makeup—even with the skintight lime-green capris, sequined high-heeled san-dals, and ruffled blouse. According to everyone who knew them both, Callie was a younger—and, she hoped, less flamboyant—version of her mother. Along with gratitude, that compliment always sent a tingle of horror down Callie's spine.

"I'm willing to take my chances, Mom, and I'm not thirty for two more years." Callie took a long sip. Damn, her shop served good coffee.

"You'll be sorry, sweetheart. You only have one face; I taught you better than that."

Before Callie had time to be highly annoyed with that comment, her employee and unapologetically gay best friend burst through the kitchen door into the front of the bakery.

"Barb, what a surprise." His eyes met Callie's, and unbeknownst to Barbara the two of them exchanged an entire silent conversation in a fraction of a second with that one look. It went something like this:

Holy shit, what's she doing here?

I know, right?

Does she know?

Yep, she knows.

Shit. You okay?

I will be.

What the hell is she wearing?

Oh my God, I know!

Eric grinned and pulled Callie's mother into a hug.

"At least someone's happy to see me," Barbara said over his shoulder.

"I'm always happy to see you, Mom." Although Callie was certain her words went unnoticed as she watched Eric gush over the woman. He always handled her like a pro, saying just the right things, but not too much, for which Callie was grateful.

"I swear every time I see you, you look a year younger, and those shoes are perfection."

Barbara laughed and feigned embarrassment. Callie knew her mother was eating his comments up and she couldn't help but smile because she knew that Eric genuinely loved Barbara. So did Callie, but her mother was a woman best taken in small doses . . . and, Callie hoped, not unexpectedly. It was best to have all your wits about you when Barbara was around, because she sniffed out weakness and secrets like a bloodhound, desperate for a way into your life. She wanted to be needed and in on the action. That was all well and good, but Callie liked to do things her own way, which usually turned out to be the exact opposite of her mother's way. They were just . . . different people.

"Now, Eric, why didn't you make Callie call me right away when she got the dance coach job?"

"Barb, please. You know how our girl is. Go, go, go, all the time. I'm sure it just slipped her mind."

Barbara turned to Callie, looking stricken. "Oh, honey, you're working way too hard here. You have to join me for a spa day. I insist."

"Thanks, Mom. But I'm good. Promise."

Her mother reached around to Callie's ponytail and grabbed the end of one of her riotous curls. "Are you sure, baby girl? These ends are fried. You haven't had a cut in weeks, have you? Amazing hair like yours cannot be neglected."

Callie hadn't had a cut in months, and she couldn't

help the fact that she'd been born with unruly curls. "It's fine, Mom. I'll schedule a haircut soon."

"You can't be the dance coach with split ends, sweetie. You must put your best face forward. How will you find the man of your dreams? If you're lucky you won't have to work at any job after that."

"Mom, I can assure you that the state of my hair has no effect on my ability to do this job, because it's not about my looks. It's not about me at all. It's about the girls on the team. And I've told you a thousand times, I like what I do. Even if I met the guy of my dreams— which is unlikely—I would still be running this bakery."

Barbara gave a pouty lip. "Goodness, you don't have to get excited. You're so much like your father. What am I gonna do with you?" She turned to Eric. "When was the last time she had a date? Or a haircut?"

"Don't get me involved, Barbara. You know I love you, but I'm always Team Callie, and if she wants to rock inch-long split ends and a cold bed, that's her business."

Callie shot Eric a dirty look. Her love life was a constant source of contention between her and her mother. Callie was happy to be single and Barbara didn't seem to understand that. She loved being a wife; in fact, Callie was certain her mother's entire identity was wrapped up in being Mrs. Daniels. She saw herself as adornment to her successful husband. At least that was the way Callie viewed it, and that was not her style. At all.

Callie never wanted to adorn anything; she'd been that girl before when she was young and trying to find her way with boys, and it did not suit her. She wasn't an ornament or a trophy; she was a human being who just happened to have breasts and could take care of herself, thank you very damn much. Callie liked to have her share of fun once in a while, but that was enough.

She needed to steer the conversation into safer waters before she said something to her mother that she'd regret. They'd had those conversations enough for Callie to know that they didn't end well and she just felt horrible afterward.

"Mom, I'm so grateful you came to see me. And I'm sorry I didn't tell you sooner about my new job. Like I said, it's just been a hectic time, but I'll be sure to let you know when the first performance is so you can come and watch."

"Well, are you sure you won't need help with costumes or hair? You know performance and presentation is my specialty."

"You taught me well, Mom; I can totally handle it. And the girls already have costumes and uniforms. We're all good." Only a tiny lie; the girls desperately needed new performance outfits. No way could Callie let that bit slip; Barbara would show up at the high school with her sewing machine in tow.

"Well, okay, but if you need help you come to me first. And the next time something big happens in your life I better not hear about it in the mani chair. You hear?"

"I promise."

Eventually, after filling Callie in on all the gossip from her hometown, eating a cinnamon roll as she proclaimed, "I really shouldn't," about fifteen times, and waiting while Callie called to schedule a haircut, Barbara finally left. Back behind the display counter, Callie let out a deep cleansing breath. Interactions with

Barbara were overwhelming. Thankfully she lived an hour away, so they didn't happen too often.

"I do adore her, but she is nuts, you know that, right?" asked Eric.

They both laughed as he leaned against the register munching on a tiny blueberry scone. Callie wasn't sure what she'd do without her best friend, and not only because he looked so fantastic with his muscles filling out the pink Callie's Confections T-shirt. And also not because 30 percent of their business was women just wanting to flirt with him—which he did very well considering he was a gay man. It was for moments like this, when he could joke with her about her crazy family and make her laugh.

He popped the last bite of his scone into his mouth and gave her a wink. "I still love you, Callie Jo," Eric said in a twangy redneck accent. "Even if you come from bad stock."

Callie sighed as the bell jingled and Eric turned to help a customer. That was their ongoing joke; he loved to poke fun at Callie and her crazy stage-kid upbringing, her mother dragging her to every talent show, recital, and beauty pageant in the Midwest. It was a surprise that Callie had turned out normal. Not that she didn't have her own set of issues. She was a ruthless overachiever, a bit on the dramatic side—although she'd never admit it out loud—had to have the last word, resorted to humor and sarcasm when she was uncomfortable, and was a little bit of a daddy's girl.

Okay, she had her share of issues. But who didn't? Truth was, she owed a lot to her parents. They were a little backwards in their thinking sometimes and Callie had been embarrassed by them plenty growing up, but they loved her and they'd taught her many valuable lessons. First of which was hard work. Pageants weren't for the faint of heart, and her mother had done whatever it took to make sure Callie was successful, like the time Barbara had worked overnight shifts for three months at the truck stop café just so they could afford Callie a new pageant wardrobe. Barbara was a force to be reckoned with beneath the façade of Merle Norman and Chico's clearance rack. Callie just wished that her mother spent more time valuing herself as an intelligent and strong woman in her own right.

According to Callie's father, both of the Daniels women were strong, but Callie knew she owed a lot of her strength and determination to him. He was the funniest and hardest-working man she knew, running one of the most well-known plumbing companies in Little Grove, Missouri, where she'd grown up. She admired him immensely and wouldn't have had the courage to start her own business without his example and guidance when she needed it.

Peeking into the display case, Callie mentally tallied what still needed to be done before she left for the day and headed to the high school for dance team practice. Her shop, Callie's Confections, made twelve different specialty treats every day Monday through Saturday and then took a limited amount of special orders every weekend. Tomorrow was the first high school football game in Preston, so she'd had a bevy of orders for blue-and-white-frosted cookies and cupcakes in addition to her usual fare.

The bell above the front door rang again and then the

small familiar voice of one of her favorite people rang out.

"Errrriiicccc."

"Clairebuggggg,"

Eric ran around the counter to sweep the little girl into his arms. A man walked in a second later and Callie abjectly appreciated the rugged manscape that accompanied Claire Edmond. Mike Everett was the best thing that had happened to Anne, Claire's mother and Callie's other best friend. Mike and Anne had only been dating a few months, but Callie knew it was the real deal. The two were obsessed with each other. Almost disgustingly so, which had really put a crimp in girl time. But it was worth it. Callie wanted nothing more than for her friends to be happy, and this man made Anne and her daughter happier than Callie had ever seen them.

"Hey, you two." Callie headed around the counter and out front, giving them a smile. "Isn't this a school day?"

"I just went to the dentist." Claire dropped from Eric's arms and came over to give Callie a toothy smile.

"Gorgeous. Cavities?"

"Nope," Claire said before yanking her mouth open with a finger hooked in each cheek.

"She was a trooper, didn't even flinch on X-rays," Mike said, stuffing his hands in his pockets. There was no mistaking the pride on his face. He truly seemed to love Claire, which made Callie smile.

"Well then, that calls for peanut butter cookies," Callie sang as she turned toward the kitchen. "Follow me to the VIP section."

"What's '*VIP*' mean?" Claire asked.

"Very Interesting Pickles," Eric said, pulling a funny face.

"Nuh-uh." Claire giggled. "What's it really mean, Uncle Mike?"

"Very Icky Pigs, I think," Mike replied.

Callie chuckled at the use of Claire's pet name for Mike. His niece was Claire's best friend and Claire had yet to drop the "Uncle" moniker.

Mike and Claire came into the kitchen behind Callie, and she got to work lifting the peanut butter cookies off the cooling rack and onto a display tray. The beauty of a perfectly baked pastry made her heart swell with pride every time.

Barbara was the queen of trend dieting, so Callie's childhood had been filled with odd desserts made with avocados or applesauce. It was no surprise that when Callie had gone away to college she'd loaded up on flour, real butter, and heavy cream so she could make the real stuff. She'd never stopped.

"These smell yummy, Callie," Claire said.

"Why, thank you, my dear. Go grab one of those pink boxes, and you can take some home and share them with Mommy."

"Yay!" Claire exclaimed as she skipped over to the shelves stocked full of paper goods.

"Thanks, Callie. I figured the dentist was cause for a treat, especially since it's the first time Claire's been without Anne," Mike said.

"I agree: I think baked goods are almost always appropriate in any situation. How's Anne's speech coming along? I assume that's why you took Claire."

Mike nodded. "This whole blog convention seriously has her stressed. She's scared to death to speak in front of a crowd."

Anne was the founder of the incredibly popular lifestyle blog *My Perfect Little Life*. It featured everything from party-planning tips and personal anecdotes to DIY furniture restoration. Almost two years ago she'd invited Callie to become a regular contributor, posting recipes and baking tips. Now they also had Lindsey Morales, whose specialty was design and repurposed crafts. Callie loved being a part of the online community that Anne had created; it was almost like being an Internet celebrity. Anne's readers loved her and had welcomed Callie and Lindsey with open arms. It seemed every day they all became more popular. Even more exciting, Anne had been asked to be the keynote speaker at an upcoming blogger convention.

"She'll be amazing. Anne doesn't do anything without doing it well. I kind of hate her for it."

"Nuh-uh. You love Mommy," Claire said matter-of-factly as she continued to load treat after treat into the pink box.

Mike finished off his second cookie. "Don't tell anyone, but your cookies could make a grown man cry."

"Flattery will get you everywhere, but the rule is no one cries in this kitchen but me." Her expression must have been a little too telling, because Mike gave her a raised eyebrow.

"Everything okay?" he asked. It was in that guy tone, the one that said he was worried but really hoped she didn't elaborate because he would have no idea how to handle it.

Callie let out a dramatic sigh as she lowered the lid on the box before Claire could clean her out. The tiny shyster had already moved on to the tray of scones and was closing in on blue and white Panther cupcakes. "Oh yeah, I don't really need to cry. Not today. But my mother did just leave, so there's that."

"Big yellow hair, Mustang convertible with 'HR HINES' written on the plate?"

"God, yes, she wanted it to say 'her highness,' but that obviously was too long to fit." Callie groaned. Barbara had sported the HRHINES license plate since Callie was six, based on the name of her father's plumbing business, Royal Flush. His advertisements featured her handsome yet rotund father in a crown and cape, holding a plunger instead of a scepter. It was quite a treat to go to high school and be known for being the princess of plungers.

Mike chuckled. "She looked . . . interesting."

"You're being sweet. Hipsters and feminists are interesting. My mother is—"

"She's an abomination. But we love her." Eric cut Callie off as he breezed through the kitchen to grab a package of napkins and head back out front.

"We do love her. But visits from her exhaust me emotionally."

"Sorry, Cal." Mike picked up the box and began to herd Claire toward the door. "Why don't you go over to Anne's tonight? She's a mess trying to prepare for the conference, and I know how hanging out together always makes you feel better. Drink wine, eat cupcakes, or do whatever female bonding shit you do."

"Uncle Mike, the *s* word is a no-thank-you word, 'member?"

Callie laughed at Claire's scolding of Mike. Their sweet little Claire was an original. In Callie's professional opinion Mike and Anne needed to get the child a sibling and quick. In a crowd she was sweet and shy, but around those she was close to she was a little princess herself.

"I seem to use a lot of no-thank-you words," Mike said quietly before he followed Claire back to the front of the store. He turned to Callie once more at the front door, giving her a serious look. "But seriously, Anne would never say so, but I think she could use a visit. She's stressed, and I'm not good with things I can't fix for her. I'd appreciate you going over and cheering her up."

Callie groaned. "Why do you have to keep being so perfect? It's really annoying."

Mike grinned. "I adore you, too, Callie."

Eric tossed Mike a bottle of chocolate milk for Claire and then before he and Claire left he called over his shoulder, "Thanks, guys. See ya later."

The door shut behind them and Callie glanced at the clock. "Oh crap!" She ran to the back, untying her flour-dusted apron. "Eric, I'm gonna be late to practice if I don't get out of here."

The dance team met immediately after school except for Fridays, which were often game days. If it was a home game the team would perform at halftime. Admittedly, this second job had turned out to be a little bit

more of a time commitment than Callie had first anticipated, but she was surprised at how much she'd instantly
fallen in love with it. So far it was worth the craziness in
her life. She figured this was the time. She was young
and healthy. Single and definitely not looking. If she was
going to live, she intended to live big and stay busy.

Plus it was dance, which had always been her escape.
Her life had always been hectic; when she was younger
it was schoolwork, pageants, and all the drama that
came along with being the daughter of Her Hines and
the King of Plungers. No matter how crazy life had
been, Callie had always made room for dance, ever since
her mother had enrolled her in tap and ballet at the age
of three. That had started a lifelong love affair. She loved
it all, jazz, modern, even ballroom, which she'd taken
in college, where she'd earned a scholarship to be on the
university's dance team. Now she'd come full circle, she
was teaching, and it was amazing.

Twenty minutes later Callie was in the high school
gym breathing in the stench of teenage sweat, hairspray,
and Victoria's Secret lotion. But she was happy. The
music was pounding, and she was joining her girls in a
hard stretch before they practiced their latest routine,
the one they'd be performing tomorrow night. She let
out a breath and felt all of her stress fade away.

Bennett Clark was late for practice, which really pissed
him off, but a student needing some extra help on a
homework assignment took precedence over football.
For at least a few minutes.

Bennett had texted his assistants to let them know,
but he hated to be late. Especially when it was only the

third full week of school. These first few weeks of practice were critical, particularly for the new players. It was when the team started to really come together and find their footing as a unit, but more than that, for Bennett it was also vital that he make sure his players understood his expectations for them as athletes and students.

He picked up his pace as he hit the hallway that ran alongside the gym, heading toward the back door leading out to the field. A loud female voice coming from inside the gym caught his attention.

"Ladies, if your rear isn't in the air, this stretch isn't doing anything for your hamstrings. I want your boobs between your thighs."

Huh? Bennett came to a complete stop and then slowly peeked into the double doors that led into the massive gymnasium. Thankfully, the girls were all facing the opposite wall, so they couldn't see him. Once again the bossy feminine voice vibrated off every shiny surface.

"Good. Hold it. These muscles need to be nice and warm."

He could only blink. This wasn't Jane, the dance team coach's voice. Had she quit? Been fired? He'd heard the rumors last spring about her sexting with an administrator but tried to ignore gossip. Maybe this was a sub.

"Okay, good. Now everyone in line so we can do the assembly kick routine full-out. Let's start on eight with chins up. Smiles wide." She punctuated the command with several rapid fire claps as the girls shuffled into place. And then . . . he saw her.

Damn.

She was on the small side, but her healthy curves were accentuated by her tight black pants. Good God, her ass was perfect, round and full but also firm. Tight. *Shit.*

This was so not Jane.

Bennett swallowed hard, his throat going dry. Her muscular legs were spread in a wide stance as she stood with her little hot-pink tennis shoes gripping the polished wooden floor, her hands grasping her hips, and her wildly curly hair pulled into a high ponytail. He wanted desperately to see her whole face, but she was also turned away from him. She began counting off, and on eight the line of dancers looked to the side and began kicking in unison.

When he realized the girls were starting to turn in his direction he took off. A male teacher appearing to gawk at the dance team wouldn't look good, so he sped up—cursing the pain that shot down his thigh—and burst through the metal doors and into the sunlight. Squinting, he took the shallow stairs with a rail down the incline, because the grassy hill was a killer on his bad leg, even though it was faster.

It had been years since his accident, but the injury never failed to get a little tender during football season, when he was frequently on his feet for long periods of time. He drew the line at taking the longest yet least painful route—down the wheelchair ramp. A man still had his dignity to protect.

The familiar and welcoming sound of grunts, and skin on vinyl, met his ears and his body released tension like a balloon deflating. The vibrant green and white of the gridiron, the stench of sweat, the growl of a pissed-off defense coach. This was his world. Coaching high school football would never have been his first choice, but of the many regrets Bennett had in his thirty years, deciding to take this job would never be one of them. Never mind that coaching was the only way he could keep football as a permanent fixture in his life after his accident.

Coaching had turned out to be a perfect fit and he couldn't have asked for a better school. Football in Preston was a way of life. Most residents would no more miss a Friday night game than they would miss church on Sunday. He was from Texas, where high school football was part of their religion, so he was familiar with the mentality. Welcomed it even.

Bennett made his way to the sidelines of the practice field and sought out his good friend and assistant coach Reggie. "Thanks for getting them started, man; sorry I'm late."

"No problem. We just finished warming up. Guys are amped up today. I can feel it. I let John take the defense to start drills, offense is stretching and reviewing the playbook with Ted, and now that you're here I'm taking my guys. I'm sure they're done running in this heat. I figured you want to work with Tate and Lane."

"Sounds good."

They stood and watched the boys for a minute until Bennett couldn't help himself anymore. Her cleared his throat and tried to sound nonchalant. "Hey, uh, what happened to Jane? She get sacked over the shit from last year?"

Reggie was no dummy. His deep chuckle told Bennett the man knew exactly why he'd asked, yet he never took his eyes off the boys on the field. "I wondered when you were gonna see her. She's a treat, isn't she?"

Bennett didn't respond, but he didn't have to. He and Reggie had been coaching together for six years. They had a bond that didn't require eye contact or even speaking, most of the time. It reminded Bennett of the relationships he'd developed with teammates over the years. Football did that, created a brotherhood. Reggie had played college ball and then gotten married and become a family man. Not every player with heart and grit was destined for the pros, just as not every player who made it to the NFL ended up a celebrity or even a success story.

"At least now I know why you were late. You got a look at the new dance coach," Reg said with a smirk and a little hip shuffle that he was known for.

"Please, you know me better than that. I was with a student," Bennett said, and Reg finally turned his way and raised an eyebrow. Bennett shrugged. "Okay, obviously I did see her. Might have held me up for a minute. Just a minute."

"Yeah, I bet." Reggie chuckled. "Why don't you talk to her? I'm sure she's dying to meet the beloved Coach Bennett. Do you some good to spend some time with a woman, you know? Just something to think about."

Bennett shook his head in response before blowing on his whistle. He headed out into the field toward his quarterbacks, trying not to dwell on Reggie's comment. Yeah, it had been a while since Bennett had been with a woman. Eight months, and then a year before that. And then probably a year before that.

He tried not to think about it, because it was downright depressing. But in his defense, he had a lot on his plate with teaching and coaching and there wasn't room in his life for a relationship. Casual or otherwise . . . because despite the implied intent in the word *casual,* those often ended up just as messy as the real deal. There'd been a time when he'd thought he'd found his one and only woman. How wrong he'd been.

Like so many things in his life, he'd lost his fiancée, Ashley, due to his accident. Apparently once a professional football contract was no longer part of his future, neither was she. In retrospect it probably shouldn't have come as a shock, but at the time it had thrown him. Hard. Yeah he'd been in a dark spot at the time, but wasn't that when the people you loved were supposed to prove it? She'd up and left him when he needed her the most.

Luckily, teaching and football helped to remind him that all was not lost. His life in no way resembled the one he grew up imagining he'd have, but it was good. Respectable, if not a bit lonely.

Okay, a whole lot lonely.

However, this season there was no reason to have a damn pity party. This team was going to be amazing. He could feel it, and he'd learned to trust his instincts.

Bennett stood under the goalpost for a while, shifting his weight off his bad leg while he watched his offense run a few drills. As a coach he knew every position was important; each played its role in a win and was necessary. But as a former quarterback himself, he couldn't help but be a little partial. His starting senior quarterback, Tate, was outrageously talented.

Bennett watched the kid throw a perfect spiral down the field straight into the wide receiver's hands. All the work Bennett had put into molding Tate Grayson for the past three years had paid off and the coach was incredibly proud. They were all great kids, but there were always a couple who shined. The ones you knew were going to be something.

Tate wasn't without his faults. He had a problem carrying his emotions onto the field, but his arm was amazingly consistent and strong. He could run fast and size up the opposing defense in a matter of seconds, and he had reflexes capable of keeping up. Bennett had a feeling it had been drilled into Tate from a young age, because the kid's dad was an overbearing ass. Tate Grayson Sr. never failed to remind Bennett how to do his job and that Grayson's son deserved to start every game now that he was a senior.

Tate wouldn't start every game, however, because not only was that unfair—there were, in fact, other quarterbacks—but also it wasn't healthy. A player needed to rest during a game. But Bennett couldn't deny that he had a winning combination between Tate and his best friend, Jason Starkey, the best left tackle Bennett had ever had.

The two boys had grown up together, played Pee Wee, rec, and club league as teammates. They executed plays like they shared a brain; Jason always seemed to know where Tate was going to end up even before he did. He made Tate nearly untouchable, and whatever magic it was, it was a beautiful sight. It was what state championships were made of.

Bennett tossed out a few pointers to Tate from the

side, nodding his head when he nailed it and encouraging him when he didn't. Reggie and the special teams guys had grouped in the side field and stopped to watch the last pass, cheering when the receiver caught it and immediately rolled into a somersault.

Bennett grinned. He enjoyed hearing the players interact with one another, not only cheering but also even yelling insults and innocent threats. He knew well that this kind of fraternizing was critical for the guys to trust one another and be successful. Add hard work, skill, and determination, and you had a winning team.

Luckily for his players, Bennett's time in the pros had earned them some extra attention from university scouts who had already started contacting him for visits. There were quite a few players—not just Tate and Jason—who could very well catch someone's eye this season. Time to get to work so that could happen.

A quick blow on the whistle and then Bennett bracketed his hands around his mouth and called Tate over to his side. Sweat dripped down Tate's overly long hair as he pulled off his dirty white helmet and let it dangle from his fingers.

"You see that pass a minute ago, Coach?"

"You bet I did. Nearly eighty yards, wasn't it?" He grinned.

"Baker's on fire, too; he's been catching everything I throw," Tate said, his breath ragged.

"I saw his gymnastics moves. Nice." Bennett cleared his throat, not liking what he was going to have to bring up next. "Listen, as much as I don't want to get into your personal business, I'm going to have to ask you a question. I heard you may have a problem with one of the guys on the South team." Tate looked away instantly, and Bennett knew he'd hit a nerve.

Teenage drama was inevitable; it penetrated all facets of their young lives and teaching and coaching meant Bennett wasn't immune to it. Usually drama with his players was centered on one of two things: family and girls.

Despite Tate's dickhead of a father, his problem usually seemed to be girls. He was a good-looking kid, weight trained constantly, was way too cocky for his own good. Reminded Bennett of himself as a teen. But this time it wasn't about a female—well, not that kind anyway. Bennett had overheard some girls in his second hour gossiping and caught enough to know that Tate's little sister—a sophomore—had suffered an ugly breakup last weekend. It just so happened to be with one of the linebackers from tomorrow's opposing team. From what Bennett could gather from the conversation, Tate hadn't taken it well, which hadn't surprised Bennett one bit. The guy was seriously protective of his little sister.

Bennett figured the best plan was to get Tate's best throws in early, before the shit talking had time to turn ugly and get the team all riled up. There was no doubt Bennett would be pulling Tate off the field at some point, hopefully before a fight broke out and the kid did something he couldn't take back. It didn't happen often, but these young guys were all muscles, aggression, and raging hormones.

"I won't give you any trouble, Coach." Tate finally met Bennett's eyes.

They were both silent for a moment. Bennett finally

cleared his throat and spoke. "You need to talk about it?" he asked gruffly. "You know I'm here for you."

"Yeah." The young man nervously dug his cleats into the ground. "I know you are, but no. I can handle it. I swear I'll leave it off the field."

Bennett nodded. "Listen, I know you can't turn your feelings off, but learn to use them to your advantage; don't let your anger control you. Got it?" Bennett asked, wishing he weren't speaking from experience. Tate nodded. "Well, now that we got that squared away, I wanted to officially let you know you're starting tomorrow."

"Thanks, Coach, I appreciate it." A genuine look of intense relief washed over the boy's face. And that's what he was, a boy, not even eighteen, but the pressure on these young athletes was incredible. "My dad's been giving me hell this week."

It killed Bennett to hear it, but he wasn't surprised. Why couldn't some parents understand that it wasn't healthy or wise to live, eat, and breathe only one thing? Football was a game and only a game.

"I'm sorry to hear that, Tate. I know you wanna make your dad proud, but you play ball for you, no one else. It's not all about being the star of the show. No one wins football championships on his own."

Tate's padded shoulders slumped. "My dad doesn't see it that way."

"No disrespect to your father, but sometimes he's got shit backwards in his head." Bennett wanted to add a few other choice phrases but managed to hold them in. Tate's father was the only parent in the house, unfortunately. Bennett was pretty sure Grayson was also an alcoholic. "Now go long and show me what I'm dealing with tomorrow. Put your frustration behind that ball."

Nearly two hours later, the team was exhausted. Bennett's favorite hat was soaked with sweat from his standing under the early September heat, his forearms looked a little red, and his leg ached like a son of a bitch.

Afternoon practices were long and intense but much better than they'd been when Bennett had started at Preston. The coach before Bennett had held practice twice a day, morning and afternoon. That had been his first change. He switched to two-a-days only during spring ball. He figured the pressure of schoolwork, winning games, and normal practice was enough for the fall season.

That had been accepted begrudgingly, but his other changes? Not so much. He'd completely thrown the community for a loop when he started preaching to the boys that football wasn't everything. Yeah, he knew that wasn't always the norm for coaches, but he took this concept seriously. Another unpopular change was mandatory 2.8 G.P.A on Friday afternoon or they couldn't play that night. He knew it was higher than most schools, even higher than the NCAA, but this was high school and if they couldn't handle high school work and football how could they ever manage college? He even lectured all the teachers about favors. His boys didn't need special treatment. They also had to serve the community instead of their community serving them— as was so common with small-town athletes.

Bennett could only assume that considering his background, the town hadn't expected his ideals, but everything had turned out for the best, and he'd gotten them on his side eventually. The state championship his first year had helped considerably. And the two since then. It also didn't hurt that the team always won their division. If any of them had stopped to consider Bennett's own personal situation, they would see exactly why the coach felt the way he did. Working hard was great. Passion was important. But things could be ripped away from you at any time.

These young men needed something else; their whole life couldn't be football. If it worked out for them, if they were one of the very few lucky ones who ended up in the NFL making millions? Great. If not, a backup plan was in place. Statistically speaking, all of them would probably need it. Bennett did have two former players just starting their first season in the NFL and about three more at universities and on their way. But he wanted every boy in college after they left his program. He wanted to be more than the guy who taught them plays and ran drills. He wanted to make them into well-rounded men. Be a positive influence in their lives. Try to keep them from making some of the mistakes he did. His biggest of which had been thinking that football was everything and the only dream worth striving for was making millions in the pros.

A backup plan was necessary.

Two

Callie knocked on Principal Jensen's door. He'd peeked his head into the gym during practice to ask if she'd swing by his office on her way out. So here she was. Curious and, admittedly, a little nervous. Getting called to the office normally wasn't a good sign.

"Ah, Callie, thanks for coming by." He lifted his hand and motioned to the chair across from him. She sat and folded her hands in her lap, trying to show confidence she wasn't really feeling at the moment.

"I hope nothing's wrong," she said with an awkward smile.

"Heavens no, of course not. Relax." He chuckled, his bearded double chin shaking against his tie. "Sorry, I should have made that clear earlier."

Callie let out a breath and laughed along with him. "Well, that's a relief."

"Let me assure you that everyone's been very happy with you so far. The girls winning that award at camp . . . what was it?"

"Actually, there were several. They received a Superior

rating for their home routine, our captains won a Silver Award, the team received a Spirit Stick for every day of the camp, and we had two All-American nominees." She smiled. She knew the man probably had no idea what any of that meant, but it didn't matter. She was just impressed he knew anything at all. In her limited experience, it wasn't unusual for the dance team to not get the respect they deserved. Many schools didn't even consider it a sport. Instead it was labeled as an activity or club, even though the girls were incredibly dedicated and worked their asses off not just for a season but for the entire year.

"Of course. Wonderful job. On that note, I actually have a favor to ask you, and I'll state up front that it's asking a lot, but I need help."

Well, that sounded grim. "Okay, I'll do my best."

"Are you familiar at all with the Millard Country Club?"

"Sure. I mean, I'm not a member," she teased, and they both laughed. "But yeah, I've delivered some baked goods there before. That is, before it flooded this spring."

"What a shame that was. Well, in October they will be having a huge fund-raiser. They do an event every year, but being as this is their grand reopening after the remodel, this one is extra-special. This year's theme is some sort of TV dancing competition. Do you watch those shows?"

She couldn't help her grin. "Are you kidding? I love them, never miss."

"Perfect. I was hoping you might say that. Maybe this will just work out perfectly. Here's the thing: they want the event to bring a lot of support from the community and so they're trying to get some local celebrity types to participate. You know how these things are. Anyway, they've asked our beloved Coach Clark to participate. Unfortunately . . . he said no."

Principal Jensen gave her a knowing look. Except she had no idea what he was implying. "That's too bad. It sounds like fun."

"Oh good, I'm glad you think so. You see, I assumed maybe Coach Clark wasn't interested because, well, you know, he's a guy. But then I thought maybe it's because he's afraid he wouldn't win. He likes to win things."

She couldn't figure out what his refusal to do the fund-raiser had to do with her. Callie didn't know a thing about Coach Clark; in fact, she'd never even met the man. She only knew he was the head football coach because everyone in town was obsessed with the team. Of course, football teams never lacked in the respect department. So typical.

"Well, I'm going to be frank with you, Callie. The past two dance team coaches were fired for inappropriate behavior."

She jerked her head back. Whoa, that was quite a left turn they'd just taken. What was he implying now? She felt her inner defense start to rise.

"I'd heard the rumors about Jane before me"—and how they had also included a district administrator funny Jensen didn't mention that bit—"but I can assure you that I—"

Principal Jensen put up a hand. "Callie, you've given me no reason to worry about you. My point is this: The school has not been shed in the best light the past few years in regards to some of its coaching and administrative staff. On top of that, Coach Clark has failed to win the Evan Award from the coaching association the past three years that he's been nominated, and I know he deserves it. I really believe that if he'd do this community fund-raiser it would clinch it for him. And . . . well, it would look good for the school, too. Maybe help our state ratings."

"Yeah, that sounds like a great idea. I mean, if he likes to win, it sounds like he better put his dancin' shoes on." She chuckled, beginning to get a little uneasy.

Principal Jensen grinned. "Yes. That's where I thought you could come in."

Oh shit. "Oh?"

"I was hoping that if *you* agreed to be Coach Clark's partner, he would participate."

Her eyebrows hit the ceiling. "Be his partner?" This guy had to be joking. The football coach? Surely he had a wife . . . or even a daughter who could dance with him? "I'm not so—"

"I'd consider it a huge favor."

Oh no. She just couldn't. Life had gotten stressful enough as it was. As much as the idea of a *Celebrity Dance Off*–inspired competition appealed to her, she just really couldn't commit. She opened her mouth to say just that, but he cut her off.

"I really need this favor, Callie. You know, at the last PTA meeting some of the moms were complaining that the dance team's budget had been awfully small the past few years. I got a small grant reserved. I might be happy to pass it on to the team to use for some new uniforms."

Callie chewed on her lip. Now things were getting

sketchy. Bribery had never sat well with her. She'd been
a witness to all kinds of manipulation and backstabbing
on the pageant circuit, and she hated it. But damn it, this
wasn't just about her but also her girls. They had a fund-
raiser in a few weeks—a dance clinic for younger
girls—but this being her first year coaching, Callie had
no idea what kind of money to expect. She swallowed.

He smiled. He had her, and he damn well knew it.

"If Coach Clark already said no to the country club,
why do you think he'll change his mind now?"

Principal Jensen looked sheepish. "The problem is
that . . . I took it upon myself to go ahead and sign him
up anyway. Told them he'd changed his mind and said
yes. They even scheduled it on a Thursday evening so
he wouldn't miss a game. They were so excited, and
if he turns them down now it will make us all look
bad."

In other words, it would make Principal Jensen look
bad. Callie didn't know what to think. This was quite a
manipulation for something that seemed rather insig-
nificant to her . . . school ratings, a coaching award. But
the thought of announcing new uniforms to her team
made her happy.

Could she win a dance competition? Hell yes, every
day of the week and twice on Sundays. Did she have
time for another project? Absolutely not. Never mind
that this coach would probably be a horrible dancer, old
and uncoordinated . . . oh lord. Just thinking about it
made her wince.

"He'll need himself a partner, one that will give him
a good chance of winning," Principal Jensen interrupted
her thoughts.

Callie blew out a breath. "This could backfire on you; have you considered that?"

"Absolutely, but I have faith in you. When you talk with him I'd start with all the positives, let him know that you're a very experienced dancer. He should feel better about it then. His plan period is seventh hour."

"Wait a second." Her eyes went wide again and she pointed at her own chest. "You expect me to break this news to him?"

"I just thought maybe he'd be more likely to say yes to . . . well, you know. You're a cute girl. I don't mean that in any inappropriate way, I'm just thinking since he's a man—"

Callie lifted a hand to stop Principal Jensen from going any further. It was always mind-boggling when a man didn't even realize how offensive and sexist his comments were. Even more mind-boggling that women were used to putting up with their idiocy. And to think he'd just reminded her of the last two dance team coaches' *inappropriate behavior*. Poor women, they hadn't stood a chance. "Listen, I make no promises, but I'll try."

She should refuse, Callie thought to her herself as she made her way down the science wing of Preston High School. She was running behind and now had only ten minutes until the first Pep Assembly started. A harsh reminder of why this was a bad idea: she didn't have time for it. But here she was, with ten minutes to convince this no doubt masochistic and old-school coach to be her dance partner.

She'd lain in bed last night stewing over it. It went

against everything she believed in, because at the end of the day Principal Jensen had asked her to do extra work just to make a man look good. Not even just one man . . . but two! Unbelievable.

Part of her wanted to march into the office and give Principal Jensen a piece of her mind on not only his style of asking for help but also his assumption that he could so easy manipulate and bribe her.

The problem was the other part of her, the one that heard only "dancing competition" and immediately went into *let's win this bitch* mode. That part was in the lead, and she couldn't help it. Whether she liked it or not, she thrived on competition—damn her mother and all those pageants.

The only way Callie could handle it was to do things on her own terms. She knew she could easily whip this old dude into shape and make him at least good enough to get them a win. Not that she wanted to have an ego about it, but let's face it: the man was often the foundation of a dance, while the woman made it look good. This was doable; the coach would just have to let her make all the rules and she would make sure they won, which was what both of them would obviously want.

Callie blew out a deep breath as she scanned the nameplates on door after door. She was prepared to turn on the charm, and yet she wouldn't beg him either. If he adamantly said no she would just take it as fate intervening on behalf of her sanity.

Finally locating Coach Clark's classroom at the end of the hall, she peeked through the small glass window. It looked just like every other science room gracing

America's schools. Tall tables, stools, and soapstone countertops. Boring.

She glanced down at her skirt and sandaled heels to make sure she was in order, gave the wooden door a rap with her knuckles, and made her way in.

At first glance the room appeared to be empty, but after a second she heard the faint sound of a football game and turned to the head of the classroom. A man sat at the desk, head down. He was watching something on his phone and hadn't heard her enter.

"Excuse me," she said, hoping not to startle him. No such luck. His head jerked up in surprise and their eyes met.

Holy. Shit. This man was gorgeous.

"Can I help you?" he asked. She shivered at the deep timbre of his voice, low and rumbly, with just a hint of a southern accent. This could not be who she was looking for.

"Umm, yes." A grin played at her lips and she gave her head a light shake as she walked closer to his desk. "I'm sorry. I'm looking for Coach Clark. Do you know where I can find him?"

He stood slowly and stepped in her direction. She was almost certain he winced just the slightest bit as he rounded the desk, but he concealed it quickly with a tight smile. "You've found him. I'm Bennett Clark."

Oh my goodness, things just took a wicked turn. For the worst? She didn't know yet, but she was definitely knocked off-kilter. He looked down at her, and all she could think to do was stare.

He was breathtaking. Built, yet lean, tall and broad-shouldered. His dark hair was cut short, his brown eyes deep, with full lashes. He was the complete opposite of everything she'd imagined the notorious high school football coach to be. This sexy thing could grace pages of magazines wearing nothing but briefs and a bad attitude.

"What can I do for you?" he asked, tilting his head to the side, and she was pretty sure he checked her out for just a second, his eyes quickly sweeping down the front of her. She realized she needed to regroup, and fast. She knew how to handle hot jock guys with roving eyes, had done it plenty of times in her life.

"I'm Callie Daniels. I'm the new Pantherettes dance coach."

Thankfully her voice came out steady, and she took a few confident steps forward, dropped her dance bag on the floor, and held out her hand. He reciprocated, taking it into his own firm grip. His skin was warm and slightly rough. "I know who you are. It's nice to meet you."

"Oh? Well, then you have me at a disadvantage, Bennett, because you are not at all who I expected you to be."

He raised an eyebrow. "I apologize. Who *were* you expecting, if I may inquire?"

"Let's just say you're about twenty years younger than I assumed."

"Ah, I see."

"Can't say that I'm disappointed." She grinned. But when he only stared at her awkwardly, she felt an embarrassed blush travel up her neck. *Well, shit.* She cleared her throat. "Anyway. I came by to give you some news, and I have a feeling you're not going to be very excited to hear it."

He crossed his arms, his brow furrowing just a bit. "Okay."

"I'm just going to put it out there. Despite your initial reservations, Principal Jensen took it upon himself to go ahead and sign you up to compete in the celebrity dance-off at the country club in October and he asked me to be your partner and coach. So to speak. So . . . surprise!" This time her grin was wide and over-the-top.

He sucked a deep breath into his nose, his wide chest expanding as he did. He let the breath out slowly, never taking his eyes off her face.

Oh my. It's a little hot in here.

He remained silent as her grin fell.

She'd made a huge miscalculation. Before she walked in, it hadn't even occurred to her for one second that this man would be, well . . . hot as hell. She'd only known old coaches, the kind who wore embroidered team polos, yelled a lot, and patted their players on the butt. Her plan had been to come here, be adorable, throw down the rules, and make this happen.

She now realized that Coach Clark was not the type to be handled and spending the next few weeks doing the vertical nasty with him would only lead to trouble. Not to mention that he looked ready to knock someone into next week after hearing her announcement.

Here it was, fate was about to intervene—and yet, being the competitive spirit she was, it suddenly irked her to no end that he would be the one to reject her.

"You're pissed, right? I knew it." She dropped her shoulders. "We could basically shut this down right now if you just march down to the office and tell him it's not gonna happen. Because to be honest with you . . . I have a lot going on this season. I run my own business as well as coach, and I'd just as soon not have to worry about helping you win."

As soon as the words left her lips she saw the kink in her plan. Callie knew a challenge when she heard one and that was just what she'd done. She'd just challenged the big, hot, brooding man. *Stupid.*

"Helping me, huh? You sound pretty sure you'd win," he finally said, and yep, there was definitely the trace of an adorable twang to his speech. He stuffed his hands in his pockets and she jerked her eyes away from his pants, tough as it was.

"Oh, I know I'd win." She gave him a wink. "Winning is what I do. And a dancing competition? Yeah, no-brainer."

He leveled his gaze on her. "But you don't want to dance with me, apparently."

Her mouth dropped open. "Okay, now you're just putting words in my mouth; I never said that. You obviously didn't want to dance with me, since you immediately got all pissed."

"I never said I was pissed."

Callie yanked her head back with a scoff. "Like you had to. That whole breath sucking in and death stare were all I needed." She did a quick impersonation of him, puffing up her chest, glaring at him.

He shook his head a little and she was almost sure that he wanted to laugh. He pulled himself together. "But I'm right. You were doing this out of obligation for some reason, but the truth is you don't want to dance with me."

Was he for real? Were they arguing about this? And

how did he keep managing to throw her off her game? "Why are you making this about me? Principal Jensen told me you said no from the beginning, I'm just trying to do you a favor, but by all means, if you want to dance, then we'll dance." She threw her arms up in frustration, annoyed that she'd just fallen for *his* challenge this time.

"No. I won't be dancing."

"It sounds like you want to."

"I don't. I was just trying to point out that you sounded very opposed to the idea of dancing with me."

"Nope," she said matter-of-factly, shaking her head. "No I didn't."

"Hmm," he said, continuing to stare at her.

Callie crossed her arms and scrunched up her face for a minute. "You're making this kind of complicated. Sort of unusual for a man."

The expression on his face made her want to laugh. She'd pushed his buttons all right; he looked completely baffled and offended. "This is not complicated. At all." He was starting to sound very flustered.

She could only shrug. "You want to; you don't want to; you're mad; you're not mad." She put her hands up surrender-style, trying desperately to make it appear that she wasn't getting as amped up as he appeared to be. She hoped it was working. "Just saying, usually a man knows what he wants and doesn't want."

"Unbelievable." He ran his hand through his hair, his gaze going serious on her. "Let me make myself very clear then. I'm not participating in any dance competition and I will be having a talk with Jensen for going behind my back."

"Okay, I'll let you deal with it from here on. But you know Jensen is hoping this will be your ticket to winning some coaching award. Apparently, it would be good for the entire school."

Why was she still talking? He'd said no and that he was going to talk with the principal. It could be done and done. She should walk out of there, go to the gym, and forget about this mess. So why was she still goading him?

His face changed slightly, tensed. "I don't coach for my own recognition and no award given to me will change anything about my process or how I feel about what I do here. So that has no bearing on my decision."

"So you don't think that all those young men that look up to you would be proud and excited if their coach was given a huge award? Not only that, but think of what you'd be teaching them about hard work and being willing to put yourself out there. Don't you want them to see that even big strong manly men can have fun, do something for a good cause? Give back to the community?" Apparently she was incapable of shutting her mouth or not thinking about how lickable his neck looked in that dress shirt.

"Are you trying to *shame* me into saying yes?"

She shrugged. "Not at all. Like I said, it would be best for me if we didn't do this."

"Look who's being complicated now."

"I'm always complicated. No objections there," she said straight faced.

"Well then, it's a good thing we won't be partnering, because I only like easy women."

"Classy, Coach Clark," she said, loving the wince on his face the minute he'd said those unfortunate words.

"You know damn well what I meant."

"It's settled then. We won't be partners. So I guess we're done here."

"I guess we are."

She stood there a minute longer, his eyes never leaving hers. Unable to stop herself, she licked her lips and watched his gaze follow the movement. He reached out and rested his hand on a soapstone counter, almost as if catching himself from falling. *Interesting.* And what the hell was she doing playing with him like this?

And was he playing with her? None of this was normal conversation. It all felt . . . heated. Intense. Crazy. Their eyes met again, his darkening. *In what . . . fury?* Surely not desire after they'd just gotten each other so worked up and frustrated.

She picked up her dance bag, hefted it over her shoulder, and turned to go. But because she was Callie Daniels, daughter of Her Hines, she couldn't leave well enough alone. "Well, I'd say it was nice to meet you, Bennett . . . but nope. I don't think I will." And she walked out just as the bell rang, her heels clacking against the linoleum.

Three

Railroaded.

There was no other way for Bennett to explain what he'd just been through. He couldn't make sense of the encounter if he tried. Callie Daniels had walked into his classroom, hot-as-you-damn-please, and completely knocked the wind out of him. And then after challenging him, taunting him, and confusing the living hell out of him, she'd turned and walked out in the sexiest little huff he'd ever seen.

Neither of them had so much as raised their voice, but he felt exhausted. The woman was more than a handful not only physically but also emotionally.

As much as the thought of dancing in front of a crowd, or even at all, horrified him, he was almost shocked that he'd managed not to say yes. As ridiculous as the past five minutes had been . . . he hadn't wanted them to end. It was insane. He could have gone on bantering with her for the rest of the afternoon.

Never mind that the thought of spending hours of practice time with his arms full of her lush little body had made him want to agree to whatever she demanded. A thought that irritated him even more, because if anyone knew how much trouble a woman like that could be it was him. Mouthy, gorgeous, and smart. The kind that was looking for a man to give her exactly what she wanted: everything.

Bennett pulled himself together and went back to his desk to shove some papers that needed grading over the weekend into his bag before he headed down to the assembly. He was certain he'd see her there. Would she look at him? Pretend nothing had happened? Nope, he was certain she wouldn't be able to forget because she'd made certain that he wouldn't with that little tease of her tongue. Right before she stormed out. Damn, it shouldn't have worked the way it did.

He groaned and paused at the classroom door, willing his body to get its shit together before he walked into the hall. Thinking about how mad he was at Principal Jensen did the trick. What a slimy bastard, sending a woman like that down to do his dirty work.

Bennett had made it beyond clear to the man that he wasn't interested in doing the country club fund-raiser. Not only because he didn't pander to the town's rich families, but mostly because he didn't fucking dance. He barely walked some days with his bad leg. He couldn't even imagine what he'd look like trying to be graceful in front of an audience.

He shook off thoughts of humiliation and tried to focus on dodging the masses of students idling in the hallway. He urged them toward the gym, convincing himself he didn't catch the scent of weed on one kid's hoodie.

The band was already playing, the reverberation of the drums bouncing off the lockers that lined the hallway. Game days during school hours had an energy all their own, and he never knew if he loved it or hated it. It was good for the students, however, and got the team in the right frame of mind, but for him it was stressful. He couldn't help thinking about the coming game while he was trying to teach, which was why he was watching a few last-minute play videos during his plan period when Callie Daniels had come in and blown his concentration to pieces.

Damn, she was still doing a number on his thoughts, because he kept imagining golden-toned legs, little high-heeled shoes, and those blond curls that had framed her face. The majority of her big hair had been pulled back, just like it had been the first time he saw her in the gym. He couldn't stop thinking how much he'd like to see it loose and wild.

He turned down the hall that ran along the back of the gym near the locker rooms. The football team congregated there, waiting for the moment when they'd be announced to an adoring crowd. A few guys called out to Bennett as he approached, and he found himself smiling, finally able to get his thoughts in check.

"Coach, it's packed in there," Jason said, his grin wide and his eyes sparkling from the adrenaline rush.

Unlike Bennett, the boys loved the pep rallies. It was a thrill to get so much attention, and while he didn't begrudge them their time in the spotlight, he was always there to knock them down a few pegs when it was over. Nobody got far with too big of an ego, how well he knew.

"Better make sure your fly's zipped." Both Jason and Tate instantly lifted their jerseys and looked down at their jeans. Bennett laughed and ran his hands through his hair.

The part about these assemblies he hated most was speaking in front of the crowd. Students, parents, aunts, uncles, staff. It made his insides twist. But they all expected a few words from him, especially the first game of the season.

At least the local news media had stopped coming like they had his first couple of years of coaching. Everybody wanted to get a look at what Bennett Clark had done with himself after he came out of hiding and took a high school coaching job in a small Missouri town. A few videos and stories had even shown up on *Sports Illustrated* online, exactly what he'd wanted to avoid. What was worse were the few brave reporters who had sought him out, wanting interviews. Bennett would do just about anything for his players, but it didn't take a psychic to see that the reporters weren't interested in hearing about the team, and he refused to talk about the accident and his recovery. Not an option.

The bleachers in the gym began to vibrate with stomping of students as the assembly got under way. Bennett stepped around some of the players and peeked into the gym. It was standing room only in the corners, but he just barely caught sight of the Pantherettes' double kick line forming. The boys would be announced one at a time and run through, a tradition at Preston High.

A large hand clapped onto Bennett's shoulder. He

turned to find Reggie grinning at him. "You ready for this, my man?"

Bennett nodded and some of the tension drained from his body. Reggie's good-natured outlook and laid-back style always helped Bennett's stress level. He said to his friend, "Can you believe this will be our sixth season coaching together?"

"Crazy, isn't it? And you still single." Reggie laughed and shook his head. Bennett's chuckle died in his throat when he caught sight of Principal Jensen from the corner of his eye. The man was standing off to the side in the gym, clapping along with the music. Bennett knew the idiot meant well, but his tactics pissed him off. He'd be having a long talk with the man very shortly.

Before the coach knew it, only Tate and another senior boy were left to be called, and once again Bennett's nerves were humming. When Tate's name was finally called the crowd went nuts.

Reggie chuckled. "That kid. His ego's gonna be insane by the time this season's out."

"Yep. Can't say he hasn't earned it, though."

"For sure," Reggie replied. A minute later he was jogging out as his name was called.

Bennett took a deep breath, his heart hammering. *Just another part of the job.* He swallowed hard as he heard the announcing cheerleader's voice begin again.

"And now make some noise everybody for Preston's favorite coach. Coach Bennett Claaaarrrrrrkkkkk."

Callie watched in wide-eyed wonderment as the hot-assin Bennett Clark sauntered down the center of the kick line. His face looked a little smug and a lot overwhelmed at the incredible reception he was receiving. The students stomped on the bleachers and hollered, like he was a wrestler entering the arena. It was outrageous, and she found herself smiling in spite of herself.

How did a small-town coach become such a celebrity? She recalled Principal Jensen saying Bennett had been in the NFL, so that had to be part of it. It wasn't a surprise she'd never heard of him; she was completely ignorant when it came to professional sports. Even when she was on the dance team in college she didn't keep up with any of the sports beyond her own school, and even then she wouldn't have wanted to be quizzed on it.

Bennett made his way over to his team in the center of the gym floor, who instantly met him with back pats and fist bumps. What did it feel like to be so beloved, and how had she not known that this was happening in the small town she'd called home for nearly two years? All this time, this man was breathing in the same air that she'd been. Had he ever entered her shop? She didn't think so; Eric would have known if this level of sexy had been under his nose.

Speaking of which. Callie sucked in a hard breath as the yelling began to die down and turned to find Eric's head in the crowd. Luckily, he'd been looking at her, too, and instantly he mouthed, *Wow*. *Wow* was an understatement.

She turned back to the gym floor just as the head cheerleader—also the announcer—handed Bennett the microphone. He put up his hands in a shushing gesture and then lifted the mic to his lips. Before he could get a word out a trio of female voices yelled out from the student section behind Callie's head, "We love you, Coach Clark!"

The crowd laughed and cheered and Callie had to stop her mouth from dropping open in shock. Three teenage girls had just inappropriately declared love for their teacher, and the crowd had *laughed*.

And they thought the female dance team coaches were the problem.

Bennett's face turned an adorable light shade of pink and he smiled down at the gym floor, the round top of the microphone rested against his lips, close enough so that his breathy chuckle could be heard huffing through the speakers. The sound sent warmth straight to Callie's toes.

When he finally looked up, his eyes instantly met hers and held for just a second. His lips pursed just the slightest bit before he finally looked away.

What was that about, and why had that warmth inside her body suddenly turned to a low simmer?

"Y'all are too good to me, Preston," Bennett said. His slight accent rippled through the loudspeaker, making everyone quiet down.

There was no denying that he commanded attention, and here she'd planned to go into his classroom and tell him how it was. That was laughable. And yet . . . as she watched him shift his weight onto the other leg carefully, she sensed there was a subtle vulnerability to him. She couldn't quite place it, but she knew it was in there. Something in his eyes, which landed on her once more.

Callie couldn't help her lips' inching up just a fraction. She was pretty damn sure he reciprocated, as if they'd just passed a secret message, which was bizarre, because they'd just been at each other's throats a few minutes ago in his classroom.

"It sure is good to see y'all here," he said, his eyes still on her. Finally he turned around and took in the bleachers from all four sides. They were packed to the rafters; apparently this was the place to be on a Friday afternoon in Preston, Missouri. "Before we get any further, I need to acknowledge a few people standing here with me."

He looked behind him and then to the other direction behind the players. "My assistant coaches, Reggie, John, Will, Jim. We wouldn't be the team we are if it weren't for these guys."

Another round of applause radiated through the crowd and Bennett waited for it to quiet down once more before going on. "And also to the parents of these fine, *fine* young men, I thank you for your continued support and dedication."

More cheers. Bennett waited, stuffing one hand in his pant pocket. It was such a simple movement, but Callie couldn't help thinking that every little gesture he did came off as more manly than the average guy. She noticed that he'd rolled up the sleeves of his shirt, his forearms tanned and lightly covered in dark hair.

Holy shit, she needed to *look away,* if for no other reason then her own sanity. He lifted the mic again.

"It's time for another year of football. I'm ready, the guys are ready, we had an amazing spring ball program, these boys look fantastic, and y'all know me, I'm not an eloquent speaker. In fact, my team knows that I'm not a complicated man."

Callie laughed to herself. That comment was *so* directed at her. He went on.

"I believe in less talking, more action. So I'd better see all of you tonight, and let's do this thing."

The entire room took to its feet as the band kicked into the school fight song. Callie refocused on the festivities as the cheerleaders and dance team formed four lines and began their versions of the accompanying dance. The football players took the opportunity to find their seats in the front row of bleachers that had been reserved for them.

Callie made it through the rest of the assembly without glancing down the row even though it killed her. If she and Bennett made eye contact at this point it would get awkward, plus she needed to focus on watching the girls perform today's routine—which they ended up nailing.

Eventually, after a student council skit and some random announcements from the principal, everyone stood and began to exit through the four sets of doors. Realizing that funneling this amount of people out of there would take a while, Callie focused on getting her bag together and then stood to find Eric in the chaos. She was grateful he'd wanted to come and support her at the first performance in front of the entire school. She knew the girls were good, but she'd still been incredibly nervous.

She felt a big hug from behind and smiled as Eric kissed her on the cheek and spun her around to face him.

"Amazing. The kicks were high as hell and in perfect sync. I'm impressed."

Callie beamed. "They did look fantastic, didn't they?

I'm so glad it's over. Now we just have to get through tonight's routine. I didn't think I'd be so nervous."

"You're a perfectionist, Callie Jo. Your only fault."

She squeezed Eric's hand; he was such a good friend to her.

"Speaking of perfection," Eric went on. "I'd heard Coach Clark was hot, but holy hell, he is a ten."

"You knew he was hot? Why didn't you tell me?" she asked in shock. Eric had been out on a date last night and he'd taken today off, so she hadn't been able to fill him in on the developments of the past twenty-four hours. "You will never believe this, but the principal wanted us to partner up for the Millard Country Club's dance fund-raiser competition."

"Seriously? Lucky girl." Eric grinned. "You should totally sleep with him. Then tell me everything."

"Shhh, good lord, Eric, can you scream that any louder?"

He shrugged. "It's noisy in here."

And it really was, hundreds of voices pinging off all the wooden surfaces as they lingered and waited for their turn to exit and start their weekend. "Anyway, it doesn't matter, because he said no."

"You're kidding? That sucks. I talked to Jill Monser in the parking lot just a few minutes ago and she mentioned the fund-raiser. I will admit your sexy coach looks a little too cavemannish to be into ballroom dancing. I got the feeling she was going to ask you to be part of it. Maybe you can dance with someone else."

Well, there was an idea, but suddenly the whole thing had sort of lost its appeal. "No, I think it's really for the best. This second job has already taken way too much of my time away from the shop, and I hate leaning so much on you and Emma."

"Don't worry about me, and if you haven't forgotten, you pay us both by the hour, so it's all good."

She was ready to thank him again when his eyes went wide and he grabbed her head with both hands and leaned down to kiss her just to the right of her lips.

"What the—ew." She grasped his biceps to keep from falling backwards under the weight of his sudden assault.

Eric just laughed and whispered against her cheek, "This should be interesting. Twelve o'clock; look breathless. I'll catch you later." He stepped past her and groped her butt as he did. Callie turned in shock and annoyance, her gaze landing on a very irritated-looking Bennett Clark. It almost looked like he'd been coming her way. Instead he turned and got lost in the crowd.

Four

Bennett winced in pain as he sat up in bed Saturday morning. They'd won the game last night, but being on his feet for nearly three hours had done a number on his leg. At least it hadn't been an away game. Those were the worst, he hated to travel. Whoever had invented the seats on school busses was evil, and Bennett suffered every time for it.

He grabbed some aspirin from the nightstand and downed them dry.

Saturday after a game was the one and only time Bennett took a break from the home gym in his basement. He was dedicated to staying in shape, keeping the muscles in his legs and hips strong and flexible, but this was his treat to himself. It was nice to just relax after the stress of Friday night football when he woke up feeling like he had a hangover. Once he was up and showered, he would be much better. At the very least, functional.

A fluffy head pushed at his hand until he conceded and stroked it. "Morning to you, too, Misha." His voice was raw from disuse, but Misha didn't mind, just rolled over onto her back so he could rub her white fluffy belly. After a moment the dog turned and stared up at him with black beady eyes.

Bennett still remembered Ashley bringing her over one day, not much bigger than a cotton ball. Ashley had named her Misha and said the dog was their first *fur-baby*. It was still hard to believe that the woman had left not only him but also Misha, whom she'd claimed to adore. But he couldn't complain. The dog had remained his constant companion through a lot of shit over the past eight years.

Bennett gritted his teeth as he stood, grasping his headboard to help pull himself up as a dull ache raced down the back of his thigh. A slight pause, then a deep breath, and he made his way to the shower. He turned the water to may-lose-a-layer-of-skin hot and let it beat on his body.

This shower—with its natural stone tile, six shower- and three rain heads—was one thing he'd never regret paying too much for. His favorite part was that there was no door; you just walked around a partial wall straight into heaven. It was a handful of things that he had left to show that at one time he'd made serious money, ridiculous money. And it had only lasted for one year.

Bennett tilted his head back and let the hot water pummel his face.

Following his father's guidance, Bennett had used most of that first year's pay to create a versatile investment portfolio. Thank god for his dad in that regard, because Bennett had turned out to need it more than he would have ever anticipated.

Being drafted to the NFL had been his dream. As any young athlete would, Bennett had assumed there were many years of multi-million-dollar salaries ahead of him. Didn't happen. But those investments had made it possible for him to take a normal-paying job that he wanted and still purchase and remodel this home out-right. Even left him with a nice cushion. Or, he hoped, retirement. Nothing crazy, but he couldn't complain.

After some time in the hot water, Bennett's muscles had turned to liquid and the steam had collected to the point that he probably wouldn't be able to see another human standing at the other end of the shower stall. That was okay, he had a good imagination, and right now his thoughts turned to picturing *her*. The complicated woman he'd been trying hard not to think about. And failing, because something else was hard all right.

In the shower her long blond curls would be wet, heavy against her full breasts. He imagined touching them, her nipples firm and slippery. Her lips would part as he let his hands run all over her body. She would moan and push herself against him, her slick, warm skin flush against his.

"Shit." Bennett swiped his hair back off his forehead. This was insane. *She* was insane. And she clearly had a boyfriend, which Bennett had found incredibly irritating. He'd really thought that maybe she'd been flirting with him a little in his classroom. The energy between them had been charged, and the way she'd smiled at him in the gym made him want to seek her out again.

It certainly wasn't the first time an unavailable woman flirted with him. Or maybe it had been so damn long he'd lost touch with what real flirting was.

He'd been able to forget about the troublesome woman during the game last night because there hadn't been time. Also because thoughts of women didn't belong in a man's head during a football game. He'd learned that lesson early on. But as soon as he'd gotten home and lain down, yep, there she'd been in his mind, taking up way more space than necessary, boyfriend be damned.

Turning off the water, Bennett grabbed a towel from the heated rack and ran it over his face and then his body, rubbing gently against the tenderness of his left leg and hip.

He had big plans for today, which included grading papers and spending some time with a heating pad, his favorite weekend routine every spring and fall when the pain got worse due to standing. If he was honest with his doctor about his lingering pains he would be recommended to continue physical therapy. Yeah, that wasn't happening. Not because he didn't see the value of therapy—he'd had plenty. In fact, he owed the fact that he walked as fast as he did to an amazing occupational therapist after his accident, but he didn't have time for that shit now. Plain and simple.

After dressing in some worn jeans and a dark-grey Henley, he went to the kitchen to let Misha outside. He grabbed a bottle of water out of the fridge and opened his laptop on the kitchen counter.

His home page was all sports and he quickly glanced through the highlights. He didn't maintain much contact with friends from his time as a player, but he still liked to keep track of how they were doing. His first year of coaching, an old friend had come to a Preston game when he was in town to play the Chiefs. He had caused quite a stir in the little town. Bennett still smiled when he thought about it.

He clicked to open his e-mail. Most of it was junk or things that could wait until Monday morning, but one email from the Missouri High School Football Coach Alliance caught his eye. It was about the Evan Award, and he inwardly groaned. He'd been nominated several times and never won. Bennett told himself it didn't matter, but it did rankle a little.

He couldn't quite figure out why they bypassed him every time, but they did. Principal Jensen seemed to think it was because Bennett didn't kiss enough people's asses, but that just wasn't his style. He worked hard at his job, he did the best he could for his guys and his coaches, and he made them into damn fine football players. He also made sure they did well in school and were upstanding members of the community. If that wasn't good enough, then fuck 'em.

He skimmed through the e-mail until he got to the heading "NEW FOR THIS YEAR'S EVAN AWARD WINNER."

We are happy to announce that Baylor Ford Dealerships, Altman Grocers, and our own Board of Directors have generously come together to offer our Evan Award winner a $50,000 grant to disburse as scholarship money to his qualifying senior players.

Bennett couldn't believe what he was seeing. Fifty thousand dollars. He had six qualifying seniors. How amazing would it be to hand them each eight thousand dollars to take to college? It wouldn't cover a full education of course, but it would get them headed in the right direction. Give them hope. And damn if he didn't know a couple of those boys who needed some financial hope.

Bennett stared down at the counter, contemplating. He'd never before had an incentive to win the Evan. He didn't need a trophy or even the title. Didn't give a shit about things like that. But damn, when it came to helping his guys out, that was something else.

He glanced back down at the donors. *Altman Grocers*. They were a regional chain, but he knew for a fact the owner lived in the next town over. Bennett had even taught one of his daughters three years ago. A million thoughts traveled through Bennett's brain at once.

He opened a new Internet window and typed "Millard Country Club board" into the search bar. He clicked on the first link, scanned through some bullshit, and then he saw it. Sure enough, Dan Altman was a member of the club.

Bennett shut the laptop and sucked in a breath.

It was official; he had to win that Evan Award, dammit. What could he do to guarantee a win? He closed his eyes and pictured Callie strutting out of his classroom, so confident. He remembered how certain she'd been that she could win the dance competition.

Didn't she know nothing was certain?

Jensen could be wrong about the entire thing. Bennett could make a fool of himself in front of a room full of rich bastards all for nothing. But damn, he would enjoy putting his hands on Callie Daniels in the process.

Now all he had to do was let her know that the game was back on.

Callie slid a piece of caramelized onion, chicken, and goat cheese pizza onto her plate and took a long drink of her strawberry wheat beer. Heaven. Complete and utter bliss. It was Sunday evening and she, Lindsey Morales, and Anne Edmond had just toasted to another month of plans finalized for the *My Perfect Little Life* blog.

Anne was the official creator and owner, but Callie and Lindsey each posted about twice a week as permanent contributors and the truth was, Anne made them all feel ownership. That was just her style, one of the many things Callie adored about her friend.

Recently they'd taken to meeting at the local pizza and brewpub, Pie Mia, and Callie loved this time with them where they could just reconnect, support one another, and be creative.

Also overindulge.

"I seriously think I could eat this every day of my life," Callie said as she held the pizza up to her lips. "Who needs a man when this pizza and strawberry beer are available?"

"Hear, hear." Lindsey took her own bite, her eyes nearly rolling back in her head.

"Not sure if I could eat it quite every day, but certainly once a week," Anne said with a wink. "But definitely never in place of a man."

Callie let her pizza droop from her fingers as she gave Anne a wry look. "Anne, since you have a big sexy man at your house as we speak, probably doing something disgustingly precious like making your daughter a grilled-cheese sandwich or reading her a book, you automatically forfeit your right to add to the *man situation* banter." Callie punctuated her statement with a big bite and then continued, mouth full. "I'm happy for you and all; I'm just sayin', we're no longer interested in your opinion regarding men."

Anne just laughed and took a bite of her own pizza, a tiny moan escaping her lips. "It is so good, though, you're right. Maybe twice a week."

"So, speaking of man situations." Callie sat back and eyed Anne. "How long till the guy just moves in with you?"

"Oh no, he wouldn't do that because of Claire." Anne shook her head. "He's made a few little hints at marriage, but we haven't had an official conversation. It's only been about four months. We're happy right now, so I'm certainly not going to push."

Callie had a feeling Anne was probably right. Mike Everett had a way of doing the right thing, especially when it came to Anne's daughter. How could you not like a guy like that? A man who put your needs above everything else? Callie had never had that; she'd always specialized in attracting selfish dickheads.

Callie listened in silence for a while as Anne and Lindsey talked about children. Lindsey's sister was pregnant with her first child and Anne was helping to plan a big baby shower for her. The whole process and planning had been showcased on the blog and the shower was in a few weeks. Discussing babies always left Callie a little melancholy. It wasn't that she wanted children; her biological clock hadn't even been wound yet, so it was nowhere near a countdown. She wasn't dying for a man either. She considered herself independent, and she had strong opinions on who the ideal mate would be—she'd decided he didn't exist. But sometimes the gushy stories of love and babies just made her feel a little lonely.

Yeah, she had her mom and dad, but that didn't really count. Neither did her best friends. There was just something about having someone to call your own that sometimes appealed to her. Someone to come home to. It was almost hard to picture.

She didn't want a relationship like her parents'. They seemed happy, but Callie didn't want a man who saw her as an assistant. She wanted to be her own person. She wanted her and the man to be partners. She couldn't function without someone who respected her as his equal.

With a sigh Callie motioned for another beer from the server and took her third slice of pizza. She was only twenty-eight; it wasn't like it was too late for her. Plenty of friends from college still weren't married. But then again . . . the ones who were seemed a lot happier. She saw them on Facebook, beautiful weddings, new houses and new babies. Eric was always telling her she was afraid, and while she would never admit it, he might be a little right. Afraid of feeling helpless and vulnerable. She worked hard and she took care of herself.

"Ooh, guess what?" Anne's eyes went big and round. "I can't believe I forgot to tell you. The new Junior League president is Jill Monser. They are mixing their fund-raiser this year with the Millard and she called Friday morning to see if I'd be interested in emceeing, and get this . . ."

Callie tensed. She knew exactly what was coming.

Anne continued. "They're doing their own version of *Celebrity Dance Off*. It will be their first event after the remodel from the flood. How fun does that sound?"

"Oh, Callie." Lindsey's eyes shone with excitement. "You should do that. You would be so good. It would be like your ultimate fantasy."

The three of them enjoyed watching the real *Celebrity Dance Off* together on television; in fact, they were looking forward to the premiere next Monday evening. Big plans had been made to meet at Anne's house and eat lots of unhealthy food while they feasted their eyes on their favorite dancers. As much as Callie loved the show, the thought of the Preston version only added to her slightly bitter mood.

"As a matter of fact, I was already asked to participate, but it didn't quite work out."

"Oh no, how come?" Anne sounded genuinely worried. "Jill had hinted none too subtly that she really hoped you would dance. She was a Crimson girl at KU, you know."

Callie stifled an eye roll. "She's told me. Many times. Expects Jessica to follow in her Jimmy Choo–clad footsteps and become a Rock Chalk Dancer."

Anne gave Callie a knowing smile. "I'm sure. So why didn't it work out?"

Callie gave them a very brief rundown of her visit with Jensen and subsequent conversation in Coach Clark's classroom.

Lindsey took a drink of her beer and then tilted her head, her long brunette hair slipping over her shoulder. "He's hot, isn't he?"

"What?" Callie was befuddled. "Why would you say that?"

Lindsey and Anne looked at each other and then Anne spoke with a shrug. "You just had this . . . look. And your tone. I caught it, too. The whole story was laced with interesting tension."

Callie just chuckled. "You guys are crazy. I mean, is Coach Bennett hot? Um . . . yes. Does it matter? No, because he's a dick. So there."

Callie tucked back into her dinner, not meeting the eyes of her friends, although she could feel them on her. How had they read her so easily? Interesting tension? No, it had definitely been angry tension. Sexual angry tension, maybe. *So what.*

Unable to handle the weight of their stares and the awkward silence any longer, she dropped her pizza on her plate. "What?"

Lindsey bit at her bottom lip, clearly holding back a laugh. "Nothing."

"It's really too bad he said no," Anne said. "It would be such great publicity for the bakery."

Huh. Callie hadn't thought of that. The incentives for this thing were certainly piling up. Too bad it was never going to happen. "No biggie; the business has been steadily growing."

"You could find a different partner," Lindsey said. "Maybe Eric would dance with you."

"He would if I begged, but no, it's really for the best."

She'd thought several times about that little smile she'd shared with Bennett at the Pep Assembly and couldn't help but wonder if he had any regrets over turning down her offer.

She guessed not a one.

Five

Bennett had been standing in the gym doorway watching her for five minutes. She hummed the music to herself while she danced. It wasn't an all-out performance; she was obviously working through a routine, her movements quick and incomplete. But good lord, she was turning him on. The way her stomach shifted and her hips moved. She clearly knew what she was doing, her body moving effortlessly.

He glanced at the clock and realized he was running out of time to speak with her alone and entered the room.

Bennett was halfway across the gym when she turned and saw him. She gasped mid-spin and nearly fell.

"Sorry," he said as she quickly collected herself. "I should have spoken."

"You think?" She widened her stance and swiped a curl from her eyes before locking her hands on her hips. A defensive position. Point taken.

Callie was slightly out of breath from dancing, her chest rising, pushing her black tank top toward him with each inhale. He forced himself not to let his eyes wander south; he'd spent enough time admiring her tight-as-hell pants from the doorway.

"Do you need something?" She obviously wanted to get this conversation over with. Well, that made two of them. Sort of. He found that he sort of enjoyed being near her.

"I do." He glanced toward the bleachers. "Can we sit?"

She stared at him for a second, obviously trying to figure him out. "Sure. Come into my office."

She walked over to where her bag and a stereo system sat on the front bleacher and plopped down. He sat beside her as she grabbed a water bottle and took a long drink. He didn't sit too close, but near enough, and even with that slight sheen on her skin she smelled delicious. Like a piece of fruit mixed with vanilla ice cream.

She finally let out a deep sigh and looked at him. "Do you need a prompt?"

He chuckled, partly out of nerves, another part out of this ridiculous attraction he was feeling, but also because she was just adorably funny. "No. I came here because . . . well, first I want to apologize for Friday. I don't usually behave like an ass."

She looked genuinely surprised but quickly pulled herself together. "Apology accepted. I guess I'm sorry also. I was *slightly* out of line."

She gave him a little wink, which did nothing to calm his nerves. He scratched at the back of his neck, unsure of what to do with his hands. "There's something else. I can't believe I'm about to say this, but I'd like you to reconsider."

Her expression didn't change for a long moment; she

just looked at him, her eyes narrowed. Finally, when he was close to getting up, she spoke. "Why?"

"Like you mentioned Friday. I'm hoping it will increase my odds of winning the Evan Award."

"You said it wasn't that important to you."

"It still isn't . . . for my own sake. But things have changed this year. If I win, it could help my players, and for that it's worth it."

"Help them how?"

"Well. Apparently this year the winner of the award is given fifty thousand dollars to disburse as scholarship money to his senior players going to college."

Her eyes widened and she stared at him thoughtfully for a long moment. He wondered what she was thinking. "That's really nice. Sounds like a good motivator. You're a good guy, Coach Clark. I don't know much about coaching football, but I think you deserve to win an award."

"I don't *deserve* anything, but I'd like to try." Damn, her words warmed his insides. People congratulated him on wins all the time, told him he did a good job, cheered for him. But something about this woman's honesty made him feel genuine pride while at the same time a desire to be even better.

He swallowed hard as she took another long drink and turned to face him, looping one foot over the seat so she could straddle the bleacher. Bennett squeezed his fists together, forcing himself not to look at her legs spread like that. It would be obvious and ungentlemanly.

"So this is official? We're doing this?" she asked.

"If you're willing."

"I wasn't lying when I said how busy I was. But I am willing."

He nodded his head. "Okay. Good. I'm glad."

"Want to know a secret?" she said, a mischievous smile playing at her lips.

"Sure."

"I was a tiny little bit disappointed when you said no."

"Huh." He smiled down at his hands. Her admission surprised and pleased him, and he considered his next question for a moment. "Will your boyfriend be okay with this?"

She laughed. "First off, I don't have a boyfriend. And second, if I did I wouldn't need his permission."

Relief settled into Bennett's bones. "I just thought—"

"If you thought the guy from Friday was mine, I can assure you that's nothing. If I recall, he was wearing his favorite T-shirt that day. It says: 'My Boyfriend Is Cuter than Yours.'"

It all made sense now. "Well, I guess you can't get any clearer than that."

She gave him her full smile and the only thought that registered was how beautiful she was. Her confidence was real and refreshing, and he was suddenly really glad he'd made this decision.

"One thing we probably *should* get clear is that if we're gonna win this, we have to do things my way. I know dance and I know how to win."

He scoffed. "Not that I doubt you, but you know, I do have a few wins under my belt as well."

She pulled a face. "This ain't football, big boy. This is dance."

"I'm sure if we compared notes we'd find that they have some things in common."

She considered him for a moment. "Maybe. Would you consider dance a sport?"

He shrugged. "Sure. It involves physical skill, dedication, training."

The corner of her mouth lifted a bit. "Good answer, Coach."

"Am I being tested?"

"What if you were?"

"Then I'd want to pass. And I'd insist on equal play." He considered his own question. "Do you believe winning is everything?"

Her lips tightened, but she didn't look away. "No. Working your ass off, finishing with dignity, and respecting your team is everything."

"Nice. I would agree," he replied.

"My turn." She tilted her head to the side. "Would you date a woman that made more money than you?"

He was surprised and it probably showed on his face. "I guess, although I'm not sure why that's relevant." Did she want it to be?

She shrugged. "It's not, really."

"Okay, my turn. Are you glad I didn't turn out to be twenty years older?"

She bit at her lip, considering her answer. "Talk about irrelevant."

"Is it? I don't know." He wanted to tease her; in fact, he was sort of missing the charge from their last heated discussion. He liked her scrappy side. It made him want to see her when she finally let her guard down fully.

"Honestly? And I'm a very honest woman, by the

way. But yes. I was very happy to find that you were not some feeble old guy."

Bennett froze. *Feeble.* He wasn't quite there, but he was far from 100 percent. In fact, he wasn't looking forward to the physicality of dancing. But he wouldn't let her know that. He cleared his throat before he spoke, intent on changing the subject. "Last question. Did you really just call me big boy a few minutes ago?"

She laughed, throwing her head back, the column of her neck glistening with perspiration and begging for attention. She was so uninhibited, so free. *Happy.* Even when she was giving him her smart mouth she did it with relish. This girl was passionate and he found himself laughing along with her.

She let out a breathy sigh, staring into his eyes. "I did call you that. You're big. You're a boy. Only seems appropriate."

He knew their time was limited, but he wanted to keep her talking. "You should know, you'll have your work cut out for you. I won't be good at dancing. And if *I'm* being honest, I really am not looking forward to it," he said.

She tilted her head to the side. They locked eyes again; hers were so blue, so knowing, as if she could read his thoughts. "If you give me everything—and trust me—it will be fine."

He swallowed, the depth of her words hitting him hard. She didn't look away, clearly waiting for his answer. "When it comes to this? I can do that."

She nodded, clearly satisfied with his response. "Well, we should get started as soon as possible."

Without thinking he said, "We can start tonight."

"You're eager; I like it. However, I do have to come up with a routine."

"How long do you need?"

"A few days. I think I have an idea already."

"How about Thursday night? You can come to my place," he said.

"You sure? I mean, I could probably arrange for us to come here."

He shook his head. "No, my property is secluded. If I'm gonna make a fool of myself I don't want witnesses."

"Also sounds like a good place for you to murder me and hide my body." She grinned at him.

"I never considered it, but yeah, it would be good for that, too."

They laughed together for a moment—something he was suddenly realizing he didn't do all that often, certainly not with a woman, but she was so easy to be around. They fell quiet and he decided he should go before things got awkward. "I guess I'll see you Thursday."

"Okay. Are you going to tell me how to get there?"

"Oh yeah." He glanced around, looking for something to write on; instead, she held up her phone.

"Why don't you just text it to me? That way I can call you if I get lost."

He nodded and pulled his phone out of his pocket, and she quickly begin to rattle off her number. That was easy. He typed out his address, hit send, and waited until she received it.

"Perfect. Thursday it is." She squeezed his arm, her touch shocking and soothing him at the same time. "Stop worrying, Coach. This will be great, and the best part is that whether you like it or not, you're going to love hanging out with me."

That was certain, because he already did.

At a quarter till seven Callie turned off the highway and onto Buckle Road. A wooden sign announcing the neighborhood, Oak Hill, sat off to the side. She'd seen it several times but never driven up. In fact, she was shocked this was where Bennett lived. With its mani-cured lawns and estate-sized homes, Oak Hill was pop-ular with the country club crowd and the tastefully rich. Definitely not the place a public school teacher lived, but who was she to judge? Bennett *had* played for the NFL at one time, so maybe he had some money.

She was still a little surprised about his sudden change of heart. He'd seemed so certain in his classroom that day, but the fact that it had to do with his players made sense. From what she could tell he was incredi-bly dedicated to them. It was kind of sexy to see a man be so passionate about something. The fact that it was teenagers was even more adorable. She could also re-late to that. Even in such a short time as dance coach she already had such immense pride and connection with her girls.

She also liked to think that he wanted to dance with her—even if it was just a little bit—because she was ex-cited to dance with him. The past two nights she'd been up late, tweaking a routine she'd done in college and making it work for this competition. It was fairly easy, a little bit sensual, and of course lovely. Now all she had to do was keep her body in check while she put her hands on this sexy beast of a man. No big deal.

Callie rolled down her window, loving the crisp scent of the air and the sound of the trees' rustling in the breeze. This was the best time of year, late summer with just a hint of the chill to come.

Large houses dotted the fields and the trees thickened as the road began to wind up the hill. After a minute or so she realized she hadn't seen another house in the last half mile. Bennett had said his was the last one on the right; had she missed it? She decided to go a little farther and finally spotted another house nestled among several oak trees. So she really had been right on the mark with the secluded enough to murder someone jab.

She pulled into the long driveway, and her mouth dropped open as the home came into view. It was gorgeous. Not massive, but beautiful, with brick and stucco. A large wrought-iron door was bracketed by several low-pitched gables on the roof. The landscaping was well maintained and three garages took up almost as much of the front façade as the rest of the house. One of the garage doors opened as she pulled up and parked on the cement pad out front.

As the door lifted, a small white fur ball of a dog darted out to Callie's car, yapping all the way. She smiled as she opened her door, the little dog pushing her nose in to bark at her.

"Well, look at you," she cooed, leaning down to scratch the dog's little white head. "You're about the sweetest little thing I ever saw."

She was fairly certain the dog was a Maltese; a friend of hers had one growing up. As show dogs they had long white hair that hung to the ground, but this one was cut in an adorable little puppy cut save one tiny fountain of longer hair on the top of her head. Callie looked closer and saw that it was adorned by a blue bow dotted with tiny footballs.

She felt Bennett's presence even before she looked up and saw him watching her pet his dog. She stepped from the car and smiled at him.

"I'm quite shocked, yet another surprise from you, Coach Clark. Does your team know that you have a sweet little bow-wearing pocket dog up here for a companion?"

He stuffed his hands in his pockets. He was wearing a long-sleeved T-shirt and sport pants. "They do. She sometimes comes to summer practices. And the guys have camped up here several times. She gets lots of attention."

"I bet she does." Callie leaned down and gave the little dog one more scratch behind her ears, trying hard not to imagine cuddling against Bennett's large, naked body in a tent. An amazing visual, but a bad idea. If for no other reason than she refused to be the next dance coach in line to be reckless in the man department. "What's her name?"

He looked a little bashful and then muttered, "Misha."

"*Misha*? Oh my." Callie laughed out loud. "It just keeps getting better, doesn't it?" Her last words were directed at Misha herself, who jumped up and rested two tiny paws on Callie's knees.

"You obviously take her grooming very seriously," Callie teased. "I love your taste in bows."

Bennett sighed. "One of my players from a few years ago's mother is a groomer in town. She hooks us up. Misha has a standing biweekly appointment."

Callie could tell that he was having fun with the conversation, and she liked that he wasn't above talking about his girly dog.

"That is really adorable, Coach Clark. If you're not careful I might start liking you."

The looked at each other for a moment before Bennett finally nodded down at Misha.

"*She* obviously likes you," he said.

"She is much better with first impressions than her grumpy owner. Misha can tell right away that I'm completely likable."

"I've never had a problem finding you likable, Coach Daniels." His voice was low, almost as if he'd rather she hadn't heard the comment.

She met his eyes—*oh, I heard you all right*. She wondered what *likable* meant to him, but whatever it was, the sound of his voice and the look on his face had her stomach clenching. She didn't want to make him uncomfortable before they even got started, so she decided it best to change the subject. "So should we get on with things?"

He turned and began to lead her through the garage and into the house. "You hungry? I made a little something. If you're not, no big deal, but I hadn't eaten."

Matter of fact, she was starving, and the second she entered the house a hunger pang struck in reaction to the incredible scent. She could detect garlic and basil, and it was like walking into an Italian restaurant.

"Oh my gosh, Bennett. It smells amazing." She couldn't see his reaction as she followed his beautifully wide shoulders down a narrow hallway.

His body was so large and muscular, it now made

sense that he'd been a pro football player; he was made like one. And he'd managed to maintain his physique years after. Even through his shirt she could tell that his back would be well formed. The way he walked was sexy, straight and confident, gait smooth. She loved how his hair was neatly trimmed short on the back of his neck. His butt was firm and tight, moving perfectly with each stride. Good lord, if Eric were here he'd have passed out by now. Callie smiled at the thought as she was led into the main part of the house.

It was as gorgeous as its owner.

The modern galley kitchen boasted high ceilings, dark wood, and stainless appliances. It was sparse but tastefully decorated with a big oak table at the end, surrounded by floor-length windows. Across an expansive island she could see a leather sectional lined up perfectly with a massive flat-screen television in the living room. It wasn't a huge house from what she could tell, but the amenities were top-of-the-line and the design was clean and masculine.

She was speechless as she walked over to the wall of windows, taking in the view. The scene was truly spectacular and the focus piece of the room. Callie could see for miles, looking down at the entire valley where Preston was nestled, the subtle changes of the coming autumn spread out before her like a warm patchwork quilt. "This view is incredible."

"Isn't it? Pretty much why I bought this house." His voice wasn't nearby and for some reason she'd hoped it would be. Suddenly, with this brilliant picture before her, she wanted to plaster herself to the glass and feel him lean into her; how wonderful would that be?

Stupid, she mouthed to herself. Her warm breath left a small foggy patch on the window and she quickly rubbed it off with her sleeve, hoping he wouldn't notice.

She turned around to find him in the kitchen dishing up food onto a plate. He dropped Misha a piece of something, which Callie found adorable. She walked to the other side of the bar that connected the kitchen and living area and leaned against it. "How long have you lived here?"

"About six years. Since right after I got hired at Preston High."

She wanted to ask him more about his past but didn't get the sense that he'd be open to that. He saved an awkward pause by setting down a plate in front of her. "Wow, you know, I never expected dinner. This is very nice." *And oddly romantic.*

"No big deal."

"Well, you're wrong. No one ever cooks for me, and this is . . . fancy." Sautéed vegetables, chicken, and pasta were tossed with a light cream sauce. A dusting of Parmesan cheese was on top.

Callie sat down at the counter and he came around to join her with his own plate. "This is not fancy. I enjoy cooking, it's dinnertime, and like I said . . . no big deal."

"A man that likes to cook? I'm sure you're not hurting for dates," she joked, even though the thought was a little irritating. And he was wrong; this was so not *no big deal.* When he was settled she took a bite of her pasta, and her shoulders slumped as she tasted it. It was pure ecstasy. Creamy, a little spicy, and the chicken cooked perfectly. "Holy crap, Bennett, this is so good."

She looked over and caught him glancing at her from the corner of his eye. "I'm glad you like it. I don't usually use cream, but . . . I just thought you would enjoy it."

"Well, good call. Everything is better with dairy." She couldn't help thinking that was the sweetest thing. He'd used cream just for her.

They ate for a few minutes in silence until he spoke again. "You want some wine?" He gestured at an open bottle near the stove. "I used a little for the pasta, but you can have some if you want."

"Do I sense a hidden agenda?" she teased.

"Absolutely not. I just thought you might be thirsty." He looked genuinely discomfited by her choice of words.

"Calm down; I was kidding." She made her way around to the bottle and he told her where she could find a glass.

When she got a second one out he shook his head. "None for me."

"You sure? Pasta and wine are two of my favorite food groups."

He gave her a small smile. "I don't really drink."

"Oh, okay. Well, then I don't have to either."

"No, please . . ."

She shushed him as she put the wineglass back in the cabinet and pulled out pint glasses. "I don't need wine. Besides, like my very ineloquent mother always says, 'only drunks and stay-at-home-mothers drink alone,' and since I'm neither of those . . ."

Callie poured them each a glass of water and sat back down to finish her meal. Realizing that soon she was going to have her hands full of Bennett Clark, she began to feel flushed. She assumed that she'd have her work cut out for her, teaching this giant football player to be graceful, but now that she'd seen his little girly dog, his beautiful home, and his perfect skills in the kitchen, she didn't quite know what to expect. This man was many things, and she couldn't wait to see what other surprises were in store.

Torture was inevitable. Bravery was imperative, because brave was what he'd have to be very soon in order to get through this evening, holding her close and not letting his baser instincts take over. The same instincts that right now wanted him to thrust his hands into her hair and taste her lips. Just once. Maybe twice.

Not going to happen.

After giving Misha some water, Bennett began to rinse his and Callie's dishes in the sink, anything to avoid his impending doom. That might have explained the meal, a distraction. But also because he simply liked to cook. Felt he was good at it and stupidly had decided he should make her dinner. It pleased him immensely that she enjoyed it, and he loved how she kept him company in the kitchen as she stood by the stove picking vegetables straight out of the pan with her fingers.

Every once in a while she'd lick the sauce from her fingertips, which he tried not to focus on. Instead he listened to her as she went on and on and on about why she'd chosen the dance she did. A waltz. If he wasn't mistaken, two people danced very close in a waltz, but it wasn't necessarily sexy. Good. Very good; he didn't want sexy. He wasn't even capable of sexy dancing.

After she'd cleared the pan of every remaining

mushroom—interesting, he'd almost left them out since Ashley had hated them—he put it into the sink and began to scrub. He found himself stalling, washing it longer just to keep hearing Callie speak. The woman liked to talk and she was really funny. Open. Humble but also incredibly sure of herself. He'd never considered that so appealing, or maybe he'd never known a woman like her. Her personality was as attractive as she was.

After their first meeting, Bennett hadn't expected to be so comfortable with her. The teasing and bantering was still there, but Callie wasn't pushing or prodding at him. He'd dated a little over the years and found that many women thought stroking his ego was the way to go. They wanted him to talk about himself, about his time in the pros. Or they wanted to talk to him about him. How much they knew about his stats, how nice his house was. It was maddening and never ever felt genuine.

Not Callie. She was happy to chatter about anything and everything as she got herself some more ice from the refrigerator. She talked about her favorite dances, the girls on her team, how much she liked the digital display on his oven. She was just so easy to be around. Never once did she ask him uncomfortable questions or hint for information. He needed to remember that she wasn't trying to impress him and didn't have a hidden agenda. She wasn't into him, and this wasn't a date. She was doing him a favor.

Nothing more. And yet watching her laugh as she talked about the crappy oven in her duplex, he couldn't help thinking that maybe she liked spending time with him, too.

When the last dish was loaded and he'd started the washer, she walked into his living room and flopped down on the couch.

"So, we could practice in here to start, but it's a little tight. And a smooth floor would be better."

"There's the basement, or we could go outside."

"Let's do that. It's nice out and the driveway's big." She jumped up. Where did she get all of this energy? And why did it have to be so adorable?

He followed her out the front door and released a deep breath. He was about to well and truly put his hands on this woman, and on top of that he was starting to panic about his leg. It felt pretty good today, but he had no idea what this dancing would require. He'd decided not to go into it by telling her he was incapable; he wasn't interested in her babying him or making concessions. He could handle it, deal with the pain later. He'd been doing that for years, but experience told him he'd better pop the pain pills before he went to bed.

Bennett showed her to an outlet in the garage so she could plug in her little iPod speaker system. She kept a small remote in one hand and then grasped his finger with her other. He was surprised but let her lead him to the middle of the concrete drive. She let him go and then immediately got to business, her expression going serious.

"Okay. So I was thinking about the best way to go about this, considering you have no dancing experience. I think first I'll do the routine and let you watch, just to get a feel for it."

He nodded. "Okay, but how will you do it by yourself?"

"Well, obviously you'll have to use your imagination. I'll pretend I'm dancing with a partner." She gave him a wink.

He swallowed when she stepped close to him. Really close, her chest brushing against his. Yeah, he'd certainly be using his imagination all right. Now, tonight, in the shower, and probably every day for the next month. He really needed to get his thoughts in check or this was going to be a very uncomfortable practice.

She placed a palm on his cheek in a light caress and he froze. She didn't seem to notice or care, just kept on talking. "So this is how we'll start. I chose this song because it has a lot to offer as far as rhythm. It's six-eight time, but it also has a great upbeat that is perfect for making it a contemporary waltz mix. It will make it a little sexier and the judges and the audience will love that."

Bennett's eyes went wide. "Sexier? You sure that's a good idea?"

She laughed, low and throaty. "Sexiness is always a good idea in dancing. I have a feeling you'll be able to pull it off."

Was she implying that he was sexy? He wouldn't ask her to clarify, but he hoped that was it. Instead he made a joke. "I wish I was that confident in my dancing abilities."

"Have you watched the actual show *Celebrity Dance Off*?" she asked, but didn't wait for his answer, which would've been a firm no. "You really should. I love it, and the sexy factor is always high. At least in my favorite dances."

Good to know. This close her eyes sparkled and she

had the tiniest little freckles on her nose. She still had her hand on his cheek and it took all of his willpower not to lean into it as she spoke. "Okay. I trust you."

"Good. I'm going to go through my part so you get a feel for what the dance will look like in the end. So, watch what I do and relax. This will be fun."

He couldn't respond; suddenly he was past the point of nervous. He was downright scared shitless. Not only to see what was in store for him physically but also to dance in front of an audience. In front of her. Funny for a guy who had played football in front of thousands, but this was definitely nowhere near similar to running and throwing a ball through the air. This was supposed to be . . . pretty. Creative. And as she mentioned so nonchalantly . . . sexy. He was in serious trouble.

She shifted her hand on his jaw and the music started. He recognized the song right away, but his brain stopped thinking altogether when she ran her hand down his neck seductively and then bent her knees in front of him, palm sliding down his chest all the way to his stomach. She jerked back up suddenly, and before he could process her movements she spun away from him.

Her face jerked in his direction and she stared into his eyes for a moment before she spun back toward him, her chest flush against his. The song had a strong drum-beat that her body seemed to have memorized and she shifted back and forth against him, making him feel ridiculous for standing still. She only smiled at him before pushing off again into a spin.

He couldn't take his eyes off of her hips, her legs. Then her body leaned back as if someone were holding her. Would that be him? Oh shit, it would have to be.

He had to physically hold his mouth shut as she put her arms up to imitate how they would rest on him as she circled.

"This is where we transition into a traditional waltz," she said over the music.

He couldn't respond; instead he slowly pivoted around like a statue on a turntable, unable to take his eyes off her as she stepped around the driveway. Her feet moved so fast he could barely keep up.

"Don't worry, you'll learn the waltz steps; it will be easy."

Her feet went forward and back, side to side, and she turned this way and that. Suddenly she did several small steps backwards across the driveway. "This is where you would drag me across the floor," she said breathlessly.

"Drag you?" His words were a whisper and she didn't stop; she turned right, left, arms back up in waltzing position. Her expression was so serene as she moved fluidly around him. Oh god, there was no way in hell he would ever get this.

He watched for another moment, completely enthralled by her. She had those damn yoga pants on again, and he could see the muscles in her thighs working with each step. The movement of her ass was going to put him in a trance. He forced his eyes back up to her face.

"A lift right here? Step . . . step . . . step." She spun around a few more times. Had she just said "lift"? Bennett tried not to feel nauseous, the weight of his decision to dance with her hitting him full force.

She paused and bent back a little. "Death Drop there . . . and then back up. Step . . . step . . . step . . . together . . .

twinkle . . . half turn . . . turn out . . . walk under . . . step . . . step . . . step." She came close to him again, placing her hand once more on his face.

"And dip." She grabbed him on each shoulder and leaned back; he reacted instantly, gripping her waist as her spine arched, her head thrown back, exposing her neck to him. She laughed and then looked up, eyes on his. "You did it. The end."

He pulled her up with a jerk. "A warning would have been nice. I could have dropped you."

"I knew you wouldn't." Her chest rested against his, rising and falling with her deep breaths. "So what do you think?"

For a moment he couldn't speak at all, his thoughts lost in how beautiful she looked right now glancing up at him. Her smile began to fall a little at his lack of response. When she went to pull away he tightened his grip on her waist.

"It was . . . amazing, Callie. You were beautiful."

She stared at him for a moment, her lips lifting at the corners. He wanted to kiss her like this, his arms full of her warm body. Then it dawned on him that next time he would have to dance *with* her. She'd memorized all of that, which meant he'd have to do the same. And figure out how to do it without looking like a complete fool.

"I can't imagine me doing any of that," he said.

She grinned. "Well, luckily you have me. I've made it a little easier on you; I get to do most of the hard stuff."

Still didn't settle his nerves. Not at all.

"Relax, Coach Bennett. I can feel your stress from here, and I want you to know it's going to be fine."

He sighed, knowing that his tension was a lot more

than stress. He reluctantly let her pull away. "Okay, let's try and do this."

She situated his hands on her body exactly where she wanted them. One on her hip and the other snaking around her back near her breast. Gosh damn, this was going to be difficult in so many ways.

"I'm not going to start the music yet so I can teach you the first part. This is a waltz, so I'm going to count off in sets of six. Probably teach you six beats at a time. Now when I go down you need to watch me. Dancing tells a story. We have to make it believable. So look at my face and let your hand slide up to my temple as I go down."

She was going to fucking kill him. Like he'd need to pretend to look at her lustfully when she was kneeling in front of him and after saying things like "go down." But he did as she said, his fingers lingering near her hair as she let her hand slip down his chest and stomach. She counted the beat the whole way down. When she popped back up she jerked her head away and looked at the ground.

"Why'd you look away? I thought we were supposed to look at each other," Bennett said, confused and frustrated.

"I *did* say that, and usually we will look at each other, but sometimes I'll look away. It's all emotion, sensuous, flirty. You'll get the feel of it. Promise. Now you look down in the other direction and then I spin away. As soon as my foot taps out you jerk your hand out to spin me back. Ready . . . go."

He was already lost, watching in bewilderment as her body twirled away from him. "What?"

She sighed but smiled at him. A total teacher move, trying to be positive and not let frustration show. "Let's try it again." Her hand was on his face once more; then she was sliding, jerking, spinning. This time he managed to put his hand out, grab hers, and pull her body back into him, but he knew it was on the wrong beat.

They repeated the same thing for nearly twenty minutes and still hadn't moved past those first twelve beats. The only thing he'd mastered was when to look away.

"Why don't we try it with the music, might help you to feel it." She put them into position again, her fingers on his cheek, his hands on her hips. "I'll count six beats off when it starts and then I'll began to slip down on the second one. So basically we don't start moving until the second measure."

He nodded, barely understanding what she meant.

She pointed the remote over his shoulder. The jazzy rhythm began and then she was counting. "One two three four five six, one two three four five six, look away, two three."

She stopped and killed the music. "Okay, let's try that intro again."

They did it about six more times. Then seven. By the tenth time her fingers trailing down his chest no longer felt sexy. He was irritated. He was pretty certain he was off beat every time, and the look on her face said she agreed. They moved on to the next part, where she spun away and he pulled her back. He would need years to get this entire dance right.

"Okay, good. Why don't we call it a night at that? I've thrown a lot at you and it takes some time to sink in," she said.

"We haven't gotten very far."

Her smile was tight. "It's an intense process. Doesn't really make sense to proceed until we get one part down. How about I come back Saturday?"

He thought about what he had going on, which was ridiculous because he knew damn well the answer was nothing. They had an away game tomorrow night, so he'd probably be sore, but there was nothing to be done for it except deal. "Okay. How about that afternoon. Like two or three."

"Can't do that early. My shop closes at five. How about six?"

"Okay, that's fine." He definitely didn't have Saturday night plans.

"You mind if I just leave the stereo here?" she asked.

"Yeah, sure. Might as well."

He watched as she picked up her stuff, patted Misha on the head, and then looked back at him. "Well, good job, Coach Clark. I'll make a winning dancer out of you yet."

She gave him a wink and then headed for her car. The mood had changed dramatically from when she'd arrived. God damn, he felt stupid. He knew what she was thinking right now, that she'd gotten herself into a mess by agreeing to be his dance partner. He didn't like to fail at things and he sure as hell didn't like to do it in front of a beautiful woman.

She waved over her steering wheel as she backed out and he did the same. One thing was clear: this was going to be hell. He was in store for a lot of hard work, and football season was not the right time for distractions. Maybe he'd made a mistake. He owed all of his attention to his guys and his assistant coaches. Between learning to dance and trying to keep his mind off his partner he was in trouble. Of course that might get easier after every practice. Turns out there was nothing sexy about dancing and after his horrible performance tonight he could only hope that she didn't decide he wasn't worth the time.

Callie placed the final pink cupcake into the giant box and gently shut the lid just as Lindsey came through the swinging kitchen door of Callie's Confections.

"Happy baby shower day," Callie said.

"I'm so ready for it to be over," Lindsey said. "I love Mel, but she's been so high maintenance lately. Is that normal for pregnant women?"

"I have no experience with pregnant women, but it sounds about right. If I was pregnant I'd want everyone taking care of me," Callie said with a grin. "When is she due again?"

"Thanksgiving Day."

"Seriously? That's funny. So you may be eating your turkey dinner in the hospital cafeteria."

"Oh no, she's having a home birth." Lindsey popped open the cupcake box and peeked inside.

"Home birth?" Callie asked. "Why would she do that?"

Lindsey shrugged. "It's kind of a thing these days, I guess. They have a midwife all lined up and everything. Of course if they felt they needed to, they'd go to a hospital."

"That sounds terrifying. Then again, giving birth period sounds terrifying."

"These are beautiful and they smell delicious," Lindsey said as she inhaled deep.

"I hope everyone enjoys them." Callie nodded to a box against the wall. "I loaded up all of the cake plates for you to display them on. I'll carry them out for you."

"Thanks for doing that. I can't wait to put all of the decorations out."

Callie had no doubt it would be beautiful. Anne and Lindsey had collaborated on the shower for Lindsey's sister, so there was no way it wouldn't be gorgeous. Between Anne's organizational and party-planning skills and Lindsey's ability to make anything look beautiful, Mel and her friends were in for a treat.

"Wish I could come. Between work and dance practice I don't think I'd have time."

"That's okay. You don't really know Mel and I totally understand. How is dance practice going? Is the coach getting the hang of it?"

Callie sighed. "Our first time was Thursday. Let's just say I underestimated what it would take to make this happen."

"That bad, huh?" Lindsey winced.

Callie put her hand on her hip. "I really don't understand how some people can't hear a rhythm. I mean, doesn't your body naturally *feel* it?"

"I think it's like anything else: For some people it comes naturally. For some it doesn't. Like creativity or athletics. I can't hit a baseball to save my life. Some people can't match colors together."

"God, you're right." Lindsey was so good at seeing things positively. She was a total peacekeeper and tended to make Callie feel overdramatic. "I really had to force myself from freaking out on him. It was just so irritating, I mean, I was teaching him the easiest part and he looked so clueless."

Lindsey gave her an understanding smile. "I have faith in you. I'm sure he's frustrated, too. Maybe try a new angle. There's more than one way to skin a cat."

"Gross. But a good idea." Callie reached over and picked up the box. "Let's get your car loaded up."

At closing time Callie rushed home to take a quick shower—sans hair wash, her curls would look crazy if she didn't take the time to style them—and then shuffled through her dresser. She'd had trouble moving correctly in her tennis shoes, so she donned her black Capri leggings, a tank top, and her nude T-strap character heels. Once her hair was in a ponytail she grabbed her favorite studio jacket and headed out to Bennett's house.

The sun had been warm that afternoon, the sky a deep blue, and she had a good feeling about today. Lindsey was right—as she so often was—that Callie just needed to be cool and try something new. She wasn't quite sure what that was yet, but it would come to her. Anyone was teachable. She hoped.

She repeated that to herself as she pulled into Bennett's driveway. The garage door was open, but he wasn't outside, so she went up to the front door and rang the bell. Misha's yapping could be heard from the other side.

A moment later he opened and immediately Misha dashed out and put her paws up on Callie's legs just as she'd done before. Callie rubbed behind the dog's ears. "Hello again, sweet thing."

When Callie stood up straight she met eyes with

Bennett. He looked tired, but he gave her a tight smile. "Hey."

"Hi, you ready? I'm feeling good about today." She grinned. Best to start throwing the optimism and positivity out early, she figured.

He nodded. They could do this. She glanced at his athletic shorts and sweatshirt. Gracious, the man looked hot in anything he had on. His legs were incredibly muscular, as if he still trained as a professional.

"You must have a gym in there, Hercules."

He looked surprised at her comment but smiled as he followed her gaze down to his calves. "I do. It's in the basement."

"Nice. Let's teach those sexy legs how to dance."

He shook his head and followed her out to the driveway. "We can try. Last time was brutal. I was betting you might not even come back."

She turned and put a finger into his firm chest. "From this point on we only think positive thoughts, Bennett. Got me? And I can't believe you doubted me."

"I know that I was terrible."

"Yeah, you kind of were. But that's normal. When's the last time you took a dance class, Coach Clark?"

He gave her a hooded stare.

"Exactly, so don't be so hard on yourself." She picked up her remote off the garage floor and met him in the middle of the driveway. "I know this isn't easy, but we'll get there. Trust me."

"Trying," he said, but she wasn't entirely convinced. He already sounded defeated, which wasn't really a good sign, but she couldn't really blame him. If he'd been trying to teach her football she would feel the same way.

They got to work, starting where they'd left off last time, which was, unfortunately, at the beginning. She had them do it a few times without the music, and to her delight he remembered everything.

"Good! Maybe it just needed to marinate, huh?" She laughed. "Okay, with the music this time."

A half hour flew by as they repeated the intro over and over. Callie was sick of counting but delighted with their small progress. She took a long drink of water and then clapped her hands together. "Okay, let's move on to the next part. After you pull me back from your left side we're going to do a similar motion toward your front."

She started to go through the motions as he watched. "I'll do it again; watch me."

"I haven't quit watching." His words were clipped. She stopped and looked at him.

Her eyes softened and she blew out a breath. "Okay, listen. Let's try a different approach. I should have warmed you up first."

That sounded like a bad idea, Bennett thought to himself as Callie circled him. He'd done okay on the first part. He'd actually spent an hour before she got there practicing on his own and he was already sore. And frustrated.

When she finally stood facing him once more, she lifted his left hand and slipped her right one into it, grasping firmly. Holding their joined hands out to the side, she gently laid her left hand on his shoulder. "Now grasp my waist, ballroom-style."

He hesitantly did what he assumed she meant. "I've never ballroom danced in my life."

"Well, you are today." She reached down and adjusted his hand to sit lower on her back, closer to where her body curved. She stepped into him, her head resting just under his chin.

The scent of her shampoo and the feel of her breasts pressed against him made him feel dizzy, but her nearness caused some of his tension to lessen.

She swayed back and forth for a moment and his feet shuffled along with her, trying to keep up with the rhythm. Damn, he couldn't even get this right. But it felt nice.

"I should have done this Thursday," she said. The feel of her words rumbled against his chest. "We just need to get used to the feel of each other."

Yeah, he wasn't sure if he agreed with that. He definitely shouldn't get used to this, because if she had any idea what he was feeling she would see the danger in what they were doing.

The music came on again and she began to count, moving from side to side, pulling him along with her. Reluctantly he tried to relax, as much as could be expected, considering their bodies rubbed together with nearly every movement.

"Sway on the down beat, the one, and then again on the four." She dipped more dramatically from side to side to show him what she meant. This had to be as basic as dancing got, which was humiliating. He hadn't danced like this since middle school.

But he liked it, being this close. Eventually he loosened up, his arms relaxing, legs finding the rhythm. He finally began to pull her body with his. Back and forth, back and forth. He even managed to turn them as he did so.

"Look at you," she said. He could hear the smile in her voice, which made him smile in response. "Eventually you'll just feel the beat inside you. Do you feel it now?"

"I feel something," he bit out.

She gasped and stared up at him, mouth hanging open. "Are you being dirty, Coach Clark?"

"Won't happen again."

"I should hope not," she teased. But he saw a hint of something more in her eyes. He chuckled and prayed to the Gods of Unwelcome Boners to grant him mercy as she leaned back into position and resumed counting.

The sun was low, easing into a golden dusk. Crickets and cicadas filled the trees around them, and the scent of the air was a heady mix of nature and woman.

"This isn't so bad, is it?" she asked quietly.

"No, this is pretty good." If you didn't consider the warmth of her small hand on his shoulder, the softness of her skin where one of his fingers brushed under her hoodie, and the feel of her chest brushing his. No, it wasn't so bad. It was torture, just as he knew it would be.

Six

A week ago Callie would have argued any person into the ground that the best smell in the whole entire world was that of chocolate chip cookies baking in the oven. *Her* cookies if you wanted to be specific, and they smelled pretty good right now as she removed a tray from the oven and took a big whiff.

Last night, however, she'd realized there was something else that could compete for the best smell ever. Bennett Clark. After leaving his house, she'd gone to sleep with her hoodie just so she could dream with the light scent of him lingering. It wasn't anything out of the ordinary, a touch of laundry detergent with an earthy aftershave chaser. But it made her think of being in his arms. Stupid, but she couldn't help it.

Practice had gone better and she'd been happy to see him loosen up a little. They'd spent some time walking around to six-eight time just so he could continue to get a feel for it. There was still a long ways to go and the hardest part was still to come, but she felt much more optimistic today and she hoped he did, too.

The best part was that last night had been fun. There was no denying the man was pure eye candy and that made things enjoyable for sure. But it was more than that, something she couldn't quite put her finger on. She was always excited to see him again and thought about him when they weren't together. She wondered what he was doing now. It was Sunday. Did he go to church? Grade papers? Watch football? Yeah, that was probably it.

Callie loaded the oven with a second batch of cookies—this time peanut butter. Did Bennett like cookies? She should take him some.

He was easy to be around, and she liked that he listened to her talk. It was her favorite thing to do and she made no apologies for it. Bennett let her, without interrupting or trying to one-up her. He didn't finish her sentences or go on and on about himself. Interesting, because of all the guys she'd dated or known, he was probably the only one who had the right to brag about himself. She sort of wished he would, because she wanted to know more.

She'd Googled him, obviously, and she didn't feel bad or stalkerish for doing so: it was a common enough thing to do these days. He'd been a Heisman candidate, drafted in the third round by Dallas straight out of college, led two games his rookie year when the starting quarterback was out injured. Basically, all info read like Bennett was on track to be a star. Except that's not what happened. She'd known that going in, obviously, since he coached high school football and taught biology, but reading it had broken her heart.

His career had ended when he'd been in a devastating accident . . . with a woman. That part had shocked Callie, just a little bit. The Bennett she was beginning to know appeared to be such a solitary creature, it was hard to even imagine him as a half of a duo—excluding Misha of course. The pictures told the story, though, and there were a few photos of the two of them before the accident. They were perfection. A Ken and Barbie couple. That is, if Ken was built for the gridiron and ruggedly handsome. But the woman, Ashley, she was gorgeous. Gorgeous enough to be a sports newscaster in Houston apparently.

Not that it made any difference to Callie. She wasn't looking to have a relationship with Bennett. She was just . . . curious.

Callie set a timer for the cookies in the oven and clipped it onto the apron around her waist before heading out front. The shop was hopping, the line at the counter six deep, with at least four more lingering around and talking. Callie grinned; this was what she loved.

Fall was a great season for Preston. There were several craft festivals and the local farmers market drew a crowd on the weekends. People just liked to day-trip when the weather was so lovely, and Preston was close enough to the Kansas City metro area to make it a great destination. Antiques, restaurants, a small winery, and great little boutique shops lined Main Street. Callie felt incredibly lucky to be a part of it.

She got to work behind the register, ringing in orders, while Eric boxed up cinnamon rolls as he laughed with a customer. Callie smiled as she gave the man his total, then went to work making change, not bothering to look up right away when the bell jingled.

"Mayday, mayday, we've got a Barbara off the port bow," Eric whispered under his breath as he handed Callie the box of cinnamon rolls.

"Great," she whispered under her breath. She thanked the man in front of her, handed him his change, then stepped around the counter to peek down the line.

And nearly threw up.

There near the front door, speaking to her mother, was Bennett Clark. Callie was sure she let out a whimper before returning to the next customer. She plastered her smile back on and resumed the task at hand. "Just the one pecan roll, then?"

So it went, the line maintaining its length toward the door. After a few minutes she was able to sneak a glance and found that her mother had taken a seat by the window.

And Bennett was sitting with her.

How had that happened? Neither would know who the other was. Unless Callie's mother knew who he was, but that did not seem likely. The most obvious explanation was that she had begun bragging to the nearest person within earshot that this was her daughter's business. Barbara had done it before.

Eric sidled up to Callie and whispered, "I don't want you to panic, but did you—"

"I saw it," Callie said.

"You better get over there. She'll have him invited to Thanksgiving dinner, bridge night, and Christmas Eve church service if someone doesn't intervene."

Callie inwardly groaned. She couldn't leave the register, but then she heard it. Her mother's laugh rang out over the small crowded room, followed by the most horrible words Callie had ever heard: "The tiara was as big as she was. I'm not even kidding."

Callie and Eric turned to face each other at the same time, both of their eyes wide.

"Oh thank goodness," Eric said as he glanced over Callie's shoulder.

She turned and there was Emma, right on time for her shift.

"Go. Go, go. We got this." Eric shoved Callie out front.

She smiled at the people waiting in line as she squeezed through. "I'm so sorry; if you'll just be patient Emma will have you helped in just a moment."

Callie walked around the line and toward the front window table. The minute she saw Bennett's face, she assumed the worst. He was laughing. Not just a chuckle, like he'd given her. No, this was an all-out that-was-funny-as-hell laugh. Whatever story of her past Barbara was retelling, Callie would probably never live it down. He grinned and then stood when he saw her walking over.

"Bennett." She sounded breathless. "What a surprise."

She glanced down at her mother. Massive purple and teal peacock earrings dangled from her ears. "Mom. Another surprise . . . yay!" There was no masking the sarcasm screaming in Callie's tone.

"I agree," Barbara said with an unmistakable twinkle

in her eye. "What a great day this is. I'm so happy I chose to stop by when I did."

Callie didn't even know where to begin. What was her mother doing here? What was Bennett doing here? Why in the name of all that was holy did they have to show up at the same time? Callie glanced down at her timer. Two minutes. "How do you two know each other?"

"I was in line and she struck up a conversation. Told me she was your mother," Bennett said.

Yep. Just as Callie had assumed. It would be best to see what Bennett needed and get him out of there before Barbara could embarrass her any further. Callie had no idea why her mother was there.

"Mom, will you excuse us for a moment?"

"Actually, sweetie." Barbara stood "If you're busy I'll be on my way. I just came by to bring you these for the girls."

Barbara never made it quick, so her offering to shoo caught Callie by surprise. Something was up. Barbara handed Callie a reusable grocery bag, and when she peeked inside Callie nearly gasped. "Oh, Mom, these are wonderful."

Callie pulled an item from the bag. Her mother had crafted all the girls matching blue and white hair bows. One ribbon end said "Panthers". The other had each girl's name. It was so thoughtful and so . . . perfect.

"The secretary at the school was very sweet when I went in there and told her who I was. She wrote down everyone on the team's first name for me."

"They're great, Mom. The girls will love them for game days," Callie said. And she meant it: the bows were perfect and she was already imagining how the team would look in them.

"What do you think, Coach Clark?" Barbara held one in front of him for inspection.

"Well, I'm not really the one to ask about bows, but I sure do appreciate the Preston pride it represents."

That was good enough for Barbara; she absolutely beamed. "Can't get a better endorsement than from the football coach himself, can you? So, are you two *friends*? Is that why you were here, Coach Clark?"

Guilt bubbled in Callie's stomach. Her mother would just die if she found out about the dance competition from someone else. Callie recalled the mani incident from a few weeks ago. As if on cue, Callie's timer went off. "Oh shoot, sorry, Mom—"

"I'm going, I'm going," Barbara said as she headed for the door.

"No, wait. You can't go. We need to tell you something."

Barbara's eyes went wide, darting between Callie and Bennett. "Well, of course."

Callie led Bennett and her mother toward the kitchen. She caught Eric's questioning gaze and shook her head. They had one of their silent conversations.

Everything cool?

Yes, fine. Don't worry.

If you say so, but you're heading into a confined space with a hot guy and your mother. I'm scared for you.

Makes two of us.

She pushed open the swinging door and quickly removed the cookies from the oven before she proceeded.

There was nothing more disheartening than burnt cookies. As she worked, Callie realized that for once in her life Barbara had gone quiet. When all the cookie pans were resting on cooling racks, Callie found Barbara waiting patiently for whatever it was that was to be said, her hands neatly folded in front of her.

As soon as Callie opened her mouth Barbara put up a hand. "Wait. Just tell me. Am I going to be a grandmother?"

Bennett's eyes bugged and Callie's jaw dropped open. "Oh my god, Mother. No. And I'm a little insulted that you assumed I might be pregnant before you assumed I might be engaged."

Barbara shrugged. "Sorry. I couldn't blame you if it was true. Look at that man!"

Callie rolled her eyes and then made the mistake of looking at Bennett. He was grinning down at the floor, a pink tinge traveling up his cheeks. "I'm so sorry, Bennett. My mother lacks subtlety."

"I'm just honest, that's all." Barbara said. "And for the record, Coach Clark, I would have been just fine with that."

"Mom, please!" Callie cried, trying to get things back on track. "What I wanted to tell you is that Bennett and I are partners in an upcoming dance competition."

Her mother gasped, her hand going to her chest. "What?"

"Breathe, Mom," Callie said.

"Dance competition?"

"It's sort of a local knockoff of *Celebrity Dance Off.* A fund-raiser for the local country club."

"Oh, honey," Barbara crooned . . . to Bennett. "My baby is going to look so good dancing with you. You'll win, did she tell you?"

"She did seem certain on that front." Bennett smiled down at Barbara. He handled her very well. "It won't be easy, though. I'm not naturally inclined to dancing."

"Well, what's the plan?" Barbara instantly sprang into action.

"No, no, no. Mom. There isn't a plan. We got this. I just wanted you to know so you didn't find out in the mani chair. Remember?"

"Well, of course, but who's making your costume?" Barbara said, confusion and concern etched into her face.

"I figured Bennett could wear a tux or something and I'd just purchase a dress."

Barbara practically swooned. "Oh no, Callie Jo. You will not wear an off-the-rack for a performance. That's for amateurs."

Callie sucked in a breath. "Mom. Please."

"Yes. 'Please' is what I'm saying. *Please* let me make you a dress."

Callie glanced at Bennett. He raised an eyebrow. "Might as well," he said. "She wants to help."

Barbara walked over and squeezed Bennett's arm. "Listen to you, handsome and smart." She glanced at Callie. "Callie Jo, he is so wonderful."

Callie gave Bennett an apologetic smile. "Yes, he is, Mother."

Bennett gave Callie a little wink, and she was relieved that he was taking this so well. Then again, if her past was any indication, guys always loved Barbara Daniels. She treated them all like they were the most important things in the world.

Allowing Barbara to get involved in this competition was risky. Even a little bit of leeway was incredibly dangerous. Before they knew it she'd be insisting that Bennett get a spray tan and Callie go on a diet. But she *would* need a dress. "Fine, Mom. Make me a dress. Nothing flashy. Simple. Long and flowy maybe. But that's all; we have the rest covered. Promise me you understand that."

Barbara clapped her hands together. "I got it, promise." She ran over to Bennett, rose up at the same time she yanked on his collar to pull him down. She planted a big red kiss on his cheek.

"I'll see you two soon. Don't skimp on practice time."

And she was gone, finally letting some of the oxygen back into the room. Callie immediately went back to her trays of cookies. "I'm sorry about that."

Bennett laughed. "Don't apologize; she's great."

Callie leveled a stare at him. "She's crazy."

"There's nothing wrong with crazy. I'm from Texas, so I'm familiar."

Callie smiled. She already knew that thanks to her internet search, but wasn't about to admit it. "Well, that explains that cute little accent of yours."

Bennett cleared his throat. "Are you sure those are done?" he asked, changing the subject.

"Are you doubting the professional? This is my secret for the perfect cookie. If you wait until they look done to take them out, then they're already overcooked."

He raised an eyebrow. "Huh, interesting."

"The batter will continue to bake under the crust even after they come out of the oven. So you take them out when they're just golden and slightly crisp on the edges, let them sit a minute on the warm pan. And voilà. Perfection."

"So they finish cooking with the residual heat."

"If you want to get technical, then yes."

"You know, baking is pretty much science at work," he said with a small lift of his lips. He stood across the stainless-steel island, watching her work.

"Yes, and the only kind of science I find interesting," she said with a wink. "The delicious kind."

"Ah, come on, science is fascinating. You just haven't been in my class. I'd make you love it. Classifying organisms, gene regulation, cells and neurons. Do you know that when you touch something, the signal travels from your fingertips to your brain at a hundred and seventy miles per hour?"

She laughed. "Really. Actually, I'm not at all surprised that your knowledge of the human body is impressive."

A shocked laugh erupted from his lips. "I guess I'll take that as a compliment."

"You should. My high school science teachers only inspired me to take a nap. I would guess the young ladies in your class give you their full attention."

"Okay, not something I even want to consider," Bennett said with a cringe. But she was pretty sure he might be blushing. A little. She loved how complex he was. One look at him and all you thought was *big-confident-tough guy,* but the truth was more interesting. He was somewhat quiet and shy, but there was a strong presence about him. She knew he was capable of commanding others, but he just saved it until it suited his purposes.

In some ways they were alike, but in many they were opposites. The truth was she found him very appealing. She liked making him laugh, and when he did flirt or joke it was so adorable and she found herself trying to pull his personality out.

Callie began to remove the cookies from the first pan and move them to a cooling rack. "Are you going to tell me why you're here?"

"Besides getting the pleasure of meeting your mother?"

Callie groaned and switched to the second row, methodically moving each cookie one at a time. "I had no idea she was coming. I mean, I had no idea you were coming either, but I was happy to see *you* . . ." Callie faltered, realizing what she'd just said.

She lifted her eyes across the metal worktable to meet his gaze. Neither of them spoke for a second, so she quickly moved on, pretending she hadn't just made herself vulnerable and so obvious.

"I assume you want to set up our next practice?" she said.

"That, yes, and I was curious about your bakery."

That definitely warmed her insides, which admittedly didn't need much warming in Bennett's presence. "You were? That's awfully nice of you."

He shrugged. "I wasn't expecting to get a private viewing of where the magic happens."

"You are very lucky, that's for sure. This is where I guard all of my secrets. Here, try this."

She handed him one of the warm peanut butter cookies and then waited for his response.

"That's . . . really good."

She smiled, loving the way his throat moved as he chewed and swallowed. It was the weekend and it appeared he didn't shave then, which was pretty damn hot.

He put the rest of the cookie in his mouth and Callie handed him another one and then proceeded to tell him what everything was for, what she made every day, what her favorites were, how she got started. Just talking about it made her happy; she was proud of herself. She even pulled the *My Perfect Little Life* blog up on her laptop and explained what it was about.

"I'm not sure how you manage to do all of this. The bakery, the blog . . . me."

"Well, teaching you to dance has proven to be a quite an undertaking, but I have to admit that I've been enjoying myself."

Bennett's eyes crinkled with the sexy little smile he gave her. "Yeah? Me too."

Oh my, this man. He was all kinds of trouble. She enjoyed being in his company, even during practice. She imagined what it would be like if he could really learn to dance well. How fun would that be? It gave her an idea.

"Hey, I just had a brilliant thought. Tomorrow night a few of my friends and I are getting together to watch the premiere of the real *Celebrity Dance Off.* Seeing as you've never seen it, maybe it would be good for you to come watch it with us."

He looked surprised. "I don't know . . ."

"Oh, come on, girls in tiny outfits, lots of good food. Plus my best friend's boyfriend will be there; he's supermanly and he's not ashamed to watch dancing. Oh, and Eric, who is . . . eh, sorta manly."

Bennett laughed. "Okay. If you think it will help."

It would certainly help him get a feel for ballroom dancing, but she feared it wouldn't do much good for her growing desire for him. That was definitely becoming a problem. Now Callie just needed to inform Anne that she had to force Mike to be there tomorrow.

"No, this is not a date. It's a research get-together," Callie said for the third time.

"We completely understand, Callie. I think it's a smart idea," Lindsey said as she cut tomato slices at the island in Anne's little kitchen.

"Thank you, Linds."

"Lindsey's just being nice," Eric said. "I don't beat around the bush and I'm starting to think you keep saying that more for your own benefit."

"I'm not responding to that." Callie shook her head as she cut the buns in half.

The back door banged open and Mike called out, "Perfect, hand me a plate to put these burgers on, will you?"

Callie had to stop herself from rolling her eyes at Anne's pet name. Out of all the "sweeties," "babes," "darlings," and "sugars," Mike had somehow settled on "perfect" for Anne. Callie had given up perfection when she'd given up pageants, and she certainly didn't want all those unrealistic expectations brought into a relationship. To be fair, maybe that wasn't how Mike and Anne saw each other. They were smart people; maybe the pet name was more symbolic. What they had seemed to be working, so it was possible Callie just had a small case of bitterness and jealousy.

Glancing at her phone, she considered the time. Bennett should be there any minute. She felt her heart thumping as she took in the chaos around her that she usually adored. These were her people, her chosen family. She loved them, but Bennett was going to feel claustrophobic in this madness; she was sure of it.

After adding some more cheese to the salad, Callie whispered to Lindsey, "What have I done? This is way too much for Bennett to take in. This is a zoo."

"Cal, he teaches high school. I think he can handle this group of heathens," Lindsey whispered back.

"You're right. You are *totally* right; I'm being ridiculous." And why did she care so damn much? She was turning this into something it wasn't.

"Someone's here in a big truck!" Claire yelled from the living room.

Callie's stomach did a somersault as she put down her salad tongs and headed for the tiny hallway that led to the living room. At the last minute she turned to face her friends. "Give me five, everybody, and then you can descend. No, forget that. I'll bring him in here. Everyone be natural."

She made off for the door again, just as Claire was turning the knob. "Hang on, sweets; you know how Mommy doesn't like you to answer the door. What if it's a stranger?"

"But we're having a party," Claire argued. "These are our friends."

Callie opened the door and smiled. Bennett looked amazing in jeans and a button-up flannel. "Hey. You found it."

"Well, you weren't kidding when you said 'cute little house on the corner.'"

"Right? Anne is kind of amazing at everything, including home beautification. Come on in."

Callie turned to the living room to find Claire staring up at Bennett.

"Bennett, this is Claire. Anne's daughter."

"Hi, Claire. It's nice to meet you."

"Nice to meet you," Claire responded, her eyes never leaving Bennett's face. "Callie's right: you are really big."

And now Callie wanted to melt into the carpet. She didn't dare meet Bennett's eyes. "Um, Claire. Why don't you go find Mommy."

"Okay." Claire bounded through the living room and into the kitchen and Callie turned to Bennett.

"Sorry, that was awkward."

He didn't laugh, but his eyes were bright with humor. "Don't apologize. It's fine."

She nodded, deciding it best not to say anything more. More talking would probably lead to more embarrassment, and she was not used to feeling that quite so often in regards to one person.

She led him into the kitchen, where everyone greeted him with warmth and kindness, like she knew they would. And it wasn't awkward at all; she'd been worrying over nothing. The little kitchen was full to bursting with people and preparation, so she pulled him outside to meet Mike. It was another beautiful evening, and with the scent of grilling meat in the air it was perfect.

"Mike, I want you to meet Bennett Clark. He's the head football coach at Preston High and, strangely enough, my new dance partner."

Mike turned from loading the burgers onto the platter. "Hey, man, nice to meet you." His eyes narrowed as soon as he saw Bennett. "Wait. You can't be the Texas Longhorns' Bennett Clark."

Bennett grinned. "That's me. Long time ago, but yeah. Surely you're not a Longhorns fan up here in Jayhawk territory."

Mike set the platter down on the patio table and stepped forward to shake Bennett's hand. "Absolutely. My father went to Texas, so I grew up watching Longhorn football. He passed about ten years ago, but I'm pretty sure one of the last games we watched was you scrambling that touchdown at the last minute and winning against Nebraska."

Bennett was nodding his head in remembrance. "I'll never forget that moment for as long as I live."

"How did I not know you were coaching up here?"

"I kind of fell off the radar not long after my accident. And if you don't have kids in high school . . ."

Mike laughed. "Definitely not. Not yet anyway."

Callie was stunned as she watched the two men talk for a few minutes about Bennett's time at Texas and in the pros. Within three minutes Mike managed to learn more about the man than she had in three hours. Maybe she should have just asked him. She couldn't believe that Bennett could become so animated, his face smiling naturally and so expressive. He definitely had some confidence when it came to his time playing ball. She found herself slack-jawed as she took it all in.

"Well, shit, it's good to meet you," Mike said. "If I'd have known I was feeding a celebrity I might have been a little more particular about grilling these burgers."

Bennett just smiled. "I'm sure they'll be great."

"You want a beer?" Mike asked as he walked to the back door with a tray full of meat.

"No thanks, man."

Mike nodded and went into the kitchen, leaving Bennett and Callie alone. She turned to Bennett, grinning.

"What?" he asked.

"You didn't expect to come here and have a fanboy, did you?"

He shrugged. "It happens occasionally. Not in a while, though, I admit."

"I've never seen Mike get that excited over anything except an old car. Or Anne of course, but that no longer counts."

"The more time goes by the more people don't know who I am."

There was something about the way he'd said that. "Is that how you want it?"

"It's easier, that's for sure."

"Why?"

"Nothing to explain, no awkward questions. No pity."

She paused for a minute, looking into his eyes. "I guess I won't ask any questions then. Even though I'd really like to know more about you."

She almost swore when she said it his expression fell a little. The only reason she knew about his accident was because she'd been nosey; they'd never spoken about it with each other and she was kind of surprised he'd mentioned it so casually to Mike. If Bennett wanted to tell her his secrets, then he'd just have to offer them up; she wasn't going to beg or disrespect the wishes he'd just made clear.

"Okay, I lied. One question."

He grinned, a look so effortless and handsome it nearly melted her. "That does not surprise me one bit. What do you want to know?"

"Did the players walk around naked in the locker room?"

He laughed softly. "Seriously?"

Callie motioned to her face. "Does this look like I'm kidding? Give a girl some details? That is the thing fantasies are made of."

Bennett ran a hand down his face and then whispered, "Yes. Of course there were guys walking around naked. But don't ask for details because I was never looking at the *details*."

Callie let out a little sigh of pleasure. "That is so awesome. I'm jealous. *Details* are one of my favorite things."

"Good lord, woman." He laughed. "No topic is off-limits for you, is it?"

"Mmmm, not really," she teased.

She realized they were much closer together now than they'd been a few minutes ago. His face was angled down to hers, his gaze taking in her face, passing over her lips a long moment. He shook his head and then said quietly, "I'm trying to figure out why you think I would purposely want to fill your head with images of other men naked?"

Callie's breath tripped over her racing heartbeat. "Well, who else should I imagine naked? A girl has to have something to think about when she's lonely."

She didn't miss the way Bennett's throat worked as he swallowed, his eyes briefly traveling over her once more. "Maybe a girl should do something about her loneliness."

"Easier said than done, Coach Clark."

Just then the screen door shot open and Claire's shrill voice rang out, "Time to eat, Callie."

"Okay, sweetie, thank you," Callie squeaked.

Bennett was still watching Callie when she turned back to him. "I guess we should go in," he said.

"Yes, we should. I'm starving and you'll want to be sure to stock up on more burgers and football talk so you balance out the fact that you'll be watching men dancing in tight pants for an hour."

Seven

Every available seating space in Anne's small living room—including the floor—was full. Callie was next to Bennett on the sofa. Lindsey was on the other side of Callie. Eric and Claire were on the floor, while Anne sat in Mike's lap in an oversized chair. Despite the fact that it was crowded, they were watching an overwhelmingly girl-friendly show, and Bennett was stuffed from dinner, he was enjoying himself. A lot.

He liked the atmosphere here. The house felt like a home, even more so than the house he'd lived in for six years. Anne was a really nice woman, attractive and sweet. He knew why Mike was so into her; she was quite a catch, making everyone feel at home and welcome so easily. The two of them were openly affectionate with each other, and it made the nearness of Callie on the couch next to Bennett all the more frustrating. She was of course the biggest reason why he was enjoying himself here. Every time she moved in her seat he felt it, the fruity scent of her hair, and the warmth of her side against his.

Even the show was *okay,* despite that fact that she hadn't been kidding about the men in tight pants. The females in the room went on and on about every dancer and every celebrity. Several times he and Mike had shared looks of disbelief and confusion when the women—and one man—freaked out over something or someone. But secretly Bennett had to admit, some of it was pretty hot. There were a few moves he wouldn't mind trying out with Callie in his arms, although if his limited experience was any indication that would never happen. He'd definitely like to see her in one of those little skirts some of the females were wearing while they moved their bodies so sensually.

It was somewhat helpful, though. He now understood a little better what Callie had been saying about it being more than the dance steps. The connection between the partners was important, and even the judges commented on their chemistry or lack thereof. He was pretty damn sure he and Callie had some serious chemistry going on. He also appreciated that they showed clips of their practice time, and it was nice to see that even the best couples got irritated with each other and struggled to learn the routine. He'd been beginning to think that he was just an idiot for not being able to get it right away.

"Okay, here we go." Callie managed to scoot even closer and patted his leg. He shifted, realizing that her touch could make things very uncomfortable for him if he wasn't careful. "This is the best guy, Bax Kotze. He's from South Africa, totally hot. He's on after the commercial break."

"He really is so handsome and very talented," Lindsey said.

Bennett had learned quickly that Lindsey was the soft-spoken yet sweet voice of reason. Anne was the mother figure, naturally, and Eric and Callie bantered like brother and sister. They had fun together, and she touched Eric affectionately, rubbed his back. Clearly it was completely platonic, but it was an intimacy nonetheless, which Bennett found made him slightly jealous. It was also a stark reminder that he had nothing similar in his life. With anyone.

He was nowhere near as close to his parents, or his brother, as he used to be. His dad called a few times during the season to check in, and Bennett called them on holidays if he didn't go home—which he usually chose not to do. He'd become a different person eight years ago, and not for the better where personal relationships were concerned. For the first time in a long while, he ached for something more. A connection.

"We can only pray that Bax does this performance shirtless," Eric said, interrupting Bennett's depressing thoughts. "When that man's abs constrict I nearly lose my mind."

"That's it; I'm getting another beer. Anyone else?" Mike carefully slid from under Anne and glanced around. Everyone else declined.

Bennett felt Callie turn and he looked over at her. He'd been leaning against the arm of the couch so as not to get too close . . . although he would have liked to pull her onto his lap. She smiled when their eyes met.

"You are so hating me for this, aren't you," she whispered.

"No, of course not. But I can promise you that I won't lose my mind if this Bax guy is shirtless."

She giggled, the sound resonating low in Bennett's gut. God, she was so beautiful. Flirting with her was a terrible idea, but he couldn't seem to help himself. Her beauty and grace seemed effortless; her humor and charm were always on. She was confident, but only because she took pride in her accomplishments. She was an amazing woman and it was getting harder and harder not to touch her when they were together.

"Has it inspired you even a little?" she asked. Her eyes were hopeful and he sat up straight, their sides brushing. She pulled her legs up under her on the cushion and faced him, her right arm on the back of the sofa. How he wished they weren't in a room full of people.

He cleared his throat and spoke quietly amidst the conversations that surrounded them. "Sure, it's inspired me. But I'll never look like one of those guys. You know that."

"First of all, don't be so hard on yourself. And for the record, no way in hell I'll ever look like one of those girls."

"Ah, that's debatable. I've seen you move."

"Was that a compliment, Coach Clark?" she asked, a flirty smile playing at her mouth.

"Back on. Shhhhh," Eric interrupted everyone.

They proceeded to watch Bax, the girls going nuts as they did. The guy was good, Bennett had to admit. Bax somehow managed to be masculine yet graceful at the same time. Seemed impossible. Or like a rare gift, something you either had or didn't. Bennett definitely didn't and never would. He was big and felt clumsy. His muscles came from weights, not from jumping and lifting women over his head. Trying to teach him to dance almost seemed a fool's errand on Callie's part.

He didn't want that. If for nothing else but to make her happy, he wanted to get this right.

Finally the show was over. It wasn't nearly as bad as he thought it would be, and it was entertaining to listen to everyone talk about it and get excited. He wasn't ready to DVR the season or anything, but it wasn't horrible. He was sure the woman next to him had a lot to do with that.

The girls went to the kitchen to clean up and he talked some more with Mike, who Bennett was finding was a really cool guy, easygoing. It had been weird to be recognized. It happened occasionally, but as the years went by it happened less and less. Usually that was exactly how he wanted it. Being reminded of what could have been was painful, but this time he'd sort of enjoyed having Callie know that he'd been good at something. Been somebody.

After a while Anne walked with Mike to his car; Eric and Lindsey both said good-bye and left. Bennett wasn't sure if Callie was going to stay and therefore he should just go . . . but he was itching to talk to her alone. She'd disappeared into the kitchen once again, so he waited awkwardly on the couch, surprised when Claire came down the stairs in pajamas and walked toward him.

"Hi there," he said.

"Hi." She made her way to his side and curled up on the couch, her little pink toes peeking from her pajama pants. The material was dotted with fluffy white sheep. She angled her head to the side. "I get to be a dancer with Callie in a few weeks. At a football game."

"You do? That's exciting." Bennett assumed she was talking about the clinic that the dance team held every year for little girls. He knew about it but had never seen the performance since it happened during halftime when he and the team were in the locker room. It also coincided with the football team's Punt, Pass, Kick fundraiser. "Callie's a good dance teacher."

Claire gave him an awkward look. "Do you like Callie?"

His eyebrows rose and an awkward laugh escaped. "Uh, sure I do."

"She's pretty."

"She's very pretty."

"And funny."

"Yes, she's very funny."

"Callie usually makes fun of boys, but she doesn't make fun of you."

Bennett laughed. "That's nice to hear."

"Claire," Callie called from the small hallway that led to the kitchen, jerking Bennett's attention from the little girl. "Have you brushed your teeth?"

Claire stood up from the couch with a sigh. "No."

"Well, get to it, missy."

"It's official. Next time I'm locking her in a closet," Callie said when Claire was back up the stairs.

"She's cute," he said.

"Yes, she is."

Bennett stood up, realizing that things would get awkward if he didn't go. "I think I'm gonna head out. This was . . ."

Callie laughed. "A blast, right? I'm quite certain you will be tuning into the show from now on in secret."

"I don't know about that, but yeah, this was . . . good."

They stared at each other for a moment before Anne came in the front door. "Oh, sorry," she said. "I'll just go get Claire into bed. Bennett, it was so nice to meet you. I'll see you at Friday's game. Mike's excited about it."

Bennett smiled, gave her a wave, and then turned back to Callie.

"I'll walk you out," she said.

It was dark outside, the air chilly and scented with hickory smoke from a neighbor's fireplace.

"I love the start of fall." Callie hugged her arms to her chest. She was in a short-sleeved top and jeans, looking as lovely as ever with her curls down. He'd been right: she looked amazing like that. "Changing leaves, jeans, and everything pumpkin-flavored."

"Fall for me always means football."

"Of course. You've played your whole life, I imagine."

"Yeah. My dad played, taught me young. Football is huge in Texas. Especially high school." They stopped beside his truck; the moon was bright, highlighting her hair and her sparkling eyes.

"This was fun. Thanks for inviting me," he said.

"It *was* fun. I'm glad you could come. Now you're all inspired and ready to kill it with your dancing skills," Callie said.

He shook his head. "We'll be lucky if I don't make a complete fool of both of us."

"I promised you I wouldn't let that happen. You have to trust me." She backed up as she spoke. "Let's practice what we did Saturday."

"Callie . . . ," he warned.

"Come on." She grabbed his hand and pulled him away from the truck and into the street before stepping into him.

He stared down at her. "There's no music."

"Oh please. Music is in your soul. Close your eyes."

With a sigh he did as she asked. "I'll admit, I've been hearing you counting in my sleep." *Among other things*—but he kept that to himself.

"Ha! Then what are you complaining for? Imagine the song. We heard it over and over Saturday. We go on my cue."

"Okay," he said into the breeze. "You know we're standing in the road with our eyes closed? This is dangerous." In a multitude of ways.

"Hush, only you have your eyes closed. Trust me, remember."

He couldn't help smile at her annoyance. It was adorable. *Trust me.*

"One two three four five six," she counted, her voice moving away from him as she slid down the front of his body. Her hand trailed down his neck, chest, and stomach. With his eyes shut it felt erotic, knowing that she now knelt in front of him like this, out in the open. Her fingers brushed the top of his jeans and it was too intense. Before he could process his reaction he grasped at her head with both hands, his fingers tangling in her hair.

She stopped counting instantly and the change startled him. His eyes flew open and he looked down into her face. He pulled his hands back. He wasn't sure if he'd meant to hold her there or stop her. A little of both. "Shit . . . I'm sorry."

She stood slowly and gave him an awkward smile. "It's okay. Maybe we'll just do something else." She slipped her hands into his and positioned them ballroom-style again.

"I liked it like this. It was simple," he said. Grateful that she'd blown off what he'd done so easily.

Her lips parted for a second, her eyes wide as she whispered, "I like it, too."

He swayed them from side to side in slow motion, loving the feel of her body flush against his. He turned them, bowing them gently from side to side, taking the lead, the streetlamp lighting her eyes and then plunging them into darkness over and over. They continued to sway like that for several minutes, until just like before she sighed and rested her head on his chest.

Bennett let his eyes slip shut once more, her vanilla scent overwhelming him, the warmth of her hand branding his skin. This was perfection.

"I told you we could dance without music," she said quietly. "If you try, you can hear it."

"Yes." It was true; once they'd started the rhythm it was there in his mind, guiding his body.

She looked up, her chin resting on his chest, and he tilted his head down to see her. She looked so beautiful like that, and the way he was holding her, she felt like she belonged to him.

"Just wait until I teach you a true waltz. That will be next time."

He groaned in mock annoyance. The truth was, as

feminine as dancing was, it surely had been invented by a man as a socially acceptable excuse to get a woman in his arms.

"Tell me the truth. Do you regret agreeing to this?" she asked, and her question surprised him.

He said the first words that slipped into his mind. "No. Not at all."

"I'm glad," she said. Every time she spoke, her chin dug into his chest. He didn't mind one bit.

They continued to sway, their faces only a foot apart as he stared into her eyes. She had to know what he was thinking. Feeling. He wanted her to be feeling it, too, even though his brain was trying desperately to remind him that this was a bad idea. They had this competition to focus on and neither one of them needed the distraction.

More than anything, he wasn't ready to fall for someone. But right now, it was difficult to care about anything else. The only thing that made sense in this moment was how good she felt—soft and inviting—in his arms. He halted their movements and lifted a hand to her chin.

For a moment she was still, but then slowly her mouth turned up at the corners and it felt like an invitation. He moved on pure instinct; dipping his head, he pressed his mouth lightly to hers.

Her lips came together tentatively, firm against his. He pressed another soft kiss, then another, before lightly tugging at her bottom lip, urging her open. Just when he decided this was a mistake, her fingers trailed up into the short hairs on the back of his head and she sighed against his mouth. Her lips parted just the slightest bit and he ran his tongue against the seam.

Her only movement was the pressure of her hand on his neck, pulling him down to her, his sign that she wanted this. Finally she responded with the lightest press of her lips to his. He didn't go any further, just placed another kiss on the corner of her mouth, then the bow of her top lip.

She leaned into his body, her hand going to his face and cupping his jaw. "This feels like a bad idea," she whispered, her voice breathy and soft.

"Do you want me to stop?" He turned his head and kissed the palm of her hand.

She let out the smallest whimper of frustration and immediately pleasure flooded his body. He couldn't help himself: instead of waiting for her answer he asked her with his touch; angling his lips over hers, he took her mouth fully. This time she kissed him back, insistent and demanding.

Now she used both hands to pull him against her, their bodies as flush as humanly possible. He knew she would feel him hard against her stomach, and suddenly he didn't care; he wanted her to know what she did to him. She drove him crazy, filled his dreams with thoughts of her, his days with longing.

The tip of her tongue met his and he groaned before intensifying the kiss. It was manic and possessive, their tongues tangling with each other, and when he couldn't get deep enough he wrapped both arms around her waist and lifted her feet from the ground. She held on around his neck, fitting against him so effortlessly it made him dizzy.

He felt the pain radiate from his hip as he walked them toward his truck, but he suffered through it, drunk on the feel of this woman in his arms, unwilling to put her down or let her go.

He kissed her long and hard, holding her body against his. Finally he pulled away, breathing deep before gently setting her toes onto the street behind his truck. Their faces stayed close, foreheads meeting. Her fingers made lazy circles on the back of his neck, like her touching him was the most natural thing in the world.

"That was *almost* better than dancing," she said, her voice all teasing and playfulness.

She was constantly making him laugh, more than anyone else. And damn, she looked so hot doing it. He grinned. *"Almost?"*

She continued to smile, her face lit by the streetlight, but he didn't miss the subtle change, her lips slipping down, her eyes refusing to meet his. She was regretting what had just happened. His fear was confirmed when she whispered, "Bennett. I don't know if we should do that again."

His body went rigid in her arms. That was not exactly what a man wanted to hear after he'd kissed a woman for the first time. He let go of her and backed away. "Okay. I'm sor—"

She shut him up by grabbing a fistful of his shirt and pulling him close. "That's not what I meant. Don't apologize. I've wanted that to happen from the first moment I met you."

That helped his ego a little, but he still pulled away, unable to be this close to her anymore. If she was able to say that so easily, she meant it. It shouldn't have happened. She didn't want it to happen again.

Callie ran her hand through her tousled hair. "Bennett, please don't be upset. Just think . . . we're going to be spending so much time together, adding sex to the equation . . ."

"Shit. No. I'm not upset." He was humiliated. And pissed. "It's fine. You're right; that was a bad idea."

He stuffed his hands into his pockets and pulled out his keys. He hit a small button and the sound of his doors unlocking startled Callie. She stepped away from the truck and into the grass.

"I better go," he said.

"I don't think we should part like this."

"Part like what? Nothing's wrong. We're good." He was embarrassed as hell, but otherwise they were good.

"Do you mean that?"

The tone of her words suddenly irked him. She was fine, but she was worried about him. She might as well have patted his head and asked if he needed to talk to someone about his feelings. It fucking sucked. "What are you asking, Callie? We're good, no big deal. When do we practice again?" His words came out a little too loud and agitated.

She cleared her throat, obviously taken aback by his sudden outburst. But she was all cool and calm. "Why don't I secure the school gym for us on Tuesdays and Thursdays after our teams practice? That way we can just get it out of the way before we go home."

So she wanted to meet on neutral ground, not at his place or even her place. *Get it out of the way—nice.* She was ready to treat this for what it was. A job.

Obviously she wanted to make sure what just

happened didn't happen again. It was probably for the best, because he shouldn't want a woman who didn't want him back. *Been there, done that.*

"Sounds good. I'll see you tomorrow."

And just like that she'd shut him down like it was no big deal. She was bold and honest, raw and intriguing. She was beautiful and funny. And from now on she was off-limits.

The following afternoon Bennett was early to practice. He passed the gym well before he knew Callie usually got there, intent on not seeing her until he had to later that day.

He shoved the heavy door open and headed out to the football field. The sound of Reggie's hollering traveled on the breeze and Bennett looked out to find his assistant out on the field with his seventh-hour strength and conditioning class, made up of mostly football and soccer players. Bennett watched as Reg called out another instruction and the guys began running high-knee drills. Damn, Bennett hated those when he was younger. These days he'd give anything just to have the ability to do them.

He shuffled down the steps, his hip and thigh more sore than ever thanks to his new recreational activity. It didn't help that he'd been practicing at home. But it's just how he was: if he was going to do something he wanted to get it right.

Reggie looked and saw Bennett and then walked in his direction. When Reggie was near enough he called out, "Nobody needed homework help today, huh? We gonna start early?"

"Guess we could. Whatever you want." Bennett hit the bottom of the stands and then stepped onto the track that surrounded the field.

Reggie met him near their sideline bench. "Whatever *I* want? You feeling okay?"

Bennett laughed. "Yeah, fine. Just a lot on my mind."

"Uh-huh. I can tell. Usually the only thing on your mind is football. What's going on with you?"

Bennett pulled off his hat and brushed a hand through his hair, sweat already collecting on his head. He was also trying to ignore the way Reggie, hands on his hips, was staring at him.

"You gonna say something or pretend you didn't hear me? Because believe me, I know that game; my wife has it down."

Bennett laughed. "Come on, man. Everything's fine. I'm early, so what."

"*So what* is that it's not like you to not have students come in on your planning period so you can help them with their science work. On top of that, I didn't hear a peep from you this weekend. How long's it been since you didn't text me repeatedly Saturday after a Friday night game to discuss play changes? So by my calculations, either you were busy all day Saturday, which I can't imagine, *or* you weren't thinking about football, which I also can't imagine unless something else more important was on your mind. So now you tell me *so what*."

Bennett stared at his friend. "You feel better now that you got that off your chest?" Bennett said dryly.

"I'll feel better when you admit that something's going on with you and that dance coach. You got weird right after that all went down, so what is it? You hit it? That the problem?"

"Jesus, Reg, we're at school." Bennett glanced out to the field. The guys had finished their drill, and without their coach there to give them direction they'd all sat down near the end zone to take a break.

"They can't hear me," Reg said with a wave of his hand. "So is that it?"

"No, that's not it."

"So the problem is that you *haven't* hit it then."

Bennett shook his head. "Nothing serious has happened. We kissed, that's it. And it's not gonna happen again."

Reggie lifted an eyebrow. "Says who?"

Bennett sighed. "Says her."

"No shit." Reggie winced. "Damn, man, sorry to hear that. I'm honestly shocked. I didn't know any woman was capable of saying no to Coach Clark."

"Yeah, well, she's one of a kind, that's for sure."

"Well, good. I hope this throws you off your game so I can kick your ass with my dancin' skills."

"Not a chance. If anything, I'm upping my game."

Reggie laughed and patted Bennett's back. "We'll see about that. I'll see you out there." Reggie headed back out on the field, leaving Bennett to stand alone. He sat down on the bench and leaned onto his knees.

Bennett appreciated that once he'd confessed Reg hadn't pushed. He knew that if he needed someone to talk to his friend was there, but Reggie wasn't going to force Bennett into any conversations. Sometimes it was just enough to know that your friends had your back if you needed them.

But he hadn't been lying. Yeah, he was distracted, but he was fine. He'd decided to focus on getting through the next month by just making it all about the process. Learning the routine, perfecting it. He could do that, treat it like any other athletic goal. He learned, he practiced, and when the time came he would execute the play. And if things went right, he would win.

They would win.

And then he hoped the Evan would follow in January, his boys would get scholarship money, and all would be right in Bennett's world.

Yep, that was the plan, and nothing made him feel better than having a plan.

Callie tucked her face into her scarf and shoved her hands into her pockets as she headed out of the school parking lot and into the neighboring field for the homecoming bonfire. The high school sat on the outskirts of town, perfect for such an event, and it was an ideal night for a bonfire. The earthy scent of wood smoke carried in the crisp breeze, the epitome of a fall evening.

She passed a few tables, the Drama Club selling popcorn, a few PTA moms selling hot apple cider. She decided to purchase a cup, happy to have the warmth on her fingers. She chatted with a mom who asked her about the upcoming Little Pantherettes dance clinic. Callie was really excited about the fund-raiser and the girls had been doing a great job with the planning, for which she was grateful. Apparently it was a long-standing tradition between the cheerleaders and dance team to teach the little girls of Preston a routine that they then performed at a home game.

Callie inhaled the scent of cinnamon from her cider as she made her way toward the excited mass of students already congregating. Rows of hay bales flanked the roaring fire, and a set of movable metal bleachers faced it on the front side. Several pickup trucks had backed in along the far side, tailgates open and full of snuggling teens. She headed in that direction, only to hear the unmistakable sound of one of her girls giggling.

Between two trucks, somewhat hidden from view, Callie caught sight of Jessica Monser with a football player, his letter jacket–clad arms wrapped around the girl like a straitjacket. Callie tried to sound laid-back when she called, "Jessica, where should you be?"

"Oh, be right there, Coach." Callie watched as Jessica tried to pull herself from the young man's grasp as he whispered something into her ear that had her giggling again. Her voice was playful when she said, "You need to stop."

Callie stood and waited until Jessica finally ran off to join the other members of the dance team. Callie sighed. Why had she just felt a twinge of jealousy of a sixteen-year-old girl? Not because of the boy—*ew*—but just the blissful ignorance. Flirting and bantering with someone. Callie knew all too well what young love was like. Drama, heartache, and more drama. But there was something to be said for just going with it. Putting yourself out there and seeing what would happen.

No. An invitation for madness was what that was. It was those heated, young, and reckless relationships that taught people to wise up. Get their shit together and put up emotional walls. The kind that protected your heart.

Speaking of walls, Callie spotted Bennett across the bonfire pit on the opposite side of the flames. Apparently he was manning the fire. Not a surprise, he seemed like the outdoorsy type and had mentioned camping. She watched as he used a garden shovel to arrange some blazing logs to his liking. Sparks popped from the flames and he stepped back a foot or so. So precise, so controlled. He didn't do anything on accident or without thought.

Except maybe that kiss, that had felt very impulsive, which made it all the more frightening. The attraction between them wasn't a secret even though they hadn't come right out and discussed it, but she could tell he'd fought it. She'd fought just as hard, and to know that he'd finally given in seemed . . . big. His kiss had felt like a question: *What are we going to do about this? Can I have you? Can you handle me?*

She wasn't sure she could.

She watched him now, his eyes glowing in the firelight. She loved the way his jeans molded perfectly to his thick thighs. He looked so adorable in his Preston hoodie, and he'd even put on a well-loved ball cap. Her knees nearly buckled at the sight of him. He was so rugged and masculine but at the same time so boyish. That was the problem; she couldn't figure this man out and it made her feel out of control. A feeling she wasn't particularly fond of.

It had been a little over a week, and they'd practiced three times since *the night of the kiss*. Things were going surprisingly well with the routine. It was as if he'd decided to stop focusing on her at all and put all of his energy into learning the dance. He'd even picked up the basic waltz step much faster than she'd expected when she'd used duct tape on the floor to help teach him. And while she was happy that the dance was coming along and she loved his newfound dedication . . . she missed him. Neither one of them had teased or flirted since she'd said they couldn't kiss again.

At the time telling him they couldn't be physical had made sense. Sort of. But the truth was she'd replayed that kiss over and over a million times in her mind. It was crazy; he was in her thoughts while she was baking, cleaning the shop, driving to the bank.

She even dreamed about him.

With her mind full of Bennett Clark, practice—while going well—had become hell for Callie. The whole time she tried not to stare at his lips or imagine his hands touching her in inappropriate places. But being that close to such a virile man made things difficult. Probably the only thing that had kept her from breaking her own rule was his cool demeanor.

A log popping made her jump and her eyes met Bennett's. She gave him a little wave. He only lifted his chin in acknowledgment. They'd seen each other that afternoon for practice, cutting things short early because of the bonfire. But still, he could have seemed a little happier to see her.

She turned back to the girls, highly annoyed. With him, with herself, with her stupid hormones. What did she want? When he'd kissed her she'd pushed him away and made it very clear that it shouldn't happen again. He was doing exactly as she asked. And yet she could still imagine the light in his eyes dimming when she'd said it. He'd been surprised . . . and maybe hurt.

She was stupid. Stupid because she'd wanted it so badly, wanted it still. But it had been so amazing it had overwhelmed her. Kissing Bennett hadn't been like any average kiss she'd had before; his was the kind of kiss that you'd never get tired of. Never stop wanting.

Trying to get over herself, Callie ushered the girls over into the field to stretch. They would do their usual Pep Assembly routines, which was really what this was, a sort of kickoff to homecoming week. After five minutes, Callie counted the dancers. One was missing, so she looked at her phone and found an "I'm running late" text. She went ahead and said a few quick words before she motioned all of them to their designated spot just beyond the fire. Tonight they were wearing their blue and white Pantherettes warm-ups, their new hair bows courtesy of Callie's mother, and were doing a pom routine in addition to the usual fanfare that accompanied pep rallies.

Callie found a seat near the girls on a hay bale and took a sip of her cider as the drum line beat out the familiar beginning of the school song, the crowd instantly coming to their feet with a loud cheer. From the corner of her eye she saw the final girl arrive and run toward the group and then watched with pride as her girls proceeded to do a perfect kick routine. She clapped for them, winking as they looked toward her for approval. She was one proud coach tonight. Every night for that matter; they were all special and so very talented.

The rest of the evening went as she expected. Singing, cheers, burning a football player dummy, announcing the Homecoming candidates. All the usual ruckus. Bennett spoke quickly, as did his two senior captains, which got the crowd incredibly pumped up. Principal Jensen said a few words, and then finally things were drawing to a close.

When it was officially over the students began to disperse, some walking to the parking lot, some breaking into groups to socialize, a few even running around in the dark parts of the field, laughing and goofing off. It was a little crazy, but Callie picked her way through the bodies around to the other side of the fire. Immediately she found Bennett; no way he could be missed. He was speaking with a couple of his players, something that had them all laughing hard. God, he was gorgeous when he was happy like that. She smiled to herself just watching it.

As if overhearing her thoughts, he turned and met her eyes, the laughing gone. For a moment she wondered if he planned to ignore her. Thank goodness he didn't but instead headed directly for her. She cleared her throat and met him halfway.

"Hey," she said.

"Hey yourself."

"That went well."

He shrugged, the hood of his sweatshirt bunching behind his neck. "Went like it does every year."

O-kay. So he wasn't in the best of moods—only when it came to her apparently, since she'd just seen him cracking up with his players. "Everything okay?"

"Yeah, sure. Why?"

She shrugged. "I don't know. Just seems like . . . something's been off between us this past week."

He looked at her from the corner of his eye. "Wasn't that what you wanted?"

Callie sighed and glanced around to see if anyone was nearby before she whispered, "Bennett, I said we shouldn't kiss again. Not that we can't be friends."

"Who said we're not friends? We've spent several evenings together practicing. There's been no issues." This time he glanced around and lowered his voice. "I've done what you said, worked hard to learn even though it fucking sucks. What more do you want from me?"

She was stunned silent; it was not like him at all to react that way, and when he realized she wasn't going to reply immediately he took a step toward the flames and away from her. The strong emotion he'd just let slip only served to make Callie want to touch him all the more. So maybe his playing it cool all week hadn't been so easy.

A parent walked up to Bennett and he chatted with them briefly about the upcoming game. His voice took on a warm and friendly tone, completely different from the one that he'd been using with her for the past week. She missed that warmth.

Callie glanced around, noting that the field was nearly empty save a few clusters of teens, and despite the roaring fire in front of her, she felt cold. She wondered if he would just rather call this whole thing off. Nobody was forcing them to do this competition. No one's life was on the line, but her sanity sure was. Maybe she should tell him that it wasn't working.

She stepped a little closer to the fire and a moment later felt him beside her. She glanced in his direction; he had his tool back in his hand and was pushing at the burning wood. "You staying to help me kill this fire or what?"

Was he asking her to stay? It almost felt like an odd apology for his outburst a minute ago. Part of her wanted to think that maybe he wanted her near, and that made her wish for more. Of all the things she'd considered saying in response, the one that came out of her mouth surprised even her. "I dreamed of kissing you last night."

He didn't turn and look at her; instead his eyes pinched shut and he sucked in a breath. When he blew it out he whispered harshly, staring right into the flames, "Don't. Don't do that."

"Why—"

The sound of angry male voices cut her off and pulled their attention toward the opposite side of the fire. Through the dwindling flames she saw a group of kids circled near one of the pickups. She felt Bennett tense beside her.

"Those are my boys," he said, taking off in a run.

Callie followed, confusion mixing with panic. The minute she and Bennett made their way over to the group she heard the unmistakable sound of fist meeting bone, followed by a loud thud against the truck.

"What the hell is going on here?" Bennett's tone was fierce, with an undertone of pure fear. It frightened her and made her heart ache simultaneously.

Students parted for him as he made his way to the center of the melee and Callie pushed in right behind him. Even in the dark and shadows she knew someone was on the ground. She said a quick prayer he wasn't severely injured, but her thoughts scattered when someone began to mumble.

"Shit, oh shit, oh shit, Coach Clark. I don't—Jason—

it was an accident," one of the boys began chanting, his voice pure panic, his breathing labored.

"Tate, shut up and tell me what happened," Bennett spat, as he crouched on the ground near, apparently, Jason's unmoving form. He was a big kid, much bigger than the one freaking out above him. Callie wondered how Tate had managed to knock Jason down.

"It was an accident," Tate repeated, running his hands through his hair, squeezing his head, as he stared down at Jason.

Callie turned on her phone's flashlight and angled it over Bennett's shoulder. Jason winced and groaned as the light hit his eyes. Right at the hairline was a large bump and a gash in his head, gaping slightly. Bennett reached up and grabbed Callie's phone from her hands without a word. The dozen or so people crowded around leaned in even closer, trying to get a look.

"Everybody back off!" Bennett yelled, then his voice softened. "Jason, can you hear me?"

The boy nodded, just barely, and tried to open his eyes all the way as Bennett ran the light down Jason's body, obviously checking for further injury. Bennett brought the light back near Jason's face, highlighting his bloody forehead, and then used his fingers to hold the boy's eye open while he shone the light directly into it. Callie could only guess Jason had gone down and hit the metal bumper of the old truck on his journey toward the ground. She and Bennett had heard the crack. "There you go, bud. You're okay. How many fingers am I holding up, Jason?"

"Four. And it was an accident." Jason's voice was low and his face pinched in pain.

"No, it wasn't," a feminine voice called out. Callie jerked her head in shock. Jessica. Was this the kid she'd been flirting with an hour ago? The young girl continued, tears in her voice. "Tate sucker punched him."

That managed to give Jason some strength. "Shut the hell up, Jess," Jason growled, and then let his eyes close as if the effort had overtaxed him.

"All right, enough. First off, you don't speak to a lady like that." Bennett's voice was stern but low. "And you better start talking, because the only person that deserves to be mad as hell is me." Bennett looked up at the kid who was clearly to blame. "I'm talking to you, too, Tate. Don't you dare go anywhere."

Another student had pulled his own truck around and turned the lights on the crowd, casting the entire scene in harsh light and shadows. Callie glanced up at Tate. His breath came in shallow puffs, the blue numbers on his shoulder shivered like a man in shock. *Letter jacket.* That was the guy who'd had his arms around Jessica. Jessica, who was now crouched near Jason, sniffling and holding his hand. What a mess. Callie could only imagine what the hell had caused this fight, but she had a pretty good idea.

"I'm sorry, Coach," Tate said quietly.

Callie glanced back down at Jason, whose eyes fluttered open once more and tried to settle on Tate. "What the fuck is wrong with you, man?" Jason muttered, almost seeming to have forgotten that just a second ago he'd said it was an accident, defended his friend. Had he forgotten? Okay, now *that* wasn't a good sign.

"Don't try to move, Jason." Callie took a step around Bennett and dropped to her knees at the top of Jason's form before gently rubbing his hair from his forehead. She didn't look at Bennett. "Just relax."

"Jason, can you hear me?" Jessica knelt beside Callie, tears rolling down her cheeks. "I'm so sorry, baby."

"Just go, Jess," Jason muttered, his eyes still squeezed tight, trying to hold back what had to be a terrific pain in his head. "Please go."

Bennett cleared his throat and Callie met his eyes. He gave her a look and she immediately guessed what he wanted. Callie stood up. "Jessica, come with me, sweetie."

Callie helped the young girl to her feet just as sirens sounded in the distance, growing closer by the second. Callie ignored the sound of Bennett cursing under his breath at the sound and led Jessica from the crowd of gawkers and over toward the fire.

By the time they sat down on a bale of hay Jessica was sobbing. Callie blew out a breath and put her arm around the girl. "Okay, okay. No one died. Tell me what's going on."

Jessica cried for another minute before she tried to pull herself together. Callie remembered all too well how heavy everything seemed when you were a teenager. Like the weight of the world was on your shoulders, the feeling that this moment could change everything. Being a teenager was way too hard sometimes.

"Is Jason your boyfriend?" Callie asked quietly. Trying to get the conversation flowing. As the coach she caught pieces of what went on in the girls' lives, but she tried not to pry unless they opened up. She knew Jess had a boyfriend but not much more than that.

Jessica nodded her head and then wiped her nose on her sweatshirt like a child. Callie couldn't help but remember Jessica's lavish and expensive Sweet Sixteen birthday party this last summer. Anne had been hired to plan and Callie had been right there to help. It had been a huge shindig, because Jessica's family was incredibly wealthy. Seems money didn't save you from the drama of adolescence.

Finally Jessica calmed down enough to speak. "They're best friends. Always have been. I should have known better."

Callie considered the girl's words a moment, then decided to go all-in. "Did you cheat on Jason?"

Jessica's eyes widened and her head shook violently. "No. No, I didn't." She dropped her shoulders. "I mean . . ."

"Jessica, cheating isn't necessarily always physical. Some people might say flirting with someone—letting him touch you certain ways—that's still a form of cheating."

"I didn't mean to. I just . . . Tate is so funny. He makes me feel good about myself. He makes me feel . . ."

"Wanted?" Callie finished for her.

Jessica nodded, her eyes filling with tears again.

"I understand. That's a good feeling; everyone wants to feel wanted by someone. Doesn't Jason make you feel that way?"

Jessica shrugged. "Not anymore. Maybe at first. He's so focused on football, schoolwork, making his parents happy."

"Maybe at your age it's important to focus on other things besides a relationship. You're still so young."

She didn't respond to that, and Callie really hadn't expected her to. Nobody ever felt too young. That was reserved for hindsight. "I just don't want them to stop being friends because of me."

Callie hesitated before speaking; it was a rather mature thing for a teenage girl to say, so she let Jessica hear the truth. "It wasn't right what you did, Jessica. But it's not all your fault. Tate's a big boy. He knew you were his best friend's girlfriend and he chose to flirt anyway. That's on him. But what I don't understand is why Tate punched Jason if he was in the wrong."

"Jason found out we'd been talking. He called him trash."

Callie's eyes widened.

Jessica continued. "Told him my parents would never let me date white trash like him. The worst part . . . he's right. I mean, I don't think that, but they're going to be so pissed when they find out what happened. My parents love Jason, but Tate . . . he doesn't have a good family. His dad . . ." She didn't continue. Her tears started up again, quietly this time.

"Sweetie, your parents will get over this. Right now you need to focus on you, and let these two boys work things out between themselves."

Jessica wiped the mascara from under her eyes. "Maybe."

"I know I'm right. When it comes right down to it, men are a huge pain in the butt," Callie said, trying to add some levity to the situation. "Someday a great guy will come along and sweep you off your feet, but right now, when you're young, you should just focus on friends and having fun."

Jessica shrugged. "Boys *are* fun."

Callie sighed. She couldn't argue that one. "Agreed. But things don't always have to be serious. You're young. Right now it can *just* be fun."

Maybe she should take her own advice.

Eight

Bennett's emotions warred inside as he watched Tate walk to his car and pull out of the nearly empty parking lot. Anger, frustration . . . shock. Jason and Tate fighting, Bennett never would have guessed. Officer Abbott walked over and Bennett let out a heavy sigh. "You get much out of him?"

The cop shook his head. "A little. Sounds like he has a thing for Jason's girl. Got caught putting some moves on her tonight. Jason confronted him and Tate reacted with his fist."

"I can't believe Tate managed to knock him down."

"I was thinking the same thing," Abbott said. "Kid's a lineman; he clearly hadn't seen it coming."

Bennett nodded in agreement. Tate's emotions flared like a flamethrower. Anybody within aim better watch out. But his best friend? And on top of that, messing with his best friend's girl? *Shit.* "What the hell is wrong with these boys? Do they think they live in a bubble? That no one will find out? No one will see their actions?"

"They're teenage boys. They're not thinking at all. Not with the right end anyway. We've all been there."

"Unfortunately," Bennett said. He didn't know much about Ryan Abbott, other than he was one of the few cops in Preston. But he seemed like a nice guy.

His radio went off on his hip, mixing with the sweet sound of Callie's voice coming up beside them. Only it was directed at the wrong person. "Ryan, I didn't know you were the one on duty tonight."

Bennett felt sucker punched himself as he watched Callie walk up and put her arm around Abbott's waist. The cop's face lit up as he returned Callie's hug. As if they'd done it a thousand times. Suddenly Bennett decided the guy might be a little unlikable. Thank goodness she pulled away just as quickly.

"How are the boys?" Callie asked casually. Like she hadn't just had her hands on another man. Bennett swallowed hard, trying to focus on what she'd just said. Ryan beat her to it.

"Okay. Tate's lucky that Mr. Starkey didn't press charges. Sadly, I have a feeling when Tate's father finds out about what he did the kid will wish I'd locked him up for the night."

Bennett winced at the thought. Tate Grayson Sr. was going to lose his fucking mind when he caught wind. And there was no chance he wouldn't find out, because Tate would have to face the consequences of his actions tonight. Actually, both boys would. The school had a no-tolerance policy on fighting, and although it wasn't during school hours it was at a school function on school property. Bennett's hands were tied; the boys would be in trouble and that would dictate their ineligibility to play ball. And the truth was, Tate deserved it. What he had done was wrong.

"Well, I think I'm gonna head over to the hospital and get Jason's statement once he's in better shape." Officer Abbott frowned. "I don't know if he'll be back this season, Coach. His head took quite a blow on the bumper of that old truck."

Bennett ran his hands through his hair, completely overwhelmed, exhausted, and pissed. "Don't think that hasn't been going through my head since the minute I heard that punch."

"Well, you guys take it easy," Ryan said with a nod. He then turned to Callie. "Cal, I'll see you tomorrow."

She smiled. "Sounds good; night, Ryan. Thanks for coming."

What. The..Hell. Jealousy bubbled in Bennett's chest at the familiarity between Callie and the cop. How did they know each other, and how well? And what the hell was going to happen tomorrow? Was that why she'd pulled away from him, because she was seeing someone else? No. That couldn't be it, not when she'd announced she'd been dreaming of him.

As soon as Abbott was in his patrol car Bennett turned to walk away. "I gotta get back to that fire."

Callie followed him, thank goodness. He glanced around the field. They were completely alone now and he tried to wrangle in his emotions, to no avail. This night had taken a bizarre turn and he was not happy about it. At all. He wanted to rewind it to one specific point in time.

He stopped a few feet away from the dying blaze. She stood next to him, facing the golden light. The shushing of the nearby trees and the chirp of the season's final crickets could just barely be heard over the simmering crackle of the fire. They stood that way for several minutes before Bennett couldn't contain his thoughts anymore.

He turned to her, taking in her profile as she tucked her chin into her scarf. "Tell me again."

She angled her face to look up at him, her eyes shining. "Tell you what?"

"You know what."

She shook her head and turned back to the flames. "I think that moment has passed."

"The hell it has. Do you think I've forgotten what you said?" He cleared his throat. He was desperate for her to go back to the conversation that had been stolen from them. "You dreamed about us . . . together."

Now she turned fully, facing him. He did the same, squeezing his hands into fists. He wanted to touch her so bad, and she was now so close. "Tell me again, Callie."

Her eyes softened, voice lowering to a near whisper. "Fine. I dreamed about you. Happy?"

He wouldn't let her go so easily. Not this time. She'd started the conversation earlier; now she was going to have to finish it. "I'll be happy when you tell me. All of it."

She swallowed, and then licked her lips. His body immediately responded and he inched a little closer, his hand went to her face, and his thumb swiped against her mouth. "Tell me about your dream."

"What do you say?" she asked, teasing him.

"Please."

For a long moment she didn't speak; then he felt her

fingers grab onto his front jean pocket and hold on. It was a subtle move, but it had his heart pounding. Finally she opened her mouth. "I dreamed of *you*."

"You said that already." He stepped even closer, pushing their bodies closer, her thumb looped over his waistband meeting skin. He wanted her to keep going. "Tell me more."

"We were . . . together. Close."

"And," he pushed. He wanted her to say it.

"You were naked." She gave him a small smile. "I liked that."

"Did you? What else happened?"

Her fingers tickled his stomach as she laid her palm flat against his skin and slid it up his abdomen. "I was naked, too."

"Good, and what were we doing naked?"

She grinned and looked down at where their bodies pressed together. He couldn't believe that the loud and confident Callie he was used to was the same one standing in front of him now. This girl was unsure of herself, a little embarrassed about discussing her sex dream. It shouldn't have been such a turn-on, but damn, it was.

"What did I do to you in your dream?"

She swallowed hard and then looked straight into his eyes. "You were inside me."

Bennett's knees threatened to buckle at her words. He wanted to kiss her so badly, but despite the moment's conversation, he hadn't forgotten her rejection from last time. Leaning down, he rested his forehead against hers, his self-control on the brink.

Their breath mingled, lips hovering an inch apart. Two could play this touching and teasing game, so his hands traveled down her hips, around her curves, and cupped her ass.

"What are you saying, Callie?"

"I don't know. I just . . . miss you."

"You've seen me several times the past week."

"But it's not like it was before."

Before he kissed her. Before she told him it couldn't happen again. His eyes clenched shut. He missed her, too. The way things had been when they'd first met and started practicing. He needed to let her know what he dreamed about. "I need to ask you a question."

"Okay."

"When you dreamed about me . . . did you come?"

She sucked in a breath, her face tilting up to his. He lifted his head so he could see the heat in her eyes. She shook her head and whispered, "No."

He gave her a smirk, holding back a full grin. "I'm glad you didn't, because *I* want to do that for real. No dream, I'm gonna make you come." He began to back them up toward his truck. She let him lead, her eyes fluttering as she breathed in deep. He spoke right into her ear. "Only me. Not the dream me. Not that fucking cop."

Her head jerked back, eyes wide and lips parting as if she wanted to speak. He cut her off with his mouth, her muffled reply melting into a moan against his kiss. Her hands immediately sank into his hair as he gently rested her back against the side of his truck.

He tasted apples and cinnamon as he savored her lips. Everything about this woman was delicious and beautiful. He wanted to devour her, right here and now.

Bennett pulled back, short of breath. "Do you want me to stop?"

"Hell no." She took a handful of his sweatshirt and pulled him back down to her mouth. He traced the seam of her lips with his tongue, urging her to open, and she did without hesitation. The lower half of her body pressed against his, forcing him to lean one forearm against the truck bed to steady himself, the other wrapped tightly around her waist.

He tore away from her once again, looking around the bonfire site to make sure no one had returned. It was empty except for his truck and the smoldering embers. The parking lot was also vacant. The school was on the outskirts of town; no houses were nearby. They were alone.

His lips found hers once more and he groaned when her tongue pushed into his mouth. He caught it with his lips and sucked on it. They kissed for several long minutes, his tongue exploring her neck, her ear. She reciprocated and he loved the feel of her warm lips on his face. He pulled away reluctantly.

"Come here."

He grabbed her hand, leading her to the backseat of his truck, thank god for crew cabs. He opened the door. "Get in."

She did as he asked without question while he went to the driver's door, leaned across the seat, and turned on the ignition. He turned the heater on low and then headed to the back.

"Scoot over."

Callie lifted her butt and scooted herself to the center of the bench seat, shoving a duffel bag and two footballs onto the floor. Bennett followed, pulling himself up into the truck, and then shut the door behind him before he leaned into her. She didn't hesitate, wrapping her arms around him and pulling his body over hers as she tilted back toward the window.

Her lips found his once more, picking up right where they left off. They kissed for several moments, wet and hungry. He wanted everything right now, could barely stand how needy he felt, but he managed to focus his thoughts on one singular goal. "I need to touch you, Callie."

He lifted himself off her body in order to get his hand between them, his fingers going for the zipper on her jeans. She didn't protest. Didn't speak at all as he parted the denim and slid his hand into her panties. He hadn't made out like this in . . . shit, years. He felt seventeen, in the back of a vehicle heading for third base.

She moaned as his fingers found her wetness, applying the lightest of pressure. He didn't enter her or push, just trailed his fingertips back and forth along the slick seam. "God, you feel so good."

Bennett was rewarded with the sexiest breathy whimper he'd ever heard. His touch became a little more insistent, exploring, pressing.

"Harder. Please," she insisted.

This time *he* obeyed, giving her what she wanted, his fingers stroking. He wasn't aware he was rocking into her hip until he felt her hands slide into the back of his jeans, under his boxer briefs. Her hands were cool on his skin as she palmed his ass, squeezing and encouraging him to ride and thrust against her. Right now he wanted more and his mouth became frantic against her lips. Callie's chest heaved in and out as her lower body writhed against the movement of his fingers.

Bennett pulled back and watched as she inhaled deep, as if she'd been holding her breath. She met his eyes. "That feels so amazing."

Bennett pushed a little harder, his fingers stroking her expertly. This rhythm he knew well, and he was rewarded with the most beautiful expression on her face. Her lips parted and her mouth slacked open into a small o.

"Oh my god. Don't stop, don't stop, don't stop." Her eyes pinched shut and she let her head fall back. *Beautiful.*

He wouldn't dream of letting up when she was this close. "I won't stop; come for me, Callie."

Callie could barely breathe. She might truly die of the pleasure. Her body involuntarily jackknifed off the seat, her nails digging into Bennett's firm backside. She sought his lips as her body began to shake against him. He gave her what she wanted, kissing her deep as her release crashed over her.

When the sensation subsided, her head dropped onto the seat and she sucked in a shallow breath. "That. Was . . . so good."

She felt, rather than heard, Bennett chuckle from above her. His body was draped along hers, their legs twisted and bunched against the truck door. She glanced down, just now realizing that she wasn't sure how they'd managed to do what they just did. Come to think of it, now that her body wasn't zeroed in on an orgasm it was a little uncomfortable being shoved into the narrow backseat of his truck.

"Sorry," Bennett said, apparently following her line of thinking. He began to move off her.

"Hold on, not yet." Despite the unfortunate location, she liked his weight on her, and she convinced him not to move by squeezing his ass once more. Good lord, she wanted to see it bare. It would have those sexy indentations on the side; she could feel the muscles flexing when he'd ground into her leg. She wanted to see the front of him. Shit, he was still hard against her thigh. "I'd hate to be the only one enjoying this."

"Who said I wasn't enjoying this?" he asked, smiling down at her. Before she could answer he kissed her once again. His lips were full and wet against hers, keeping his kisses soft and searching one moment and then increasing the pressure and angle just enough to keep her wanting more. It was pure bliss.

Shifting her body, she let go of the headrest on the front seat and pressed her palm against his erection. He was so hard, the length pushing against his jeans. The way he'd been rocking into her had made her imagine it inside her, which led to an intense orgasm. She wanted that for him, too. Needed it.

He continued to kiss her as she undid his zipper and then fumbled with his jeans until the fly fell open. Never had she been so excited to touch a man, discover what he had to offer, pleasure him the way he'd done her. She couldn't believe how they'd ended up here; it was almost funny. Two grown people going at it in the back of a truck like teenagers.

Bennett changed position, lifting his body so she could shove his pants down a little and slide her hand inside. His boxer briefs were snug against the warmth of his hard length and she ran her palm up and down several times, loving the feel of the soft cotton against his hard flesh.

His breathing became more ragged and his hand flexed in her hair, almost pulling. She loved it; his response made her feel sexy and bold. She wanted more.

Callie ran her palm all the way down to the base, cupping his testicles through his underwear.

"Oh . . . shit." Bennett blew out a breath and leaned his forehead against hers. Callie gave a gentle squeeze of her hand. Bennett nipped at her lower lip before whispering, "You've got a handful of my most prized possessions."

Callie laughed quietly, enjoying the feel of his grin against her mouth. With her palm still full of him, she ever so lightly slid her middle finger up and down against the cotton. Bennett's body shivered against her.

"Do you trust me with them?" she asked, giving another light squeeze.

"God, yes. Do that again."

She obeyed, doing it a little harder this time before she finally repositioned her hand so she could slip beneath his underwear. He sucked in a deep breath as she wrapped her fingers around him. His skin was soft and warm, and Callie suddenly realized that nothing had ever turned her on as much as holding Bennett Clark's cock in her hand.

"Why didn't you tell me I was psychic?" she asked.

"What?" His voice was rough. He looked at her again. "What do you mean?"

"When I called you big boy. I was right."

Bennett chuckled as she began to stroke him, his laughter ending on a low moan.

"I'm not used to laughing so much when a woman has her hands on my dick."

Callie grinned. "I'm not used to making out in a truck, but I like it."

"Yeah? I do, too. Obviously."

They laughed again and then grew quiet as he kissed her once more. It was a little awkward to tug at him with her hand wedged between them, but he had his body angled as well as he could to make it easier for her. She changed it up, running her thumb over the tip and then back down.

"That feels so good, Callie." Bennett's torso shuddered and he began to pump into her hand a little harder. "I wish I could see you touching me right now."

They both knew that wasn't possible; it was dark save the fire outside and turning on the interior lights could draw attention if anyone drove down the road. But she agreed with him; just the thought of what her fingers looked like wrapped around his thickness made her feel achy all over again.

Her hand picked up speed, as did his shallow thrusts. She wanted to hear the sound he made when he came; she couldn't wait, her excitement urging her on even though her arm grew weary.

Just as she thought he might be getting close his arm gave, his chest crashing into hers, his free arm jerked down to his side. "Oh fuuu . . ."

For a moment she was confused, but there was no mistaking the tone of his voice—this wasn't a cry of pleasure—and instantly Callie's heart raced in a new way. She instantly let go of him and tried to push at his chest. "Bennett, are you okay?"

His head arched back, and his teeth revealed their whiteness in the dark, his lips curled back in pain. When he spoke, the words were ground out through gritted teeth. He tried to move his hips a little, which confused her even more.

"Bennett, what?"

"Holy shit, I've gotta get up. Gotta get out."

Then he didn't move, and she realized he was holding his breath. The full weight of him, mixed with her confusion, sent her into a sudden panic. Was he having a heart attack? A stroke?

Once more she tried to push him up, but he was too solid. "What do I do?"

"Oh god, hold on." With a loud groan he pushed himself up again. "Open the door. Out. Get. Out."

It took Callie a minute to figure out what to do, but then adrenaline took over and she managed to reach over her head, open the door, and shimmy her body out from beneath his. All the while Bennett was blowing out breaths quietly and lightly pumping his leg as she maneuvered herself out of the car and into the grass. Lucky she was pretty flexible. She looked into the cab; he'd fallen face-first onto the seat, his legs still bent awkwardly into the driver's legroom. Pulling herself together, she zipped her pants and dug her phone from her pocket. "Hold on, Bennett. I'm calling an ambulance."

His head jerked up. "No. No, don't do that. Just open the damn door."

She ran around the front of the truck, quickly glancing toward the fire—which was thankfully almost out—and flung open the opposite door. His right leg immediately went straight and found footing, but she realized he was squeezing his left thigh.

"What happened? Did you get a cramp?" she asked, realization dawning. As a dancer she'd had plenty of leg cramps in her day. There were nights she'd woken screaming, her calves bunched up in painful knots. Her parents would come in and rub them, help her up to walk the cramps off. Sometimes they took five minutes or more to work themselves out, pure agony.

"You need to stand, Bennett. We need to walk." She reached over his body and rubbed where his hand squeezed his thigh. It was tight enough she could actually *feel* it. He choked out his irritation with her touch. "Bennett, come on; you have to walk this out."

He slowly began to slide from the truck, then pushing himself up with his arms when both feet hit the ground. "Shit!"

She realized he was trying to move and get ahold of his pants, so she quickly helped him adjust his jeans and underwear so they didn't fall and grabbed his hand. She looked up at his face, his mouth a straight line, eyes squeezed shut. Her heart nearly gave out when she saw a bead of moisture leaking out of one eye.

"It's okay, Bennett. I've got you. Take a step."

"Not yet. Just hold on." He was flexing his foot repeatedly, his left hand squeezing his thigh.

Callie knelt down in front of him and knocked his hand away, using her fingers to rub at the back of his thigh. She knew it hurt him, could hear the pain in the way he was breathing, but they had to work the cramp out for him to get some relief.

After a second she stood up and grabbed his hands

once more. Thankfully, he was now looking at her. "Okay, now walk," she instructed.

Two wooden steps later and he finally spoke. "It's easing up."

"Good, keep walking."

And then just like that his face contorted, his mouth dropping open on a silent moan, his non-cramped leg going slack. It had come back, and Callie knew all too well that the cramp could come and go before finally stopping for good.

"Keep moving, Bennett. Let's maybe try to the side."

She continued to step sideways, then back, pulling him along with her. He blew out a hard breath and followed. On they went for what seemed like forever but probably wasn't even a full two minutes.

Finally Bennett let out a deep sigh, his head dropping forward. His fingers squeezed hers and she returned the motion as he spoke. He let out a shuddering breath before he spoke. "I'm so sorry. That was . . . that was really fucking humiliating."

Callie could barely stand the sight of him, so embarrassed and wrung out from the pain of the muscle spasm. She dropped his hands and then wrapped her arms around his waist, her cheek resting against his chest. "Don't you dare worry about that. I'm just so glad it's over. You scared me."

Slowly he wrapped her in his arms and rested his cheek on her head. She could still feel the way his chest heaved in and out as his body tried to calm down.

"I know how bad a cramp hurts. I got them a lot as a kid," she said quietly. "My parents would have to come in my room at night and help me through them."

"I've always been alone when it happens."

She pulled back and looked into his eyes. The glowing embers of the fire put off just enough light that she could see him. "Well, then I'm glad I was here."

"Me too. Thank you."

She lifted her hand to his face, stroking his firm jaw. She wanted to massage the embarrassment out of his expression—make him laugh. But she knew that wouldn't be what he wanted right now. "How often does it happen?"

He shrugged. "Maybe once or twice a month."

She tilted her head to the side. "That's a lot; is the dancing making it worse?"

"No, the dancing is fine. It's just . . . aches and pains from past injuries. I'm probably dehydrated. It's fine."

She wasn't sure if she believed that. "You need to take care of yourself, Coach Clark. That way when a woman tries to get you off in the backseat of your truck you can enjoy it."

He barked out a strangled laugh and she smiled, loving the sound of it. "Yeah, that was not how I wanted that to end. At all."

Callie shrugged. "I'm willing to give you another try sometime. If you want."

"Of course I do."

She grinned. "Good. I'll make sure to have a heating pad handy."

He shook his head, but his laugh was always her undoing.

The following evening Bennett sat on his couch, stacks of assignments sprawled out on his coffee table. Football season was overwhelming, took up a lot of his time, and always required him to buckle down at work in order to get everything done. Papers graded, copies made, lessons planned. This year it was proving to be even more of a struggle to keep on top of things.

Dance practice only added to his stress. But damn, he wouldn't dream of giving it up. Not now, even if it made life a little more difficult.

Everything he did was a little bit clouded by thoughts of Callie. Even on the days he didn't see her, he liked knowing that she was in the building, just a walk away. Sometimes the girls on the dance team would mention Coach Daniels in class and he would eavesdrop, wanting to know anything more about her. A few times students had even discussed the dance competition with him, including his players who liked to give him and Reggie a lot of shit for participating. But Bennett could tell they were supportive also, which was nice.

The hard truth was that Callie was on his mind all the damn time. Too much, and the more time he spent with her the more he thought about her. Those intimate moments certainly didn't help—but holy shit, they were amazing. She was amazing. He'd never enjoyed fooling around with a woman so much in his life. Callie was sweet, funny, and so sexy. That was the problem; he wanted more. All of it. And she obviously did too.

But the part that was driving him crazy was how caring and attentive she'd been when he'd been in pain. He hadn't expected that at all. It would have been more like her to give him shit, tell him to tough it out, man up. But she'd been gentle and concerned.

The whole thing had been incredibly humiliating.

One second he was on the verge of one of the best orgasms of his life; the next he was bent over in pain, pantless. It couldn't have been any worse, and he should have known better. It was no surprise his bad leg had seized up; after all, it was football season, when he was stressed, didn't drink enough water, and spent a lot of time on his feet. To shove himself into the backseat of his truck bed had been the stupidest thing he could have done, but at the time he'd had one thing on his mind. And it wasn't his bum leg.

He'd felt the cramp building, the muscles in the back of his thigh tightening as he'd awkwardly thrust into her hand, both legs twisted against the door. But at the time he couldn't bring himself to stop. A severe miscalculation. That's what he got for making out with a woman in his truck. Grown men were supposed to take a woman to their beds.

Bennett ran a hand through his hair and stared at the mess of papers spread out before him. The stress of the past few weeks was culminating in front of his eyes. He was behind on schoolwork. Two classes' worth of tests needed grading and his AP Biology class had just turned in research papers that needed reading. He had a lot of catching up to do before progress report grades were due, and time was tight this week with homecoming activities.

On top of that, he was still pissed as hell about the fight and the loss of his two star players in the upcoming homecoming game. He honestly still couldn't believe it had happened. Jason's physical condition made Bennett even more depressed. They'd been able to use some sort of glue to seal Jason's small cut closed, but he had indeed suffered a concussion, which they'd all figured but were still distressed to have confirmed. The doctor had said two weeks without football, and Bennett wanted a guarantee that everything was in the clear. Second-hit syndrome had become too common in football—especially high school—and he was not willing to take a chance.

Bennett sighed and dropped his head to stare at the floor. So much to do, so much shit going on, and still his thoughts turned to Callie. He looked up at all the work to be done and then chose to pick up his phone instead.

He quickly found Callie's contact and hit the call button. As her phone rang he glanced at the time on the television. Nine. Not too late; he hoped she wasn't—

"Hello," she said in a flirty little voice that informed him she knew exactly who it was and was happy to hear from him. He liked that. Bennett smiled and leaned back on the couch, some of his stress fading away just from the sound of her voice.

"Hey. How are you?"

"I'm good. How is that leg?"

It was sweet and also embarrassing that she had to ask. "It's fine."

"Good. Any time you need a Callie massage you know how to find me."

"Nice, I'll be sure and do that," Bennett said.

"I don't offer Callie massages to just anyone, I'll have you know." She laughed.

"You better not," he responded without thinking, and quickly regretted it. What would she think of that? Shit, what did *he* think of that? Acting possessive of her implied something and he didn't think that's what either of them wanted. But the only thing that had crossed his mind was the thought of her touching anyone else, and he hadn't liked it one fucking bit.

For a moment they were both quiet and suddenly he realized maybe he should have just texted her. Thankfully, she saved them from the awkward pause.

"So, did you need something or did you just miss me?" she teased. He loved how she made it so easy to talk to her. Did he miss her? Yeah, no doubt, but he wasn't sure if he wanted to admit it just yet.

Fuck it, he'd just sounded possessive; why not go for it?

"Of course I did . . . miss you. But I had a reason for calling."

"Okay." He could tell she was smiling on the other end of the phone.

"Unfortunately, I think I'm gonna have to bail on practice tomorrow night."

"Oh, okay. How come?" Her voice had lost its flirty tone and he could tell she was skeptical. Not what he wanted.

"Not because I want to; I've just got a shitload of work to get done before Friday when progress report grades have to be turned in, and I can already tell I'll be pushing it as it is."

"Do you need some help?"

He laughed. "Nice of you to offer, but I'm not sure you'd be interested in reading AP Biology research papers."

"Eh, probably not. But then again, who knows. Sometimes I even surprise myself. What are some of the topics?"

He appreciated her feigning interest and picked up the paper on the top of the stack. "Okay. First up is 'Early Symptoms of Senile Dementia.'"

"Yuck. Too depressing."

Bennett grabbed the next one. "'Biological Warfare of the Future.'"

"Yikes, no."

"'Deforestation's Effects on Parasitic Diseases,' 'Vaccinations in Third World Countries'?"

"Seriously? I expected things like . . . 'How Eyeballs Work' or 'How People Catch a Cold.' What do you say to these kids as a guideline? 'Write a paper that makes you question your will to live'? Those topics are awful."

Bennett sank into the couch, getting comfortable. Misha jumped up and sat beside him, so he petted her head as he spoke. "I find these topics fascinating and so do most students who take AP Biology. And the guideline is basically to write about biology in the real world."

"Yeah, well, I think I'll pass. Sorry I couldn't help you, but you know, life is easier when one lives in denial about parasitic diseases."

Bennett chuckled. "It might be. So what are you doing right now?"

"I am currently typing up a blog post for tomorrow. It's a recipe for the best banana bread in the whole world. Much happier subject matter than *your* work."

"True. Sounds good."

"You think? I'll have to make you some. Do you like

bananas? I don't like bananas plain, but I like them in stuff."

"They're okay. But yeah, I probably prefer banana bread to plain bananas." He smiled to himself as he considered how normal and at the same time odd this conversation was. She was just so easy to talk to. "What's your favorite thing to bake?"

"Easy, anything with a yeast dough. Cinnamon rolls, pastries, bread. It's very rewarding to have it turn out right, because yeast dough can be tricky. So many variables come into play in order for it to turn out. Moisture, temperature, even the weather outside."

"There's that damn science again. Can't seem to get away from it."

Callie giggled and then turned on a fake stern voice. "Stop making me like science, Coach Clark."

"Stop talking about how important it is then," he teased back. Bennett glanced at the coffee table in front of him loaded with work that desperately needed his attention. Damn, he hated to get off the phone with her, but he had to, considering he was already behind. He sighed. "Well, I better get going so I can get some of this done."

"Okay. So, I guess I'll see you at the game Friday?" she asked.

"Yeah. Then back to practicing on Tuesday."

"I'm looking forward to it," she said.

"Me too."

"Good."

"Okay." Why was he stalling? He was acting like an idiot by hesitating and felt even more ridiculous when he heard the sound of Callie laughing quietly on the other end of the phone. Finally she spoke first.

"Good-bye, Bennett."

"Bye, Callie."

The line went quiet and he knew she'd hung up. Time to refocus. Bennett sat up and forced himself to start reading about senile dementia. Callie was right: depressing as hell. He would much rather think of her.

Nine

This was Callie's second homecoming since moving to Preston, but it was way more exciting now that she had a connection to the school. She felt more a part of the community this year. And the little town did homecoming up right, treated it like a holiday. Most stores on Main Street had posters in their windows or a Panthers flag displayed out front just as Callie's Confections did.

She smiled to herself when she considered that last year she had no idea that the football coach was a total hottie. How were people not talking about it? Maybe she hadn't really cared to listen or ask. It could be that everyone was used to him since he had been at the high school for six years now.

Callie carried a tray of blue-and-white-frosted cupcakes into the front of the bakery and slid them into the case. She glanced at the clock on the wall and then over at Eric, who was restocking the coffee buffet. "Can you flip the sign and unlock the door for me?"

"I'd be happy to. If you give me details about what's going on with Coach Clark." Eric shot her a look.

"Eric, I don't kiss and tell."

"Are you kidding me? Our relationship's foundation is built on stories of foreplay gone wrong, one-night stands, and guys with bad breath. What gives?"

Callie shrugged. "I don't know, it just doesn't feel right. Plus you're making something out of nothing. It's not like we're dating."

Eric lifted an eyebrow and then walked over to the front door, unlocked it, and flipped the Closed sign to Open. "You're into him."

"Well, yeah. I mean, enough to fool around."

"Uh-uh." Eric walked to the counter and leveled his stare. "That's not what I mean, and you know it. So you're not dating, but is this . . . something?"

Callie considered the question, and her definitive answer was clear. "No. It's not *something*. It can't be something. I don't want to be the female coach that puts the moves on the hot football coach."

"Fair enough. Then be the hot female coach that lets the football coach put the moves on her."

Callie rolled her eyes. "You know what I mean."

"You and I both know it's too late for any of that. You've already kissed him, maybe more, and who cares what anyone else thinks."

Before Callie could respond, the front door opened. A woman with dark skin, curly shoulder-length ebony hair, and a beautiful smile walked in. Callie recalled seeing her in the shop before with two little girls.

"Good morning," Callie called out. "Welcome to Callie's."

"Good morning to you." The woman walked right up to the counter and stuck her hand out toward Callie. "I'm Corinne. Reggie Wilson's wife."

Callie smiled and shook her hand. "Reggie the coach, right?"

Corinne smiled. "And gym teacher."

"Well, what brings you in today?" Callie asked.

"Two things, really. First, I wanted to get the players a little something for tonight. I know it's a mom thing to do, but it's tradition. I usually bake myself but thought why bother when your cookies are so good."

Callie smiled and grabbed a pink box, ready to fill it. "I wish everyone thought that way."

Eric headed to the back to frost cupcakes as Callie took Corinne's order for the team. It made Callie happy to think Bennett might eat one of her cookies with the players. She hoped he did.

They hadn't spoken since Wednesday night on the phone, and she missed him terribly. Had even considered calling him again the night before but had decided it would be weird. Yeah, they had talked and flirted a little when he called, but at least he'd had an initial reason for calling. She couldn't very well do it for the hell of it. She'd hoped to see him in passing during practice after school, but it hadn't happened.

Corinne cleared her throat. "The other reason I'm here is to invite you to our annual homecoming party. It's tonight, right after the game. Teachers, coaches, and a few of our close friends. Are you interested?"

Callie was shocked. "Oh. That's so nice. Are you sure? I don't really know many of the other teachers or coaches."

"Exactly why you should come." Corinne tilted her head. "And of course you know Bennett."

Callie gave her a half smile. "I do. Thanks to the fund-raiser we're participating in." Callie wasn't normally a blusher; she hoped that didn't change right now.

"How's that going? I have to tell you, we were all so excited to hear somebody had knocked some sense into that boy."

"Well, that wasn't me, I can assure you. I think he just had a good reason to say yes."

"Whatever his reason, I'm sure it didn't hurt that you're beautiful."

Okay, the blushing was inevitable. "That's very sweet, but we're just friends. I'm just doing him a favor." Callie knew damn well that she could go to hell for that blatant lie.

The Panthers were losing their homecoming game. It was one thing to be down one starter, but two was insanity. And not just any two, but Bennett's very best. He'd been looking forward to this season for a couple of years, and here they were in a damn mess.

He choked down three ibuprofens—with yellow Gatorade, which he couldn't stand—and continued pacing the sideline. He'd been afraid this might happen with the two boys out, but the reality of it was devastating. Not because he wasn't a good loser; he'd lost many times—although he hated it. But Tuesday night's events with Jason and Tate had left a heavy cloud over the team and the coaches. Morale was down, animosity was high, and Bennett had a feeling the boys were taking sides. He just wasn't sure what the sides were. It felt like the boys were mad at him, but surely that was his guilty conscience speaking.

He had some anger of his own, that was for damn sure. He was *still* having trouble processing what Tate had done. The kid had received three days' in-school suspension for punching Jason. Obviously, that meant Tate couldn't play tonight, but it also meant he'd been unable to fulfill his role as homecoming candidate. Jason had received three days of after-school detention for being involved in a fight.

Not even being crowned Homecoming King at halftime had seemed to put a smile on Jason's face. Whatever words the two young men had spoken to each other Tuesday night had caused a rift that didn't seem to be healing. That was the biggest tragedy, and Bennett hoped more than anything that the boys could restore their friendship. If it was truly over a girl—and Bennett was pretty damn sure it was—then he hoped the boys had realized already that it wasn't worth it. Although who the hell was he to talk? Right now a female had his thoughts jumbled in his brain. Women had the power to make a man do some crazy shit, like sucker punch your best friend. And ballroom dance.

Bennett shook that thought off. This was football and he needed to focus on the game. It wasn't like him to allow such a distraction. He eyed the field and groaned as one of his boys made a ridiculous fumble on a second down. The crowd's unison *awww* was like a knife to Bennett's heart; he'd heard it again and again over the course of the evening. He bit off a curse of relief when the player managed to recover the ball. Not that it mattered, they were going to lose tonight, but damn, it would be nice to make this final score.

Bennett signaled for a time-out. The ref blew his whistle, and the boys ran over to the sideline where Bennett stood waiting. After they were all huddled he let out a deep breath. He couldn't give them a bunch of shit now: everyone was hurting; the situation was the fault of no single player on the field tonight . . . only the two who weren't. But he needed to say *something*.

"It's been a tough night, y'all. Your spirits are down; shit, mine are, too. But we're Panthers. We may lose a few, but we don't give up, and I can feel some of y'all givin' up." He hated how stress made his accent come out in full force.

Bennett glanced around. Many helmets were slumped in shame and despair. His guys hated to lose. He did, too.

"All of you listen the hell up." Reggie stepped in. He was much better at pep talks than Bennett was. They might not be poetic or even appropriate, but they were effective. "I don't know about you, but I'm not going out like this. Panthers don't take ass whoopin's, you hear me? So quit your damn cryin' and feeling sorry for yourselves. So we're down a couple men, so what. Quit actin' like you lost your manhood. Pull your shit together and give me this touchdown. Do I make myself clear?"

"Yes, Coach," rang out from the mass of bobbing helmets.

"On three," Bennett said. The boys huddled, counted off, and ran back to the twenty-yard line. Two downs and five minutes later they'd made the touchdown but lost the game. The final score was 22–14.

Bennett slugged through a morose wrap-up in the locker room, trying to find something encouraging to say, which was hard because for once he was unsure of what the immediate future held. He talked to parents—some concerned, some angry, some full of pity—gathered his stuff, and then headed to his truck.

He was completely exhausted as he made his way to the parking lot. So far this was the most depressing game of his coaching career, and he couldn't stop thinking that it shouldn't have happened.

He hated that he had so many other things going on in his life this season. He couldn't help feeling like maybe he should have sensed the strife between his two best players. But no, he'd been clueless. The fight had come out of nowhere as far as he was concerned, which was irritating, but he was even more pissed with Tate and Jason. If there was one thing Bennett had stressed to his guys it was that he was there if they needed him. Why hadn't the two talked to him about the shit that was going on between them? He hoped that it wasn't because they'd felt he was too busy for them right now.

But as much as that all sucked, Bennett had one thing going right in his life. Callie. Yeah, maybe it was all a distraction, but he deserved it, didn't he? He'd devoted all of his time and energy over the past six years to this school and this team. He was enjoying himself, and most important, he was enjoying her. All the way home he debated calling her tonight. Would it seem like a booty call? Did that matter?

Bennett pulled into his driveway and headed into the house. Misha greeted him the second he walked in, her tiny paws kneading at his legs. He dropped his bags and scooped her into his arms. "You miss me?"

The little fur ball responded with tiny licks to his chin. Bennett chuckled and set her down before heading to the back door. "Come on, Misha, let's go potty."

He smiled at the clicking of her tiny nails against the wood floor, and then she was out the back door. Bennett walked over to the fridge and pulled out something he only reserved for game nights. A bottle of sweet tea. His beverage vice, since he no longer drank alcohol. Also a reminder of his childhood.

When Bennett was a kid his mother would make a fresh pitcher of sweet tea every single day. She'd eventually stopped, realizing it probably wasn't the healthiest option, but for Bennett it was a reminder of happy times. Now on game days he always made sure to have one on hand. To be honest, it wasn't even really that great, but nostalgia was a powerful thing; it was about comfort.

Just as he was about to snap the lid open, his phone rang. He pulled it out of his pocket and glanced at the screen before answering. "Hey, Reg."

"Where you at? I thought you'd be here by now." Laughter and happy voices sounded in the background.

Shit, the annual homecoming party. Bennett blew out a breath. "I'm sorry, man. I can't believe I forgot."

"What the hell, Clark? We've been doing this for five years now."

"I know; I just . . ." Bennett glanced at the back door and ran a hand through his hair. "I've had a lot on my mind. Then tonight."

"Yeah, tonight sucked. Which is exactly why you need to get your ass over here. We won't talk about the game. Just eat some good food and shoot the shit."

"I know, man; I just think I'm going to miss this year. Now that I'm home I'm tired as hell." He also possibly had other plans.

Reggie was silent for a minute, and Bennett felt like a total ass. Reggie's wife, Corinne, went to a lot of trouble every year for this. The sounds of the party faded on the other end of the line, as if Reggie had gone into a quiet room. "This isn't about your dance partner, is it?" he asked.

Bennett's stomach knotted. "What? No. Why do you ask that?"

"I don't know. You've been spending time together; you seemed kinda into her maybe. Then Corinne talked to her at her shop this morning."

Bennett stalked over to the back door and opened it, trying to process the change in the conversation. Misha's white fur almost glowed in the dark as she pranced through the yard and inside. "She did? What about?"

Callie did not seem like the type to kiss and tell. No way.

"Nothing bad. Just that you guys were only friends. She was just helping you out as a favor."

What the hell? He couldn't really blame her; what was she supposed to say? But he definitely didn't like her answer.

"Okay. Fine, but that has nothing to do with tonight."

"All right. I believe you, just wanted to be sure you weren't avoiding the party because of her."

Bennett froze. "Is she there?"

He didn't miss Reggie's small chuckle. "Yep. Corinne invited her, and she's been sitting with McNeal for the past twenty minutes. Now I can't be certain, but it looks like he might be putting the moves on her nice and thick."

Bennett was silent. He had no words, but right now his jealousy was a living, breathing thing. He could feel it weighing down on his chest.

McNeal? John was one of Bennett's assistant coaches.

"So, uh, I'll see you in about twenty?" Reggie said, his voice full of amusement.

"You're a smart-ass," Bennett said.

"Hey, one of us has to be smart." The line went dead.

Bennett filled Misha's water bowl and then headed to his bedroom to take a shower. He had a damn party to go to.

Ten

Callie laughed at another one of John's corny jokes. He was funny, especially since he'd clearly had a little too much to drink. He was kind of cute, too. However, John's attention didn't keep her from glancing at the sliding glass doors every thirty seconds.

The party was spread throughout the Wilsons' house from the living room, through the kitchen, all the way out to the back patio, where she currently sat in a folding camp chair. One of many situated around a cute little brick fire pit. The fire did nothing to take her thoughts off Bennett. Would the smell of burning wood always make her think of kissing him? Touching him? Probably. And why wasn't he here?

"So, I heard you're teaching our main man how to dance," John said beside her. Callie turned her head to meet his eyes. He was leaned against the side of his chair—which he'd scooted closer to her at some point.

"I am. He's doing great so far. I'm really proud of him."

"I can't even imagine Clark dancing."

Callie smiled. "Anyone can dance. And he has an excellent teacher, so he's lucky."

"He is lucky. I'm a little jealous."

Okay, that was awkward. She gave him a small smile and then looked toward the back of the house once more. *Come on, Bennett.* She was a little tired of making idle chitchat. Many of the teachers she'd met for the first time tonight, and while they were nice, she hadn't come for them.

"Looks like he won't be coming out tonight," John said. "Bet Clark is pissed because of tonight's loss."

Callie wondered if it was obvious that she was waiting for Bennett. She decided to just go along with the conversation. "Well, you can't really blame him. It's always disappointing to lose."

"True. But he takes it harder than most. Blames himself when things are going wrong with his players."

"Why would he do that?" Now she was truly engrossed. If this guy would spill secrets about the man she couldn't quite figure out, then she was all ears.

John shifted in his chair. "Coach puts a lot of pressure on himself. He's got this idea in his head that he's responsible for these boys. Tries to keep them out of trouble, make sure they're doing well in school."

"I can't imagine what's wrong with that," Callie said.

"Now don't get me wrong, it's admirable and shit, it's just, you can't be everything, ya know. You can only do what you can do."

Callie nodded. John was right of course, but she couldn't help but feel a little thump in her chest to learn this about Bennett. It wasn't a shock; she sensed this about him just from things he said and what she'd witnessed herself. John turned back to her, leaning in close again.

"I mean, he forces his players to have his cell number on speed dial in case they get into trouble. Who does that? Students get themselves shit-faced on a Saturday night, I want nothin' to do with it. Know what I mean? I'm not having anyone's parents on my back." His words slurred a tiny bit.

"Well, I guess it's better than having someone end up in a ditch," she said, beginning to feel irritated. Bennett was a grown man, he didn't need her to defend him, but damn it, she wanted to. The world needed more men like Bennett Clark. Too many people wanted to turn a blind eye. Shit, she was guilty of being one of them way too often. "What do you think makes him that way?"

John shrugged and then burped a little. *Nice.* "He lost everything because of that accident. His NFL contract. His fiancée. No way that doesn't fuck a man up. I think he's just on a personal mission to make things right in his world. Who the hell knows. I don't question him."

Callie was stunned but kept her expression neutral. *Fiancée?* That was news. "No. Of course not."

Suddenly she was in the mood for anyone else's company, but before she could make an exit a large body stood in the doorway casting a shadow on the patio. Callie let out a breath. *Finally.*

Butterflies bounced around in her stomach as Bennett walked down the two cement steps. She willed him to see her, and her heart skipped as she watched him glance around the group of people and finally make eye contact with her. She stared right back at him and all she could think was that he might be the most thoughtful and caring man she'd ever met. She really wanted him to be the one telling her about himself. Maybe it was time for her to start pushing a little bit harder.

He said hello to a few people and then, thank goodness, he picked up a vacated chair and made his way around the circle straight toward her. Someone was sitting not far away from her on the right side, so she wondered what Bennett planned to do.

"Hey," she said, glancing up when he was right behind her. She had the answer to her question when he angled his chair into the space between her and John. Callie turned in her seat so she could see Bennett. His knee brushed the side of her chair as he sat down.

"Hi," he said when he was settled. He lifted his chin toward John, who had stared silently at the fire through the whole process. "What's up, John?"

"Clark," John said before taking a long swig of his beer.

Callie bit her lip, not wanting to laugh. Had some manly thing just passed between John and Bennett? She secretly hoped it had. She hadn't necessarily wanted whatever this was with her and Bennett to be public, but technically there was no rule against two staff members seeing each other. And to be honest, for all of Principal Jensen's warnings, he had made them *dance partners*. What did he expect would happen? Then again, it was possible everyone would just assume that she and Bennett had become friends over the dancing. That was totally believable.

"Sorry about tonight's game," she said.

Bennett folded his hands together and slouched into the seat. "Happens. Sometimes it's not your night. Right, McNeal?"

"Can't win 'em all. That's for sure," John said, casting Callie a quick glance before focusing his attention back on the fire.

Callie looked over her shoulder at Bennett and he raised his eyebrows in challenge. She laughed quietly and then turned back toward the group just as a conversation across the way gained everyone's attention. She listened as another teacher went on about something that had happened with some students during his class today.

The fire popped and Callie snuggled into her chair and stretched out her legs. She could almost feel Bennett's eyes on her profile. She really wished John would just get up, so Bennett could squeeze in closer. She was almost surprised John hadn't offered to, after the way Bennett had acted. Or maybe that was why John hadn't. *Men.*

Callie's pocket vibrated and she twitched in her chair before reaching into her puffy vest and pulling her phone out. She glanced around; everyone was still engrossed in the story being told. Callie held her phone down in her lap for privacy . . . she just had this feeling.

BENNETT: Has John been hitting on you?

A giant grin threatened to erupt on her face. She bit at her lip but didn't respond immediately. After a moment her phone vibrated again.

BENNETT: ??
CALLIE: Chill out, Clark. And please define
"hitting on."

She heard him shift in his seat behind her.

BENNETT: You know exactly what I mean.

This was cute. Jealous Bennett Clark. She wished she could see his face right now. She turned around to look at him. He was farther away from the fire, but she could still make him out just fine even back in a shadow. He was staring at her, one foot resting casually on his knee. But there was nothing relaxed about the expression on his face. She gave him a little smile.

Instead of speaking or returning her smile, he glanced back down to his phone, and she could see his thumbs moving over the screen. She turned back and waited.

When the message popped up her heart rate sped into dangerous territory.

BENNETT: I wish you were sitting in my lap.
Naked.

She liked this side of Coach Clark.

CALLIE: I could ride you hard in that chair.

She heard Bennett blow out a long breath behind her.

BENNETT: Let's get out of here.
CALLIE: You move fast.
BENNETT: When I know what I want I do.

She shoved her phone between her thighs. She needed to collect her thoughts. Did she want to take this all the way? Stupid question; of course she did. The real question was, *should* she? Callie hadn't come tonight so she and Bennett could roast marshmallows together. Although she now realized that she totally would do just that if it's what he wanted. She liked Bennett. Talking to him. Hearing him laugh. Learning about him. She wished she knew more, but right now a naked Bennett Clark seemed like a very good place to start.

Callie picked her phone up.

CALLIE: Let's not be obvious. I'll go in and say good-bye, etc. You meet me out front in a little bit.

Without waiting for him to respond, Callie made a show of yawning, saying good-bye to John, who already seemed to have given up on her—smart guy—said good night to several others, and then made her way inside.

Ten minutes later she walked down the street to find Bennett sitting in his truck idling beside her car. She smiled, making her way to his window, but then felt a twinge of panic when she saw the look on his face.

"What's wrong?"

"I'm sorry, I'm gonna have to go," he said, his arm resting on the window. "I know this sounds nuts, but . . . I got a text from one of my guys. Tate's trashed at some field party, threatening to kick somebody's ass. He's not taking this week's events—"

"Are you going to go pick him up?" she asked, cutting Bennett off.

He looked at her and she could tell that he seemed surprised at her comment. Did he not think she'd understand? Of course she was disappointed and admittedly a little pissed that a drunk teenager had ruined what she and Bennett had planned, but she couldn't fault him for this, especially after her talk with John.

"Yeah. I was going to go get him."

"I could come with," she said, not sure if that's really what she wanted but knowing full well she'd do it if he wanted her to.

"Might not be a good idea. If Tate's dad isn't around I may take him back home with me to sleep it off on the couch. Don't want to leave him alone drunk and angry."

"Have you done that before?"

"Once. I'm afraid that while Tate's been known to get trashed on occasion, his father does it regularly. With everything that's going on, and this loss tonight . . . I ju—"

"I understand, Bennett. If you think it's the right thing I believe you. Go take care of your quarterback and maybe . . . I don't know, call me. Let me know how he is. How you are."

Bennett looked at her for a moment before leaning out of the window a little. "Come here," he said quietly.

She stepped toward the driver's door and laid her fingers on his forearm. "I'm here."

"Thank you, for understanding," he said.

Callie went up on her tiptoes and placed a kiss on Bennett's lips. Then another. Just when she was about to pull away he took his hand off the wheel and slid his fingers through her hair, gently cupping the base of her head and pulling her harder against him. They kissed deeply for a moment, his tongue teasing hers.

Finally, her toes aching, she retreated. The heat in his eyes after their kiss made her stomach tingle. "Don't look at me like that," she teased. "Or Tate's going to have to fend for himself."

The corners of Bennett's lips quirked before he spoke. "Don't go back in there and talk to John again, ya hear?"

Callie playfully rolled her eyes. "So bossy, Coach Clark. Don't worry, I'm going to go home and dream about you again."

He gave her a sexy grin this time before he whispered, "Bye," with just enough Texas twang to make her sigh. She watched his taillights until he turned off onto a cross street. Callie got into her car and started home.

What the hell was she doing? She didn't know what she wanted out of this. Sure, she wanted the obvious, an amazing night with Bennett, but was that all? It had been a long time since she'd truly missed a man, but with Bennett it was becoming a problem. When she wasn't with him, she thought of him constantly.

Eleven

Callie walked up to Anne's front door holding a large Callie's Confections box. She kicked lightly with her foot in lieu of knocking.

It was once again her favorite day of the week during the fall. *Celebrity Dance Off* Monday. Although this week she could only think of the last time she'd watched the show, with Bennett sitting next to her. She'd been so close to inviting him again but hadn't. They'd see each other again for practice tomorrow, and she was excited to think that maybe they'd now have fun with each other again.

The door opened and Claire greeted her in sparkly pink cowboy boots and a Chevy Camaro T-shirt.

"Well, it looks like I came to the right place. I was looking for a cowgirl mechanic," Callie said.

"I'm not a mechanic; they're dirty." Claire moved so Callie could enter.

"Oh, sweetie, someday you'll appreciate how hot that is," Callie said under her breath.

"What did you say?" Claire asked.

"Oh, nothing; where's Mommy?"

"In the kitchen. Did you bring me something?"

"Of course I did." Callie lowered the pink box for Claire to remove a cookie. "Don't tell Mom; you haven't had dinner yet."

As Claire ran up the stairs with her loot Callie walked into the kitchen to find Anne cooking. This week Mike would have definitely called uncle on watching dancing again, so he was nowhere to be seen. Callie set down her box, her mouth watering at the scent of tomatoes and garlic. "What is that fantastic smell?"

"Mom's famous lasagna," Anne said with a grin. "From scratch."

"Sounds delicious. How is Marie?"

A few months back Anne's mother had had a little scare with her diabetes acting up, so Anne kept a close eye on her. "She's doing well. Just spent the weekend in Branson with her girlfriends."

"That's the life. When I grow old I want a bunch of Maries to vacation with."

"Aww," Anne said. "Lindsey and I will be your Maries."

"Of course, we'll be the coolest old ladies ever." Callie gave Anne a wink and held up the pink box. "I brought today's leftovers. And wine, duh."

"Lindsey said she's running late, to get going without her, and Eric should be here any minute," Anne said as she cut some bread.

Eric announced himself as having arrived by yelling from the front door and then joined them in the kitchen. After greetings and wine pouring they all began loading up plates of food. They had about twenty minutes before the show started, so they settled around Anne's little kitchen table.

"So, is your winning dance routine ready?" Anne asked Callie.

"Almost. The last few practices have been particularly good and things are really starting to come together. Despite the fact that my student is a grown man that has a deaf ear for music and too many muscles to keep track of."

"Problems, problems," Eric said. "I'm so sad for you. So how is it really going?"

All eyes were on Callie. "If you're asking the question I think you are, the answer is no. Not yet anyway."

"Do you mean . . . I mean . . . do you like him? Is there something going on between you?" Anne said, looking a little confused.

Callie felt kind of bad that she hadn't confided in Anne lately. They'd both been so busy, Anne with the conference, Mike, and of course being a full-time mother. And Callie with . . . all the shit going on in her life. Things had just gotten very complicated for everyone as of late. In good ways for the most part, of course, but still, beside the blog they had all kind of been too busy to just have fun with each other.

The front door burst open and they all turned to look as they heard heavy steps run through the living room and then suddenly Lindsey appeared in the kitchen, her face full of wide-eyed panic. "Where can I hide?"

"Oh my god, Linds, what's going on?" Anne scrambled from her seat.

"I just need to—"

"Lindsey Morales, you can run, but you can't hide," a deep voice boomed from the living room. The front screen door slammed and once again footsteps came through the house, but these weren't running; they were charging like an angry giant.

"Derek, what's wrong? Where's Mike?" Anne asked in shock as the man stepped into the small kitchen. The frustration emanating from his body nearly sucked the oxygen out of the room. He didn't even acknowledge Anne's questions; his eyes were focused intently on Lindsey.

Callie liked Derek—what she knew of him anyway, which was basically that he was a friend of Mike's. And also the hottest single dad she'd ever met, but the way he was acting at this moment made her question his sanity.

"Were you really going to pretend you didn't see me out there?" he asked, pointing right at Lindsey.

"Yep, that's exactly what I was going to do. But you just ruined it," Lindsey nearly growled, her body on the verge of shaking, fists clenched at her sides.

Eric and Callie glanced at each other over the table, both showing their extreme shock. They had never heard or seen sweet, quiet little Lindsey behave this way. Callie didn't know their friend was even capable of this kind of passionate behavior; she wasn't sure if she should be impressed or afraid for Lindsey.

"Well, excuse me if I'm a little slow on the uptake," Derek ground out. His voice was full of sarcasm and venom. "I guess I assumed that we had grown up a little since college. I see I was wrong."

"Linds," Callie said, her eyes darting between the angry couple facing off on each side of the kitchen. "Is everything okay?"

"Everything is fine, Callie," Lindsey bit out. Callie's mouth dropped open. Yep, she was definitely impressed with Lindsey. The girl had some spunk they didn't know about.

"Well, now we've seen each other, so you can leave," Lindsey said. Her voice was shaking, but she held her ground. Derek looked like he was mad enough to smash something, his lips thinning and nostrils flaring. What the hell was up with these two?

Callie felt Eric kick her under the table. She looked and met his eyes.

Do you know what the hell is going on?

Not a clue, but there's definite history.

For sure.

We are so Team Lindsey if we have to choose.

Obviously . . . although Derek is hot.

Callie glared at Eric.

Okay, Team Lindsey!

Derek opened his mouth to speak, but Mike came into the kitchen. "What the hell is going on in here?"

Anne stood up. "Lindsey, please tell me what's wrong. It's my fault Derek is here; I told Mike that they could come and make a plate of food and go." She sent a regretful glance toward Lindsey. "I had no idea it would be a problem."

"I'm sorry, Anne," Lindsey said. "It's fine. I'll just . . . wait with Claire upstairs." She made for the doorway, but Derek rushed forward and stood in her path.

"Are you really not going to talk to me?" Derek asked. His voice had gone soft.

Lindsey glanced around the room. Everyone pretended to get back to their food as she whispered, "I have nothing to say to you. I won't ever have anything to say to you, Derek."

Callie kept her head down but glanced up through her lashes just in time to see a flash of deep pain cross over Derek's eyes. She had no idea what the history was between the two, but history there definitely was. One that no doubt involved strong feelings and a traumatic ending, if she was any kind of expert on body language and soap operas. Which, of course, she was, thanks to Barbara, who had used *All My Children* and *Guiding Light* as babysitters.

"Hey, man, maybe this isn't the time," Mike said quietly to Derek.

Derek's jaw clenched, his eyes never leaving Lindsey, who was working really hard at not meeting them and fighting off tears at the same time. *Shit.* Callie hated that there was something capable of hurting Lindsey so easily that she hadn't known about. Callie and Anne shared a look of concern.

"You're right." Derek relaxed a little and turned to the table. "I apologize. I'll go and let you ladies . . . and uh—" His eyes darted to Eric.

"No worries, man. I'm used to it," Eric said with a shrug.

Derek nodded, obviously uncomfortable. "Anyway, I'll just go."

Callie stood up. "Hold on a minute. Lindsey and I will just go check on Claire for a moment. You boys get your dinner to go and scram before we're finished."

Grabbing Lindsey's sweaty hand, Callie led her out of the kitchen, through the living room, and up the stairs. Before they reached the top Callie heard Lindsey sniffle and turned quickly and pulled her into the bathroom.

"Sweetie, don't let that man make you cry. Tell me what's going on," Callie said as she moved Claire's pink princess towel and sat on the side of the tub. Lindsey plopped down on the toilet and dropped her head into her hands.

"I can't believe I just reacted that way. How humiliating. I've played that moment over and over in my head so many times. Never did I plan to act like a complete fool."

"Do you want to talk about it? You know I'm here for you, Linds. I had no idea there was anything between you and Derek. As far as I knew you'd never even met him."

On a groan Lindsey lifted her head and looked at Callie. "Derek was my first boyfriend, first kiss, first *everything.*"

"Let me guess, first heartbreak, too?" Callie said as she grabbed Lindsey's hand.

A fat tear ran down Lindsey's cheek. "Believe it or not, this is the first time I've seen his face since Christmas break my sophomore year of college. I can't believe it's affecting me this way. It was years ago."

"That's not *too* long ago," Callie said, unsure if the words helped or made it worse.

Lindsey blew out a breath and wiped her eyes. "Darn it. I'm so angry that I freaked out like that. Why couldn't

I have been cool, indifferent, or, better yet, married! I mean, I'm in no better of a place now than I was then. No man seems to want me."

"Are you kidding me? You're an artist that runs her own business, you're a popular online presence, and you're beautiful and smart." Lindsey's Mexican heritage had given her the most gorgeous complexion and dark hair. Anne and Callie had discussed many times how plain they felt in Lindsey's presence. "Plenty of men want you. I see them looking; you're the one who doesn't notice. And what the hell does Derek have going on that's so damn great?"

"Oh, I don't know," Lindsey said, full of sarcasm. "Maybe he's a rich architect that drives a Mercedes."

"Uh, he's also a divorced single dad that . . ." Callie struggled to find anything wrong with Derek. Obviously there was something, because no one was perfect. But he didn't have a beer belly, far from it. He hadn't aged poorly or gone bald prematurely. As far as she was concerned, he was always polite and charming. The Derek she'd just witnessed in Anne's kitchen was not the one Callie was used to seeing.

"See? He's hot. Just a big badass hot version of his young self. I saw him and just fell apart. I had no warning, just *bam,* my past staring at me across Anne's front yard. I had no idea he was friends with Mike. I didn't even know he lived in Preston." Lindsey chewed her lip, her brows scrunched before she asked. "Is he really divorced?"

Huh. That was an interesting response, but Callie didn't comment, just nodded her head. "He is. Not sure for how long, but I get the feeling that it was messy."

"I didn't know that. But it doesn't change things. I just made a complete fool of myself."

"Well, it's over now. You don't have to talk to him again if you don't want to."

"I can't believe this. Of all the people. I love Mike, and now I know he consorts with the enemy!"

Callie gave a sheepish smile. "Well, if we're being honest, so do I. Derek is a really nice guy. He brings his son to the shop sometimes."

On that note, Lindsey's lip wobbled, as she finally gave way to fresh tears. "What I don't understand is why Derek didn't seem that surprised to see me."

"Anne wouldn't set you up like that, no way. But Linds, you're gonna have to come to terms with this. I mean, yeah, Derek doesn't come around a lot, but you're bound to cross paths. He's Mike's best friend. Maybe it would help to hear him out. Get some closure."

"Oh no, no way. It took me two years to finally get over him; I can't revisit those feelings. I can barely look into his eyes."

After what had jus transpired downstairs, Callie wondered if *over him* was the right way to describe Lindsey's feelings but didn't say so. She was pretty sure that wouldn't go over well. "I can't tell you what to do, but you can't let your past define you. Take control of it. I'll be here for you. Plus, how fun will it be to show off how awesome you are now?"

"Yeah, I really showed him I'm awesome by running in the house like my heels were on fire. I came off like a total psycho."

"Sweetie, if we were judged solely by our crazy times,

I'd never have any friends." Callie grinned and squeezed Lindsey's hand.

"Thanks, Cal. I'm so glad I have you guys."

A soft knock at the door preceded Anne's entrance. "Hey." Anne knelt down next to them in the small bathroom. "I'm so sorry that happened. They're gone. Did you guys . . . date?"

Lindsey nodded, her lip threatening to quiver again. Callie patted Lindsey's knee.

"I think he really wanted to see you," Anne said.

"Well, that's too bad," Lindsey said. "I'm not interested in talking to him at all."

Anne looked a little concerned but went on. "Well, I didn't want to do this in the bathroom. But the real reason I invited him here was because Mike and I sort of arranged for everyone to stop by tonight because . . . we wanted to announce our engagement."

Anne held up her hand; it was sporting a dazzling cushion-cut diamond. Not huge, but on the healthy side of modest. It was gorgeous and looked slightly vintage. Derek drama quickly forgotten, the three women erupted into screams and hugs.

A moment later Anne collected herself and took a deep breath. "Linds, I want you and Cal in my wedding more than anything. But Derek is Mike's best friend. If you don't want to—"

"Stop." Lindsey put up a hand. "Don't say another word. I'm a big girl, I can handle this. I won't let what happened between us take anything away from you and Mike's day. I promise, Anne."

Anne teared up and then pulled Lindsey in for a hug.

"Thank you." When they separated Anne was swiping at her eyes. "I'm just so happy."

At those words Callie was shedding a tear also. "We're so happy for you both. I'm doing your cake, right?"

"Of course, oh my gosh, the whole event will be a collaboration between the three of us."

"Oh god, the readers are going to shit when they find out about this. Can we cover the entire planning on the blog?" Callie asked, ideas crashing around in her brain. "It would be amazing."

Anne grinned. "Actually, Mike and I discussed the same thing. It would be a really fun series. We even thought we could let the readers vote on some things. Of course, we'd have already approved all the options, but how fun would that be? And we're getting married at the farmhouse. In fact . . . wait for it. . . . Mike bought it for us! That's where he proposed, in the garden. He even had Claire videotape it. It was so sweet."

The tiny bathroom erupted into another round of giggling and hugs.

"A rustic barn wedding. That is right up my alley." Lindsey fanned her face. "Oh, Anne, this will be so wonderful."

Eric's voice called to them from downstairs that *Celebrity Dance Off* was starting.

The three women all held hands now. "I love you both," Callie said. "But right now, men in tight pants are calling my name. So let's revisit this moment over pizza this week."

* * *

Bennett stood up from the desk chair he'd been sitting on for the past twenty minutes and glanced at the clock. About seven of his first-hour biology students had missed that morning due to a band field trip, so five of them had come in during his planning period to get the day's assignment done. "Looks like you've got about twenty minutes left before the bell rings to get that finished if you don't want to have homework."

The distinctive sound of bodies shuffling in seats met his ears and he stepped into the supply room to check his phone. He'd done that more often in the past couple of weeks than he'd done in his life. Even crazier, he'd just enjoyed life lately more than he had in a long time. Longer than he could remember. Ironically, it had nothing to do with football. Only a woman, teaching him to dance. Unbelievable.

Practices, while hard, were enjoyable just because she was there. And he was finally getting the hang of it. They could even end up winning. But he didn't even care about that so much anymore. It was Callie who occupied nearly all his thoughts.

The way she touched him, kissed him. And especially the way she'd understood—and even known—that he would go get Tate Friday night. That had shocked him. She hadn't pouted or gotten angry; she'd just accepted it.

She played it cool, always, so unlike other women. She didn't talk about going out together, didn't invite him over, and didn't hint at more. Whatever more was he wasn't really sure. But for some crazy reason he found himself wanting just a *little* more.

More time. More talking. And definitely more touching.

Finding there were no texts or missed calls, he shoved the phone in his pocket and went back to his desk. Everyone was silent, the only sound the scratching of pencils. One of the kids stared aimlessly out the window.

Bennett began grading some papers from his physiology class. Five minutes later one of the freshman girls—Ava, she was on the quiet side, smart—brought him her finished assignment. He motioned for her to put it on a pile at the corner of his desk. She did but then lingered, edging around the desk closer to him.

He looked up at her. "Can I help you, Ava?"

She smiled back and spoke quietly. "Some of the girls and I were wondering what kind of dance you and Coach Daniels are doing?"

Bennett glanced at the other students in the room; two other freshman girls watched, waiting for his answer. "Uhh . . . well, it's a waltz for the most part."

"Oh, that's good," another student called from the closest row.

Ava was still standing at his side. "We're all excited. We made our moms buy tickets."

He laughed. "Well, don't have your expectations too high. I might look ridiculous."

"It's cool, though, I mean, that you're doing it." This was from a guy.

"I'm happy to hear I have all of your support. I'm pretty nervous about it," Bennett said, and then looked at the clock again. "Y'all only have five minutes, so hurry and get that work done."

Ava grabbed her backpack and left and Bennett pulled his phone out of his pocket again and opened a text.

BENNETT: Some of my students have bought tickets to see our dance. Better make me look good.

He hit send and stared at it for a minute. It was a Tuesday; she was more than likely really busy at her bakery. She probably wouldn't respond.

Except she did.

CALLIE: Please. We are amazing.

He smiled when he saw the tiny emoticon of a woman dancing. Callie loved using those little pictures.

BENNETT: Are we still meeting tonight?
CALLIE: Of course.

He quickly tried to think of another thing to say. He wished they were together right now, which was a completely insane thought. He was working. She was working. He'd seen her Friday night and would have her in his arms again tonight for practice.

They were still practicing in the gym, but he realized that wasn't what he wanted tonight. He wanted her all to himself.

BENNETT: Come to my place.

She didn't respond for a while and he worried he might have blown it. They were both adults. She knew exactly what he was asking. His phone buzzed.

CALLIE: I'll be there, big boy.

A stupid grin broke out on his face, but he quickly collected himself. He glanced at the students still working.

BENNETT: Good, gotta go.
CALLIE: Bye, Coach.

Followed by a tiny football.

Twelve

Callie was exhausted. Today had been rough. The bakery had been unusually busy; she'd had a blog post due for Wednesday—that she'd finished, thank goodness—and dance team practice had been incredibly stressful. The captains were attempting to teach the team a routine they'd choreographed, and while it was really good, no one seemed to be getting it.

Knowing she was sweaty and had flour in her hair, Callie ran home to shower before heading to Bennett's. It was days like this she wondered why she tried to burn the candle at both ends the way she did. It sure would be a lot easier to take her mother's advice and find a rich husband. Have 2.5 children, become president of the PTA, and spend her days lunching with other moms before chauffeuring her children to and fro.

Then again, nope. Just the thought of it was more than she could handle. She was too independent for her own good. She liked the life she had, but damn if it wasn't tiring.

After her shower, she decided to blow-dry her hair

straight. She hadn't done it in a while, but it usually made her feel pretty. A little done up. Tonight was going to be . . . special. She was nearly certain. The fact that Bennett had requested to practice at his place again was the bigger clue, but the other was that everything had been leading up to this. The next step was obvious and she was so ready.

Finally done with her makeup, Callie got in her car and headed through town toward Bennett's house. She couldn't help admiring her bakery as she drove down Main Street. Even closed, it looked so cute with its white-and-pink-striped awning, the scripted *Callie's Confections* logo so bold and lovely. She was so proud of what she'd done.

It seemed like just yesterday that she moved to the small town of Preston. She'd majored in dance and art history, a double major that led to very few job opportunities in the Midwest. Plus by the time she'd graduated she was pretty burnt-out on performance—and her parents—so she'd moved to Preston, where her best friend Eric was from. He'd always spoken so fondly about his quaint little hometown, about all the cute little shops, nice people, and lovely parks. It sounded perfect, and as Callie had grown up in a small town south of Kansas City, one up north offered a familiarity along with the bonus tranquility of being a small road trip away from her mother.

That first summer, Eric had worked for his dad's landscaping business and Callie had immediately gotten a job waitressing at a dive bar in the next town over. She made okay money but loathed the handsy creeps who were regulars and hated even more the way she smelled when she left there. Like beer, tobacco, and broken dreams. Several nights a week she'd get off and go to the all-night supercenter, load up on baking supplies, and go home and create masterpieces in her tiny kitchen.

It was Eric who'd encouraged her to set up shop at the farmers market on Main Street on Saturday mornings. She remembered clearly the day Anne had come to her booth and tried her blueberry scones. They'd come out perfect that weekend, a tender, flaky center and a crunchy outside dusted with sanding sugar. Anne had gone on and on about them and come back the next week with her daughter, Claire, and tried the sugar cookies, then cinnamon rolls the week after that. On the fourth week Anne had asked Callie if she'd do a feature on Anne's blog.

The blueberry scones recipe had rolled out on the *My Perfect Little Life* blog the following Monday and had been a hit. The rest was a blur. Word of mouth spreading like crazy, the blog gaining more and more popularity, until finally Callie had taken out a small loan from her father and opened her own shop. She didn't regret a bit of the hard work. She'd managed to pay off the loan in her first five months of being open, and the store was profiting. Not too bad for a girl with a closet full of tiaras.

Pulling out of town, Callie merged onto the highway that led to Bennett's house. Her nerves kicked up in her stomach. Silly, since they'd already spent quite a bit of time together.

It was a cool day, a little overcast. She hadn't checked the weather, but it looked like rain could fall any moment. The flat grey—nearly fluorescent—tinge of the last rays of daylight only served to make the emerging fall colors more vibrant. She was surprised how lovely the drive up to Bennett's house was, even more so than it had been a few weeks ago. Deep yellows, reds, and oranges dotted the forest. It was breathtaking.

Just as she pulled in, drops began to fall on her windshield. She glanced at the house and saw that the garage door was raised, Bennett and Misha waiting for her. Seeing that big man with his cotton ball of a dog never failed to amuse. This time the little dog stayed put right at the threshold, barking wildly.

Callie grabbed her bag and got out of the car. Misha began to whimper with excitement as Callie approached. She knelt down right away, dropping her bag on the garage floor. "Oh my goodness, oh my goodness." Callie allowed the little dog to lick her cheeks. She rubbed Misha's ears and head. "You missed me so much, didn't you, Misha?"

When Callie stood up and met eyes with Bennett, her entire body flooded with desire. She'd been thinking of him all day long.

"It's sprinkling," she said.

"I see that."

"Practice inside?" Her words were punctuated with distant thunder. Misha scampered off toward the door to the house.

Bennett picked up Callie's bag—a complete gentleman—and without speaking she followed him inside. He led her into the living room and set her bag down on the sofa.

He looked so handsome today, his short hair sticking up in spots, a slight shadow on his sharp jaw. He wore a white long-sleeved T-shirt and Nike pants.

Shaking off her desire to jump him right then and there, she began to dig her phone out of her bag. Bennett showed her where she could plug it into his stereo system and then they both began to push the furniture out of the way in order to have plenty of space. She glanced up at the ceiling; luckily, it was pretty high in the living room.

"Okay, let's do what we've learned so far and then we're going to learn the lift."

His eyes widened. "I've been dreading this."

She laughed. "Are you thinking I should go on a diet first?"

"Oh god . . . no. I just—"

"It will be great; everyone will love it."

She started the music and began to count off. They went through the beginning, then the waltzing, circling around the living room.

"You've been practicing, Coach Clark," Callie said, looking at him.

He smiled. "Maybe."

They got through most of the dance, up until the big lift, and she stopped and smiled up at him.

"That was perfect. Didn't that feel perfect?" She was elated. It was the best they'd ever done. He still had a firm grip on her hands as he looked at her. "You've become an expert dancer."

"I wouldn't go that far, but yeah, it felt pretty good."

"Okay, once more, and *then* we'll learn the lift." She restarted the music again and they went through the motions, shooing a curious Misha out of the way a few times with their toes. This time Callie didn't count the whole time, just let them feel their way through it. She loved that it had become natural. Bennett knew the steps, handled her expertly, leading her through the waltz. When she dipped he stared right into her eyes.

The rain had picked up outside, the sky dark and casting the entire living room into shadows. Thunder rattled the windowpanes, and still they danced.

They continued to look at each other, intense, and when they met in the middle she reached up and touched his face. There was no way she could be this close to this man without wanting him. She knew he felt the same, could see it in his eyes, feel it in the way he held her.

Every step felt like foreplay, his hands lingering low on her back, his large thigh moving between her legs as they waltzed. He'd found a way to make it almost inappropriate. There was truly nothing like the feel of a man leading you through a dance with sure and confident steps. It was sexy, romantic, and beautiful.

When they normally would have stopped, after the swirly dip, he pulled her back up and continued to dance them around the living room.

So much for the lift. She let her hand that rested on his shoulder slide up his neck, touching the hairs at the base of his head. She was almost certain a shiver ran through his body, and still he stared into her eyes. They never lost their footing, never slowed down, lost count, or stopped, until finally the song faded away.

They stood still, wrapped together, hand in hand and chests rising and falling against each other. She saw Bennett's neck work as he swallowed.

"I don't think I can keep doing this and not have you," he said in a low voice.

"Then have me," she said.

They stared at each other for a moment and the minute she felt the warmth of his lips against hers she knew she was in trouble. He kissed like a man starving, his hands grasping her face and neck. The slide of his tongue against her own was enough to have her entire body melt against him.

Callie wrapped her arm around his neck, lifting herself higher to his mouth. Her other hand slipped under his shirt, exploring his heated skin, so unyielding but soft to the touch. His lips made their way across her face, under her jaw, and down her neck as she began to back up toward the sofa.

He stopped, halting her movements. "Not here."

He grabbed her hand and quickly led her down the hall. She barely registered that the *tap tap tap* following her was Misha. Bennett pulled Callie into his bedroom and she watched—all smiles—as Bennett leaned down and shoved the tiny dog out of the room and then slammed the door in her face.

"Aww, you're such a mean daddy," Callie teased.

Bennett shook his head in disbelief as he stalked toward her, intention etched into his face, his voice low and gruff when he spoke. "That's enough out of you."

"Bossy, bossy." Callie's eyes went wide as he took ahold of the hem of her shirt and quickly drew it over her head. She couldn't help teasing him a little more. "Is this the part where you spank me?"

Bennett gave a strangled laugh. He couldn't help it. *This woman*. He didn't even know how to describe her. She was an enigma. Gorgeous and sexy, and yet could make him laugh like no one else. He'd never experienced this feeling with any other woman.

She was grinning up at him all the while her fingers were finding their way under the elastic of his pants. His eyes went to her bra and he cupped one perfect breast in his palm.

"Do you *want* me to spank you?"

"I'll admit, it's not really my thing." Her head tilted to the side. "But I'm an adventurous sort of girl."

"Yes, I believe that you are. But right now . . ." He turned her body to face away from him and reached for the clasp of her bra, the release of each hook punctuating his words. "I only want one . . . simple . . . thing."

"What's that?" she asked, her head dropping forward.

"You, completely naked. On my bed."

Her bra went slack and he lowered his lips to her nape, planting small kisses just below her hair, down her neck. She rolled her head to the side and he moved on to her shoulder, lightly running his tongue across her smooth skin. He didn't let up until a shiver ran through her body.

"A hundred and seventy miles per hour, huh?" she asked. "The body is so efficient."

It took him a minute to remember that she was quoting his scientific facts about touch and brain signals. "Mm-hmm. I bet you also didn't know that a man's tongue is usually larger than a woman's."

"Obviously. Mother Nature is a woman and she's no dummy."

He chuckled and moved Callie's hair aside so he could lick along the shell of her ear, giving her just a hint of all the things he wanted to do with said tongue.

Thunder rumbled outside and goose bumps broke out across her shoulders. Bennett slid her bra straps down her arms as he whispered, "Goose bumps are caused by the pilomotor reflex. They're uncontrollable, and happen when your body is flooded with adrenaline because of strong emotions like fear . . . or arousal."

"Your brain is so sexy, Mr. Clark." Her head leaned back onto his chest.

"Know what else is triggered by the pilomotor reflex?" he asked. He grasped her hands and brought them to her breasts. Guiding her fingers, he placed them on her nipples and squeezed lightly. She sucked in a breath. "This. Do you feel how hard they are?"

"Yes," she whispered.

He turned her around to face him. "Get on the bed."

They both undressed fully and she crawled onto the bed. Even in the darkness of his room it was beautiful watching her move. He walked around to the side—not wanting to put his weight on his bad leg—and lay down beside her. Callie instantly grabbed for him, her fingers wrapping around his erection, her lips finding his. She didn't ask permission, just took, did as she pleased.

They kissed and touched each other, each learning what made the other catch their breath, moan, and sigh. She didn't hold back and he loved it. Loved touching her, loved the sounds she made. He wanted to get his mouth on every part of her, wanted to feel her body vibrate against him as she came. He lay flat, lifted his head to pull the pillow out from under him, and tossed it off the bed. With one efficient movement he pulled Callie on top of him, her legs naturally falling to each side of his waist.

His hands went to her breasts, fondling and teasing them. She leaned forward so he could pull one into his mouth. After a moment she sat up straight and she looked so beautiful there, above him. Her body was so strong and supple, he wanted to know every part of it.

Bennett palmed her backside and pulled, urging her body forward, "Scoot up here." He gave a jerk of his head, letting her know exactly what he meant.

Callie didn't need any further instruction; she grabbed the headboard and pulled herself up before shuffling her body over his chest, positioning a knee on each side of his head, her center right at his lips. He inhaled deep, loving her scent, and then trailed his tongue along the front of her.

"Holy shhh . . . oh my god." Her voice was strained and sexy as he devoured her.

Callie could barely breathe. Her fingers dug into the wooden headboard as Bennett's mouth worked her into a near frenzy. Every pass of his tongue got her closer; she wouldn't last long like this.

She glanced down, wishing she could see what he was doing to her, because it had to be the most erotic sight, her straddling his face like this. Bennett's hands settled on her hips, pressing them, urging her to rock against him. "You're gonna kill me, Bennett. But please don't stop."

The rain continued to pelt against the window and when lightning lit up the sky she was gifted with the sight of him—just for a moment—his head moving beneath her as his tongue did magical things. That was all it took for her. One of her hands dropped to his head, sliding through his hair as her body went still. Her legs began to shake as she came and his hands settled on her waist to help keep her upright. Callie's mouth dropped open, a slight whimper escaping.

When the sensations ebbed she let out a long breath. Her heart was pounding in her chest, and suddenly she couldn't hold herself up anymore. She slowly fell to the bed beside him, throwing one arm across his chest. "That was mind-blowing."

"Good. That's sort of what I was going for."

She let out a strangled laugh and then finally leaned up onto his chest. Laughing and goofing off with him was her favorite part of . . . whatever this was between them.

He moved a lock of hair off her face, tucking it gently behind her ear. "Why is your hair straight tonight?" he asked.

"I straightened it. I do that sometimes."

"I like it better curly. It's more *you*."

Warmth settled into her bones at his comment. She glanced down to see him still erect, and she found the strength to get up, straddling his lower half once more. "Do you know how sweet you are?"

He gave a little huff, as if he didn't believe what she was saying.

"I mean it. You are . . . amazing."

He reached up and pulled her down, their bodies flush and warm against each other. He kissed her once and then whispered against her lips, "You're more amazing."

She felt his body grind upward, big and hard against her. She smiled. "Oh, I'm sorry, did you still need me for something?"

He gave her ass a swift smack and she gave a squeak followed by a quiet giggle.

"Condoms in the drawer." He nodded to the bedside table and Callie leaned over to retrieve what they needed. After rolling it on, she rose up and slid down onto him, slowly. He had ahold of each thigh, his thumbs squeezing gently as she took him deeper.

When her behind met his upper thigh she stilled, just wanting to take in the sight of him. He was so perfectly proportioned, his chest wide, dusted with hair across his pecs and down the center of his abs. This was what a man should look like.

The rising of his chest brought her eyes to his. "I love looking at you," she said.

The corner of his mouth quirked up. "I feel the same way about you." His palms sought her breasts and she leaned over to give him better access.

"Ride me," he whispered.

She did, his thrusts meeting hers inch for inch until, his jaw locked tight, he breathed hard out of his nose and his hands pulled her down for the most sensual kiss of her life. It was all tongue, moans, and him shuddering beneath her. They were amazing together.

Later they lay tangled up in his bed, Callie drawing circles on his chest with her fingernail. "Sex and a science lesson in one. Impressive."

Bennett's chest vibrated under her head. "Turn you on?"

Callie looked up at him. "Actually, yes. Tonight was really great."

"Yeah. I agree."

Not wanting him to think she was looking for some

sort of deeper proclamation, she laid her head back down on his chest. "You're very smart. I always thought most coaches taught gym or speech class."

"I always loved science, since I was a kid. Read a lot about it, always did well in science class. When I was seven I asked for a microscope for Christmas. I liked to look at fingernails, hair . . . scabs."

"Ewww, that's so gross!" Callie exclaimed. They both laughed and he threaded his fingers with hers.

"Boys are pretty gross. Especially when they're kids. Did you not have any brothers or even sisters?" Bennett asked.

"I have a half brother. My dad was married once before. I don't really know Lane that well. He didn't spend a lot of time with Dad, plus he's eight years older, so there wasn't much of a connection. As soon as he was eighteen he went into the Air Force. He's an air-traffic controller now in Minnesota."

"Wow, that's cool."

Callie shrugged. "Yeah, I guess. We're Facebook friends. That's about as close as we get. What about you? Brothers and sisters?"

"I have an older brother. He's a doctor in Texas."

"Oh wow, a doctor and a professional football player. Your parents must be proud."

Bennett went still. Callie looked up at him, unsure of what to say. "I'm sorry. That was insensitive. But I'm sure no matter what happened, they're still proud."

"You're right, they are. It's just . . . I don't really even like to consider that time in life. I almost wish it was wiped from my memory."

"That's crazy. Look what you accomplished. You

know how many guys would like to go through life saying they'd played for the NFL."

Bennett's lips lifted a little. "Maybe."

"Maybe my ass. I bet some guys would give their left nut for that."

Bennett shook his head, finally giving her a real smile. "You're crazy."

"It's very possible."

Thirteen

Bennett sat at his desk Thursday afternoon, wired up and ready to get the day over with—including practice. All he wanted was to get home and have Callie in his arms. If that required dancing, so be it.

After spending the evening in his bed, they'd ended up practicing late into the night. He felt good about how far they'd come—at least how far he'd come. He was still worried he would mess everything up in front of an audience, but even that fear subsided a little more each time he and Callie practiced. He was now able to do the entire routine from memory along with the music. She'd even shown him the lift and they'd done it perfectly several times Tuesday night.

His leg had given him hell the next morning, but it was still worth it. Being with her touching her. Seeing her smile and tell him he was doing a good job. It was all worth it.

It was more than the dancing, though. He hadn't stopped thinking about having sex with her, recalling very vivid memories of her perched above him. Pleasuring her. He wanted her again so badly he was close to losing his mind. The whole thing terrified him. He'd been with women, enjoyed himself. But he hadn't craved a specific woman ever. Not like this. Not even Ashley.

There was a knock on the wall and Bennett looked up to find Jason in the doorway to his classroom.

"Hey, Jason."

"Coach."

"Come on in and have a seat." Bennett motioned for a chair near his desk. "So how ya feeling?"

Jason blew out a breath. "Better, now. I came to bring you this."

He handed Bennett a note, written on letterhead. A quick glance told Bennett it was Jason's medical release to play starting today, which meant he was hoping to participate in Friday's game. Bennett couldn't believe they'd cleared Jason so soon.

The problem was, something was up with Jason. Everybody sensed it. The coaches, the players, even Bennett himself. Something was off.

Jason and Tate still weren't speaking and the animosity between the two was affecting everybody on the team. Bennett ran a hand over his face before speaking. He needed to say this right. Delicately.

"I've been really impressed with how you've been handling yourself, coming to practice, keeping your grades up. But I want the truth. How are you doing?"

"What do you mean? I'm cleared to play." He nodded to the note.

"I know what the letter says. But I'm asking *you* a question. You haven't been yourself and I want to know what's going on. Tell me how you're feeling."

"I feel fine; I'm ready to get back on the field."

"Jason," Bennett urged, "let's be real right now."

Jason looked at the floor. "I'm frustrated, I guess. Tired."

"Pissed?"

"Pissed as hell."

"You have every right to be," Bennett said. "Depressed?"

The kid didn't answer for a long moment and Bennett's heart fell. He hated seeing one of his guys like this. Bennett couldn't help consider that Jason's main job on the field was to protect Tate, the same guy he currently couldn't forgive. His best friend only a few weeks ago.

Bennett asked again, "Jason, have you been depressed?"

"If that means I fed like shit all the time, then yeah." Jason didn't meet Bennett's eyes.

"I'm sorry, man; I wish this hadn't happened. Have you and Tate spoken yet?"

"Not really."

"He's hurting, too, you know?"

"Yeah, well, not as bad as I am." Jason's eyes finally came up, full of anger. "Now he has the full attention of every scout that comes to practice. I'm sorry I said what I did to him. But he fuc—I mean. He punched me. Took me out of the game my senior year. What friend does that?"

Bennett didn't know what to say. Jason was right; it was bullshit that this had happened. Friends don't sucker punch each other, except sometimes they did. "Jason, I hope you don't think Tate had some sort of agenda; you guys are too close for that."

"Are we? Honestly, Coach, I don't really know what I think anymore. Sometimes I just don't want to think at all."

Bennett chewed on that statement for a moment. He remembered being a teenager. Emotions, hormones, and adolescent drama could take its toll, but he'd sat through enough in-service hours about teenage suicide and depression to just blow Jason's comment off as normal. Shit, he'd felt that way himself. Low enough that life no longer seemed worth living. But that feeling mixed with the head injury. It just didn't sit right with Bennett.

"You need to talk to someone about it? I mean, you can talk to me, too, but I mean, ya know . . . someone."

"Like a shrink?"

"I'm just sayin' sometimes you need to get things out. You remember who you're talkin' to, right? Look at me," Bennett demanded. Jason's eyes landed on Bennett's and he could see so much pain in that young face it hurt to look at it. "There is no feeling going through your head right now that I haven't dealt with, you understand me? Anger, sadness, self-hatred, guilt, suicide. I've felt them all. But I'm here to tell you that your emotions can lie to you and sometimes you need someone to help you figure out the lies from the truth. I talked to a shrink once. I can't say it was life changing, but it sure didn't hurt either."

Jason looked away, breathing in deep and then running a hand through his hair. "I don't know, Coach."

"Jason. We'll get through this. I'll help you. This doesn't mean football is over for you, but you have to trust me."

Jason fiddled with his jacket zipper. "Maybe I could talk to Mrs. York."

Bennett let out a breath. "I think that's a good place to start. Why don't I have a talk with her?" Bennett said. Mrs. York was the school's psychologist and Bennett liked her. She was married with kids but still young enough not to seem out of touch to the students. He'd actually already given her a little heads-up about Jason, because he'd had a feeling things weren't going well. "I think talking out some of your frustration will really help."

"I just can't believe that this has happened my senior year. I've worked too hard for this."

"Yeah, you have, and I wish I could change it for you; I really do. I won't feed you any lines about what doesn't kill you makes you stronger . . . although I just did, but I want you to know I'm on your side. I want you to come back and show these scouts what you're made of, and I know that some of your pissed-off feelings are aimed toward me. But Jason, you know my position on safety. I won't risk your health for this sport."

Jason's jaw dropped open, his eyes going wide with shock. Then anger. "What are you sayin', Coach? You won't let me play?"

"No, I'm not ready to let you come back today. Practice can be dangerous, too. You can stand and assist with me. Watch, but you're not suiting up. You're going to have to miss Friday's game."

"That's crap, Coach. I know I'm fine. My parents want me to play; the doctor says I'm good."

Bennett hated being the bad guy, more than Jason

would ever know. But Bennett wouldn't back down. "Listen. I get it. You're angry, and I'm going to have to deal with being the focus of your anger. You may hate me for it, and that sucks. But too many kids are ending up damaged from second hits. I won't let you be one of them. I know the doc says your concussion is minor, but you haven't been yourself this past week. And maybe it's nothing, but I'm not willing to risk it. A concussion is a concussion."

Jason was quiet for a long time. "What about next Friday's game? I heard Jim Rice might come."

Bennett knew for a fact that a scout for Mizzou was coming. University of Missouri was one of Jason's top picks. It would kill Bennett to keep that opportunity from the kid, but he was unwilling to make any promises. "Why don't we reevaluate next Wednesday morning? In the meantime I want you to meet with Mrs. York every school day. I'll set it up. Get a lot of sleep; continue to exercise. Feed your body some healthy food. And think about talking to Tate."

Jason wrung his hands repeatedly. Bennett let Jason sit there as long as he needed, respecting his need to let the news sink in.

Finally he looked up. "All right, Coach. I'll be back in here Wednesday morning before school."

"Hey, man, I know things look bleak, but I guarantee you, things could be a lot worse. And even if they were a lot worse, well, then they could still be a lot worse than that. Hear me?"

"Yeah, I hear ya."

Jason shuffled out and Bennett ran his hands through his hair. He didn't enjoy seeing one of his boys suffer.

As a man who had suffered to the extreme himself, he knew it wasn't as bad as they thought it was, but you couldn't tell a teenager that. That didn't stop Bennett from trying.

Callie stood at the front door and glanced around her duplex Thursday evening, trying to envision it from someone else's perspective. It was cute, if not a little small, decorated with bright colors and some great flea market finds she'd scored with Lindsey—who despite her shy personality was amazing at finding great pieces and haggling.

Callie was nervous to have Bennett over for the first time. It wasn't necessary, but she'd started to feel bad that they always went to his place. And the truth was, she wanted him here. Wanted him to know all of her. She'd even made him dinner—a recipe from Anne's mother, who had assured Callie that her meat loaf was sure to win a man's heart. Well, Callie wasn't sure about the heart winning, but she did want to please him.

She'd come home before team practice that afternoon and made the meat loaf so she could just bake it tonight. The smell in her little place was divine. She'd even made a couple of baked potatoes to go with it. She prayed it all came out tasting as good as it smelled.

There was a small knock on the door and Callie's heart pounded. Right before she opened it a high-pitched voice called out, "It's your mama. Open up."

Shit. This could not be happening. Callie swung open the door just in time to catch a large garment bag thrust at her.

"Mom, what are you doing here?"

"Doing a fitting, what else?" Barbara held her sewing bag and her purse, dropping both onto Callie's perfectly plumped sofa. Callie bit back the words she really wanted to say right now.

"Couldn't you have given me a call? Let me know you were coming?"

Barbara's eyes danced as she turned her head from side to side. "Do you have company?"

The woman looked hopeful. "Well, not at the moment, but soon."

Barbara sniffed. "Are you cooking something?"

Callie groaned. "Mom, let's get this fitting done quickly please." She grabbed the garment bag and headed for her bedroom.

Shutting the door, she quickly undressed and then pulled the plastic cover off of her dress. She nearly gasped. "Oh, Mom," she whispered to herself.

The dress was beautiful. Spectacular even. Callie didn't give her mother enough credit; the woman was insanely talented when it came to sewing. She might dress herself outlandishly, but she did have an eye when it came to performance outfits.

Callie carefully pulled the dress from the hanger and slipped it on. She stood in front of her full-length mirror and took it in.

The sage-green material was incredibly flattering on her. The straps lay perfectly on her shoulders, leading down into the chiffon bodice that fit snug through the waist before flowing into a breezy skirt that hit right at the bases of her calves. It was simple yet so elegant. Callie did a few twirls. A woman was never too old to enjoy a twirly dress.

She opened her bedroom door and headed down the short hallway. "Mom, I love it."

She stepped into the living room and found herself face-to-face with Bennett. He stood up from the sofa as soon as he saw her, his eyes wide.

He didn't say anything for a long moment and neither did she. He swallowed hard and his lips parted slightly as his eyes ran the length of her.

"It's perfect; don't you think so, Coach Clark?" Barbara asked. Callie noticed her mother had a twinkle in her eye.

"I do. It's beautiful," he finally managed to say.

Barbara's grin made Callie want to laugh. How did the woman always manage to get her way? Maybe Callie *should* aspire to be more like her mother.

"Mom, it's great. It fits perfectly. Thank you."

Barbara walked over and began to feel around at the seams. The process so familiar to Callie it was like stepping back in time. So many hours of her childhood had her standing still as a statue, arms out, as her mother poked and pinned, repinned and measured. Callie had hated it, but standing here as a grown woman, she suddenly realized what an act of love it was. The pageants were ridiculous. Extravagant. Insane. But her mother had always, *always,* wanted Callie to be happy. Wanted Callie's father to be happy. Barbara's entire life was a selfless act, and suddenly that realization made Callie want to cry, instead of judging her mother. The overwhelming rush of gratitude Callie felt for this woman nearly knocked her over.

As Barbara knelt down to check the hem, Callie glanced at Bennett. He was grinning, and when their eyes met he winked. "I love it. You look beautiful," he said. No shame, no hiding his words from Barbara.

"Thank you," Callie said.

A moment later Barbara stood. "I think it'll do."

"It will more than do, Mom. It's wonderful."

Barbara grinned. "I'm glad. Well, I guess I'll just leave you two alone to practice." Like a gentleman, Bennett helped Barbara carry her stuff out to her car. Callie used the opportunity to go change back into her Capri leggings, heels and T-shirt—better known as her practice outfit.

When Bennett walked back inside he instantly looked disappointed. "Why'd you take it off? I was looking forward to putting my hands on you in that dress."

He shut the front door, locked it, and came right over to where she stood, pulling her into his arms. It felt so easy, so natural. She looked up at him. "We don't want to mess it up before the competition."

"True. So then after the contest you have to wear that dress and let me do whatever I want to you while you're in it."

"How about that night we will celebrate our win with superhot sex?"

"Sounds good." He lifted his head. "Are you cooking something? It smells amazing."

She was beyond pleased, and also a little nervous. "I made us dinner, and the rules are, even if it's nasty you have to tell me how delicious it is."

Bennett chuckled and placed a small kiss on her nose. "I'm sure it will be fine. I'm starving."

Callie dished up the dinner, noticing that now they

were done flirting his eyebrows were drawn together like he was stressed.

"You okay?" she asked, setting a plate in front of him.

"Yeah." He immediately smiled, but she knew better.

"Liar. What's going on?"

Bennett put some butter on his baked potato. She liked watching his careful ministrations. Like everything else he did, it was slow and precise. She hadn't known there was a way to precisely use butter.

Finally he started talking. "Jason really wanted to play tomorrow night, but I told him no."

Callie felt relief flood her body and proceeded to shake a ridiculous amount of salt onto her own potato. She'd been so afraid that whatever was bothering him was about them, the competition, anything that was going to devastate her. "You don't want him to play?"

"I *do* want him to play. I'm just nervous. He had a head injury. A concussion. He's depressed." Bennett took a few bites and she did, too, waiting for when he was ready to continue. "Second-hit trauma has sort of become an epidemic and I'll be damned if that happens to one of my boys. I told him we'll see about next week, but I'm not even sure about that. The thing that's eating me up inside is that the scout from Mizzou is coming. If I don't let him play . . . shit, I'll feel like I'm robbing the kid of his dreams."

"Is a scout seeing him the only way to play for them?"

"No. But it would definitely help. A lot."

They continued to eat and Callie was happy to see that Bennett had no problem downing her dinner. Even telling her twice how great it was. But she kept thinking about his concerns. She wanted to help him, but she really didn't have much experience.

"Has his doctor cleared him?" she finally asked.

"Yep. Which surprises me, and then again, it doesn't. His dad was probably in there throwing his attitude around. But it's made me the bad guy."

"You have to do what you think is right, Bennett. You're not trying to be a jerk; you want them to be safe."

Their eyes met and he nodded. "That's all I ever want. Nobody knows better than me that you can go on without playing football. I don't want them to have to learn that the way I did."

"You're doing the right thing then, Bennett."

She was relieved when he nodded and then helped himself to seconds of meat loaf as large as his first helping.

"I'm not kidding; this is really good. I haven't had comfort food like this in a long time. Since I lived at home."

"It's Anne's mother's recipe. Meat loaf a là Marie. I guess she made it for Mike and he liked it so much that Anne has to make it for him a couple times a month. I hoped that meant you'd like it, too."

"So you made it just for me, huh?" Bennett asked; a boyish grin broke out. He was blindingly handsome when he did that.

"Well, obviously, I don't usually make a pan of meat loaf for myself." She tried to play it off as she got up to put her plate in the sink.

"Come here," he said, pushing his chair away from the table. He patted his thigh.

Callie didn't hesitate, making her way around the table to straddle his lap.

He pulled her lips down to his. It wasn't a heated kiss but a sweet one, soft and gentle, and the scent of his aftershave made her want to lick his face. He looked into her eyes as he spoke. "Thank you."

"For cooking? It wasn't a big deal."

He shook his head. "You're wrong. I've been taking care of myself for years. Worrying about everything in the world. My players, my students, Misha."

The sound of Bennett laughing was one of the sexiest things Callie had ever heard. "Misha is a handful," Callie said. "Literally."

Bennett cupped Callie's jaw. "You've been taking care of me. Teaching me, trying to help me win this ridiculous competition. Listening to me. I like it."

"I like it, too," she said, even though the moment should have been terrifying. It wasn't. It was perfect and she felt compelled to say more. "I like *you*."

"I like you, too."

They naturally let their foreheads fall together and Callie took a deep breath. Many of her fears had just played out right before her eyes. Relationships scared her, the idea of devoting herself and her life to a man. That was terrifying. But this felt right, and in no way did she feel any less herself by hearing Bennett tell her she took good care of him. In fact, it felt wonderful. Empowering.

She'd cooked for him because she wanted to please him. Satisfy him. She'd liked the way his eyes lit up when he'd seen her in the dress. When he had the leg cramp it had made her happy to be there to take care of him. She'd listened to his problems and wished like hell that she could fix them for him. Make him smile and take away all his worries. But not because she felt forced to. No, she'd wanted it, more than anything.

It wasn't all one-sided, which she'd always feared. He allowed her to teach him, boss him around. Listened to her talk endlessly and asked her questions. He'd put her first intimately, always making sure she was satisfied— sometimes more than once—before he found his own pleasure. He'd made her an amazing dinner, come into her bakery just to see where she worked. Told her how impressive it was.

They were dance partners. They were friends. Lovers. All because they'd chosen each other. Wanted each other to succeed and feel good. His happiness was linked to her own. What a terrifying and wonderful discovery.

And he *liked* her. It felt so silly for them to exchange those words. Of course they liked each other, but she knew the words held a deeper meaning. At least hers did. Callie suddenly realized that her feelings might run very deep for this man. He might be the person she was willing to be completely and utterly selfless for. And be happy doing it.

Callie ran her fingers lightly through his hair, using her nails to tickle his scalp. His eyes slid shut. "Damn, that feels good."

"I'm good at making you feel good," she teased.

"Yes, you are." He opened his eyes to stare at her. "You really are."

"I'm glad you think so." Her voice was quiet. She didn't want to ruin this moment, because something special was passing between them.

His hands slid up her sides, running up and down her torso. Finally he palmed her ass and pulled her hard against his erection. "I can't seem to get enough of you."

"Good thing I feel the same way." Callie leaned down and kissed him once more. They took their time, nipping and sucking at each other, his hands squeezing her backside, grinding her against him.

Callie's desire to show Bennett just how much she cared had her slipping off his lap and sinking down to her knees between his legs. His eyes went wide. "Callie, you don't ne—"

"Shhh. I do whatever I want," she cut him off, loving the way the corner of his mouth rose in response.

Her fingers went to his jeans, unzipping them. His breath hitched as she reached into his briefs and wrapped her fingers around him, freeing his erection from the cotton.

She looked up at him, their eyes meeting for just a second before she pressed the smallest kiss on his warm skin. His hands went to her shoulders, like he was looking for leverage. She took him into her mouth and Bennett cursed under his breath.

"That feels . . . damn . . . ," he said between shallow breaths.

She lavished him with attention, soft and slow and then fast and hungry. When Bennett finally found his release—her name on his lips—Callie experienced a rush of emotion. Giving pleasure—giving anything— to Bennett felt like caring for herself.

Fourteen

"What if tonight we try something different? How about pepperoni, roasted red peppers, and feta?" Callie asked Anne and Lindsey as they sat down at their usual table at Pie Mia that Friday evening. The football game was away, so Callie and the dance team had a glorious Friday evening off.

"Ehhhh, I don't know. I thought we wanted to eat chicken, onion, and goat cheese every day for the rest of our lives," Lindsey responded.

Callie shrugged, unsure of why she felt the desire to mix things up. That wasn't usually her style. It also wasn't really Lindsey's style to disagree. "I know. It's good. I love it; I was just thinking how it might be nice to try something new."

"But if the food that you'd like to eat more than anything else in the world is here, why would you choose something else?" Lindsey asked.

"Okay, gracious. Chicken, onion, and goat it is," Callie said.

Lindsey had seemed different the past week. Ever

since the Derek thing. They were all so used to sweet, agreeable Lindsey and lately she'd seemed a little off. She'd never really opened up about the details of her history with the guy, and Callie and Anne had agreed not to push.

"Well, wait. . . ." Lindsey held up a hand. "I was kind of warming up to the idea of pepperoni, peppers, and feta."

"Oh dear," Anne said. "That's enough, you two; we'll get one of each."

Callie and Lindsey put their menus down and went for their beers, happy with Anne's solution. Callie wondered if her own sudden desire for something different was a side effect of her warring emotions. She almost regretted having this commitment with the girls tonight. She wished she were at Bennett's game and then going home with him afterward. She missed him like crazy, and she'd seen him just yesterday.

The whole thing was a little frustrating. It was not like her to miss anyone, let alone a man. Callie Daniels didn't let men dictate her emotional state. Apparently Bennett wasn't like all the others.

"So, I've put together some idea boards for the wedding, want to see?" Anne asked. Callie smiled. Hearing about Anne's wedding was a perfect diversion.

"Of course." Lindsey scooted their beers out of the way so Anne could put her things in the center of the table where they could all see. The first idea board was gorgeous: barn wedding, rustic yet classic.

"That's beautiful, Anne," Callie said. Lindsey nodded in agreement. "Next."

This one was also a barn wedding but had a mix of

vintage art deco flair. The dress was a thirties style, the grooms and groomsmen in bow ties and suspenders.

"Oh hell no, Mike doesn't do suspenders," Callie said.

"No?" Anne wrinkled her nose as if she was unsure.

"Uh, Anne . . . can you picture for one minute Mike in suspenders and a bow tie?"

Anne appeared to think about it. "Nope. I guess you're right. He'd hate it."

"Okay, here's the last one." Anne bit at her lip as she laid the board down.

Lindsey and Callie both gasped. The dress was fitted, lace overlay with a long veil. Callie could already imagine the dress gracing Anne's curves; it would be gorgeous. The barn in the inspiration image had long white tables adorned with simple wheat bouquet centerpieces, chandeliers made of clustered mason jars filled with strings of white Christmas lights, and the groom's vest and tie had boutonnieres made of lavender—Anne's signature scent.

"Anne, you totally already chose this one, didn't you? Everything on this page is totally you," Lindsey said.

Anne shrugged. "Okay . . . maybe. And how adorable would Mike be in a vest and tie?"

Callie and Lindsey nodded. The inspiration board painted such a clear picture of what was sure to be a perfect day for her friend that Callie had to wipe a tear from her eye. She'd always pooh-poohed the notion of a wedding being the best day of someone's life, but right now she felt a twinge of envy so acute she wasn't quite sure if the tears were from happiness or sadness.

Anne reached across the table and squeezed Callie's

hand as if she knew exactly what was going on in her head. Callie squeezed back and then they both refocused when Lindsey spoke.

"Would all the guys wear this?" Lindsey asked nonchalantly. "Even the groomsmen?"

Anne nodded and then glanced at Callie for a moment. They were thinking the same thing. Lindsey was imagining Derek in this outfit, and if Lindsey's imagination was as efficient as Callie's was, the girl knew that he would look hot as hell.

When their pizzas came everyone agreed that the pepperoni, roasted red peppers, and feta was indeed amazing.

"I think it's possible that Mia just can't make a bad pizza," Anne said. They all nodded and continued to pig out, plan some blog posts, and discuss a bratty little girl who was giving Claire trouble at school. All normal friend conversation.

"I can't believe the fund-raiser is coming up so soon," Anne said.

"I know; I can't wait for you guys to see our dance," Callie said. Anne would be there to emcee, and Lindsey had purchased a ticket. Callie was beginning to feel the excitement of a looming performance. Something she hadn't experienced in years. It felt good, really good, and knowing it would include Bennett sweetened the deal.

"So, have things between you and Bennett progressed?" Lindsey said, eyes waggling.

"Lindsey," Anne chided.

"What? He's totally hot, and we could all tell how much he was into Callie."

Had it really been that obvious? "I guess it's a fair question," Callie said. "And the answer is . . . possibly."

Anne and Lindsey leaned forward, eyes wide. "Oh my god, what?" Anne whispered.

"Have you . . . you know, done it?" Lindsey asked. "He's so good-looking. And built."

"That he is. And the answer is yes. I had sex with him." Callie lowered her voice, no need to play coy. These were her best friends. She wanted to discuss what was happening, because she needed a different perspective.

"I was so hoping that this would turn into something," Anne said. "So was Mike; he's already asked me about it twice."

"Aw, someone has a boy crush." Callie said with a smile. "I thought I sensed the beginnings of a budding relationship that night at your house. Tell Mike he can come to the game Friday night."

"That's a good idea," Anne said. "We'll bring Claire."

"How about you, Linds?" Callie asked Lindsey. "The games are a lot of fun."

"Um, maybe."

They all knew why she hesitated. Anne blew out a breath. "Linds, I really doubt Mike would mention it to Derek, but . . . I hate to make him leave out his friend if he wanted to include him. I want to be able to invite both of you to things without worrying."

"I know," Lindsey said with a lift of her shoulder. She pushed a piece of pizza crust around on her plate. "I'm probably being childish about this. I just need to get over it."

"No one said you're being childish. The guy obviously

hurt you. Right?" Callie said, clearly fishing for answers. She paused to give Lindsey an opening, but she only nodded her head. "Don't let what he did affect now. Brush him off; you're the bigger person. Show him he doesn't matter."

Lindsey sighed. "You're right. I'm giving him the power, after all these years. I'll be fine, no matter what happens. In fact, it's just better if I get used to seeing him around."

Callie and Anne agreed, and they ordered another round of beer. After a while Lindsey excused herself to the restroom and Anne leaned in to whisper.

"Mike and Derek have already been discussing the renovation of the farmhouse. I really wanted to ask Lindsey if she'd be my designer, help me with the details. Find furnishings, you know how good she is at that."

"Absolutely, I think it's a great idea. Perfect series for the blog, too," Callie said.

"Right? I thought the same thing," Anne replied. "But there is no way she could completely avoid Derek if he's our architect and contractor. I hate to put her in that position if it will upset her."

Callie considered this. "It may be just the right thing to force them to get used to being around one another."

"Derek wants to see her. He's been asking a lot of questions. I feel like I'm betraying her friendship if I answer, so I just plead the Fifth every time."

"Well, Lindsey's a big girl," Callie said. "I think you should ask her. We'll be there for her the whole time."

Little Pantherettes Saturday finally arrived, and Callie was excited and also ready to get the dance and cheer clinic over with. The planning for this had been way more work than she'd anticipated, and that had been with the entire dance and cheerleading team working hard. But she was proud of what they had planned for the sixty-four girls, ranging from grades one through five, who had signed up.

It was a full-day event, three sessions of dance and routine lessons, a break for pizza, and then all the girls would perform at football game halftime at the upcoming game that Friday.

Callie smiled when Claire and her best friend, Bailey, ran up to the registration table.

"Callie, we're here!" Claire yelled.

"I'm so happy to see you," Callie said, wrapping her arms around Claire. Callie waved at Anne and Bailey's mother, Erin, who were just coming in the gym door. "Why don't you get in line and Erika will get you signed in and give you your T-shirt and hair bow."

The girls squealed and ran to the end of the line as Anne walked up. "Claire couldn't even fall asleep last night, she was so excited for today."

"Oh, I'm so glad. They are going to have a blast," Callie said.

Anne looked around. "There's a lot of people here; I'm so happy for you."

Callie whispered, "It's amazing; even after paying for everything the dance team will make about fourteen hundred dollars."

Anne's eyes went wide. "That's great. Well, I'll let you get to work. I know you're busy."

Anne went to join the others in line. Callie glanced around, noting that everything looked good, so she headed around the corner and down the hallway to the girls' locker room. She had her bags shoved into the PE teacher's office and needed a hair tie. Just as she was about to push through the door a body crushed into her from behind and then pulled her through a different door. The latch sounded as the door was closed quickly and she was shoved up against the wall in a dark room.

She might have panicked, but within a fraction of a second she'd known exactly who it was, the scent of his skin a dead giveaway. Callie also knew the football team was probably outside setting up for their Punt, Pass, Kick event this afternoon.

"Some might frown upon this kind of manhandling," Callie said.

Bennett replied by slamming his mouth down on hers, his hands cupping her face. Callie kissed him back, a whimper lodged in her throat. After a moment he pulled back, breath ragged.

"God, I love kissing you," he whispered.

"I'm glad. Do it again."

He did, several small pecks and then his tongue slid along the seam of her lips. She opened to him, angling her head and asking him to give her everything. Bennett sucked her tongue into his mouth, a low groan rumbling in his chest.

He kissed down her jaw, neck, and then finally ran his tongue along her earlobe. "Oh my goodness, stop. I have to get back out there."

"Okay, I'm sorry. I just . . . knowing you were in here. I had to come and see you. Just for a minute."

"I'm glad you did. Am I to assume you would have

attacked me like this in front of our dance clinic had I not been in the hallway?"

Bennett laughed and placed one more kiss on the tip of Callie's nose. "No. It was an amazing coincidence that I saw you when I came in the side door."

"I wish I could see you. What is this room?" she asked.

Bennett leaned over and then a fluorescent light flickered to life, the hum of the bulb filling the air. Callie squinted for a moment and then turned to make out the . . . nurse's office?

"Oh my goodness." Callie laughed and then looked up into Bennett's squinting eyes. He smiled down at her.

"There is a cot over there. Fresh paper sheet and everything," he said with a grin.

Callie smacked at his chest and then leaned her head on him, exhaling deep as her arms tightened around his waist. "You're horrible."

Bennett rested his cheek on her head and wrapped his arms around her. They stood like that for a long moment, just enjoying the nearness of each other. Callie breathed in the smell of Bennett, aftershave, grass, and sunshine.

"It's a busy weekend, again," Bennett said. "For the first time in a long time I'm looking forward to November. It will be nice when we can just . . . be together."

Callie was silent for a moment; she stared at a poster on the wall about CPR, but she wasn't really seeing it. All of her focus was on the words Bennett had just spoken. It was the first time either one of them had made any mention of what would come next, after the dance competition.

She looked up at him, her chin resting on his chest. It was quickly becoming her favorite view. "That will be nice."

Bennett leaned down and kissed her forehead quickly before giving her butt a little slap. "I gotta get back out there."

"Ow, what is with you and slapping my butt?" Callie asked.

"It's those tight little pants," he said. "Your ass is just asking for it."

Almost a week later, Bennett stood outside the gymnasium with his players, the school band blaring from beyond the doorway. This wasn't the first game of the year, so the team would be called in together. This was actually Bennett's favorite way to go in, as a group.

"Hey, Coach."

Bennett turned and Tate was staring up at him. "Hey, what's going on?"

"I just wanted to thank you for letting Jason play this week."

Bennett gave the kid's shoulder a squeeze. Wednesday morning Bennett had made the decision to let Jason practice that afternoon and Thursday. He was going to play for the first time at tonight's game. Bennett smiled. "I figured you could use him after seeing you get sacked twice last week."

Bennett was teasing, but Tate's eyes fell. Bennett tried to recover; the last thing he needed was to upset his quarterback on game day.

"Hey, man, we've already talked about this. Don't let

it get you down," Bennett said. "Their defense was insane. We learn from it and we get better."

"Nah, it's not that. I just—"

Bennett looked up. Reggie had opened the doors, the music getting louder. Taste and Bennett didn't have a lot of time. He looked back down at Tate. "You and Jason talking yet? I mean, I know you've talked during practice, but I mean real talk. About what happened?"

"No, we haven't," Tate said.

"You've been friends your whole lives. That's more important than any of this shit. More than football, more than girls. You need to fix it. You can't go out tonight and put your faith in Jason if you guys aren't speaking."

Tate nodded. "You're right. I will. I promise."

The announcer called them in and the team shuffled into the gymnasium, the roaring applause nearly deafening. On instinct, Bennett sought out Callie right away. He spotted her right where she always was, kneeling down front and center of the band so she could see her girls easily. She smiled as soon as she saw him, and he gave her a wink, hoping the entire population of Preston High School was oblivious.

Nobody needed to know that he spent too much time imagining the dance team coach naked. Or on her knees in front of him. Shit, he'd been picturing that almost exclusively for the past week. She looked beautiful today in tight jeans, tall brown boots, and some sort of fitted flannel shirt. She looked like she could use a good roll through the leaves . . . with him on top of her. Or maybe sex in a tent; yeah, he could picture that, too. He'd definitely be taking her camping, whether she liked it or not.

There were only two football games left, and it shocked even him how much he was ready for the season to wrap up so he could spend more time with Callie. He hadn't planned to tell her exactly that last Saturday, but he had, and then he'd been relieved when she hadn't acted weird about it. In fact, she'd agreed. And this entire week had been great. They'd had two great practices . . . and lots of sex. He wanted more.

One week from now and the competition would be behind them also. He didn't really care anymore whether he won or lost. It would be amazing to win—he still wanted to give that scholarship to his seniors—but lately he'd been trying to remind himself that these guys' future wasn't in his hands. It wasn't his job to protect them, save them, and make sure they were okay. It was a little freeing to give himself a break. His team had been Bennett's focus for so long.

Bennett glanced at Callie once more. All of these feelings were because of this woman. This funny, loud, and incredibly sexy woman. She smiled, clapping along to the band.

The song ended with a round of cheers and whistles, pulling Bennett's thoughts back to the task at hand. Principal Jensen turned and handed Bennett the microphone and the applause continued. He smiled at the crowd and lifted his hand to quiet them down.

"Preston, I'm happy to say that tonight we will finally be back on the field as a full team." The crowd cheered as several players lifted Jason's arms in the air. Bennett couldn't help but smile. The look on Jason's face was priceless as his fellow students let him know by their overwhelming response how much he'd been missed on the field.

It had been an agonizing decision to allow Jason to play, but Bennett had observed him closely the past few days and talked with Mrs. York, who thought that much of Jason's depression was due to his inability to play, not a symptom of a concussion. Bennett couldn't be certain, but he was going with his gut instinct, which was telling him that things would be fine.

"I hope you'll come out tonight and cheer us on." Bennett looked around the gym once more. "Because we plan to annihilate those Bulldogs."

Ten minutes later Bennett watched the dance team perform. Today was the seniors-only dance, and they were good, really good, and he could tell the difference in the performance from years past. He was certain Callie had a lot to do with that.

On that thought his mind traveled back to her. He glanced over to where she knelt, her lips moving, and he knew she was counting the beats. Studying the girls' movements. She was so damn amazing at what she did—*everything* she did. Dance, her bakery, which was incredible, her ability to make everyone around her feel good.

He needed that in his life.

When the assembly was over he headed to where Callie was seated, battling the crowd of students heading in the opposite direction. He and Callie met in the midst of moving bodies and she smiled up at him.

"Why didn't you tell me you'd decided to let Jason play?"

Bennett shrugged. "I've been questioning it, but I feel good about it."

"I'm glad. You've really been worried. I hate seeing you stressed out."

Bennett didn't like to see concern in her eyes, but knowing it was for him made it a little better. He'd almost forgotten what it felt like to have a woman genuinely care for him, and he realized how much he wanted someone worrying over him.

"I tend to be a little overprotective about those boys."

She laughed. "A little?"

He pulled on her pinky finger, trying to touch her without being noticed. Although the students were focused on getting out the door, he had a feeling that he and Callie had become an object of conversation. He wouldn't be surprised if they were being watched. She must have had the same thought, because she gave him a curious look.

"Sorry, I can't help myself when you're near. Your body calls out to me."

She grinned. "And what does it say?"

"What it says . . . is not really appropriate for mixed company."

"Good, that's what I was hoping for. What are you doing tonight after the game, Coach?"

He shoved his hands in his pockets. "Well, that depends on if we win or lose. If we win I'll be in the mood for celebratory sex."

"And if we lose?" she asked with a grin.

"If we lose I'll need consolation sex."

Callie laughed. "I think I can handle that."

"You better." He winked at her. "I'll see you tonight."

* * *

The cheerleaders, Pantherettes, and Little Pantherettes nailed their halftime performance. Everyone loved seeing all the cute little girls on the field and they'd even received a standing ovation.

By the time all the parents had retrieved their children in the waiting area at the south end of the field, Callie was exhausted. She, Anne, and Claire made their way up into the bleachers where everyone waited. Claire immediately ran into Mike's arms as he gushed over how great she'd danced. Callie smiled at the sight.

"The hair bows looked amazing," Barbara said as Callie sat down.

"They did, Mom. Thank you so much for making one for each of the kids. They all loved matching the big girls," Callie said, wrapping an arm around her mother's shoulders.

"I'm impressed, Callie Jo." Her daddy's voice always had the power to make her smile. She turned to her other side and hugged him.

"Thanks, Daddy. I'm so glad you could make it." She gave him a kiss on the cheek.

"Well, we don't see you enough; you never come home. Guess we'll have to start making more trips up this way," Ted Daniels said. "They got any plumbers up here?"

"Of course they do, Dad. Don't you even think about moving; your business down south is too good."

And Callie could never live that close to her parents, no matter how much she loved them.

Callie glanced down the row of stadium seats. All of

her favorite people had come to support her. This was the first game where everyone had been able to make it. In addition to her parents, Anne, Mike, Claire, Lindsey, and Eric were sitting in the stands.

Callie squeezed past her parents' legs to sit by her friends.

"Hey, they looked amazing." Lindsey handed Callie the rest of her nachos. "I saved you some. Extra jalapeños."

"Mmm, you're the best." Callie sat down and dug in. She was starving. The weather had turned back a little and it was a warm night for October. She'd lost the flannel early in the evening and was now sporting her blue Panthers T-shirt.

Claire came down and squeezed in between Callie and Lindsey, a giant pickle in one hand, a Sprite in the other.

"Hi, Bug. You did such a good job tonight," Lindsey said.

"Thanks." Claire beamed.

Callie looked around at the people sitting near them and saw Corinne Wilson sitting with her daughters. Callie reached down and patted Corinne on the shoulder. When she turned she gave Callie a wide smile.

"Hey, girl. Great performance tonight."

"Thank you, I'm pretty proud of them." Callie's voice went quiet. "How are the guys doing?"

Corinne raised an eyebrow, then leaned forward. "The're having problems with Jason. He almost acts afraid out there. Tate already got sacked twice on pass plays. They had to pull him."

Callie's shoulders dropped. "You're kidding. Bennett had finally felt good about letting him play."

"I don't know what's going on. I texted Reg, but he hasn't replied back. The Bulldogs have a couple of massive linebackers, so they can't afford to keep him in there if he isn't ready."

"Is that the boy that got hurt?" Anne said beside Callie, her voice full of concern.

Corinne and Callie nodded.

"It was his first night back," Callie said.

"Grayson Senior has been down there giving the coaches hell, causing a scene. I want to go down there and whoop his ass." Corinne gave them her meanest glare and Callie smiled.

"What do you think he was saying?" Callie asked.

"Oh, I'm sure he was pissed that Bennett wasn't pulling Jason sooner. The last time Tate got tackled he nearly jumped over the railing, he was so angry. I keep hoping Mr. Starkey will go down and have words with him."

The band starting up told them the second half was starting, and the team ran onto the field amidst cheers. They were down by fifteen points, and now Callie's good mood had taken a dive. She wasn't the most informed football fan, but she knew the basics, and she wondered what was happening with Jason. She wished she could talk to Bennett. She watched as he sauntered back to the sideline, his head down, his eyes looking at the ground.

While his assistant coaches were yellers, he was more like a caged tiger, pacing back and forth, back and forth. But when he did speak or raise his voice to the boys out on the field, every single one of them turned and listened. He commanded their respect and she enjoyed witnessing it, but right now she just wanted to wrap her arms around him.

A few minutes later Callie watched as Jason ran out to the line of scrimmage for the first play. She looked down at Corrine at the same time Corinne turned to look at her.

"He's back in," she whispered. "Hope Bennett knows what he's doing."

"Me too," Callie whispered.

It didn't take long for the boys to make a first and then second down. Callie began to relax a little; things seemed to be going okay. But all she had to do was look at Bennett's rigid shoulders to know that he was indeed stressed. Three weeks ago she wouldn't have been able to read his body language this way. But when he got frustrated he put his hands on his hips and rolled his neck, as he did now.

Bennett signaled for a time-out and Callie watched as a few boys ran over to the side. She saw Bennett using his hands to describe what she assumed would be the next play, his shoulders taut and wide in his blue Preston polo shirt. He spoke specifically to Jason at one point and then the boys all ran back onto the field and into formation.

This time Callie's eyes were on Tate; he was a few steps back behind the center this time and when the ball was tossed to him he caught it, and grunts and crunching uniforms filled the air. Callie's eyes darted to Jason, who was instantly crushed to the ground a few feet from Tate, and the next thing she knew a big guy came around the back side heading straight for the quarter-

back. From the corner of her eye Callie saw Corinne
jump to her feet and start yelling.

Things began to play as if in slow motion, the massive linebacker hit Tate from the back left side; his
body looked like a rag doll, head lolling and then
flopping as he went down, the other player landing on
top of him.

She knew tackling was part of football, but something looked . . . *wrong* about how it had played out.
Her feelings were confirmed by the immediate reaction
of the crowd. Some had jumped up; many had gasped.

Callie glanced at Corinne, whose hands had gone to
her mouth, her eyes wide. That wasn't good.

Players on the field began to retreat back to the line,
not realizing yet what had happened, but everyone in the
stands noticed that Tate didn't get up when the other
team's players did. The linebacker even knelt down and
touched Tate's back.

Tate was facedown in the grass, unmoving, and
Callie's eyes immediately sought out Bennett. He was
running onto the field. Reggie followed, but the coach
from the other team got there first and fell to his knees
beside Tate's head. The referees—and another man who
Callie could only assume was Tate's father—jumped
over the railing at the bottom of the seats and ran onto
the field.

Callie felt tears burning in her eyes as the paramedics ran through the side gate . . . they came to every
game and waited in the parking lot. Always prepared,
because football was dangerous.

The crowd was hushed and waiting as the huddle surrounded Tate on the field and Callie felt Anne squeeze

her hand. Instinctively she gripped back, terrified. She hadn't realized how rigid her body was until she felt Eric behind her. He'd squeezed in front of the people behind them to comfort her.

Her. When she was sitting here safe—fine. She didn't need comforting. She didn't need saving. Tate did, and Bennett. Oh god, Callie felt her heart breaking just imagining what he must be feeling right now.

Callie whispered, "I have to go to him."

"It'll be okay, sweetie; these things happen all the time at football games," Lindsey said beside her.

Callie nodded; Lindsey was right. They did. But this was Bennett's game, his worst fear coming true. If anything happened to one of his boys it would destroy him.

Suddenly the huddle parted. They were helping Tate to his feet, and the crowd cheered. He began to walk, with the help of Bennett and a paramedic, toward the sideline.

Callie let out a sigh of relief. But it was short-lived . . . suddenly Tate's legs crumpled and he went limp, Bennett's arms shooting out to catch him as they all went to the ground. The frantic gasp of the crowd filled her ears, sending her body into a panic.

"Oh my god," Callie whispered. She got out of her seat, unable to sit still anymore. She couldn't believe this was happening. She ran down the steps and stopped at the bottom railing, feeling helpless and afraid. She glanced at the student section; their eyes were all wide and frightened, hands over their mouths. One girl began to cry. Callie couldn't blame her; the sight of Tate collapsing, taking Bennett to the ground with him, was almost too much.

Within seconds two firemen were running out with a stretcher between them and it was all too real, too awful, as they laid Tate's lifeless body onto it, strapping his torso, his legs, his head. Callie stood immobile, watching as they left out the same side gate and Bennett went with them, his expression completely solemn and unreadable.

Callie ran down the aisle, sliding between standing onlookers and the railing. When she finally hit the steps she sped up, taking them quickly, and then broke into a run. The paramedics were at the edge of the parking lot, just beginning to load the stretcher into the back of the ambulance. She didn't see Bennett anywhere.

Just as she made her way around the back of the ambulance it flipped on its lights and sirens. Callie stepped onto the curb as it pulled out. She hadn't seen Bennett get into the back, only the medics and Tate's father, but it had all been a blur. Then she spotted the taillights of Bennett's truck lighting up a row over in the parking lot. He was just going to leave the game? His team?

She ran, heading around a neighboring car so he didn't back into her. He'd backed out of his parking spot, ready to go, when she ran up alongside the passenger door and pounded on the window.

He stopped—*thank god*—and rolled down the window, his eyes nearly glazed over. "Callie, I've gotta go."

"Let me come with you."

He shook his head. "No. You stay here."

She yanked on the handle, but the door was locked. "I want to come with you, Bennett."

The car inched forward.

"Bennett!" she yelled. "Let me be there with you!"

He looked out over the dash. "I'll call you. Let me go, Callie."

His jaw hardened and the minute she stepped back he pulled away without looking at her again. She couldn't believe it.

He'd left her, too.

Fifteen

Callie paced her living room, glancing down at her phone one more time. Probably the thousandth time. The game had ended two hours ago, early, both teams too shaken to continue. The spectators had filed out of the stadium, shocked and saddened looks on their faces.

She'd gone back to her seat to find everyone waiting for her, trying to be optimistic and supportive. But it didn't matter. Bennett had shut her out and she was completely devastated. After the past couple weeks she had started to believe that there was something between them. A something that would make him want her with him in a traumatic situation. But he hadn't. Even when she'd begged. It hurt way more than she ever would have guessed.

Callie glanced over at her father sitting on her sofa. Her parents had driven her home and insisted on coming in. Staying with her. She was grateful. It was soothing to see him there watching television, and as if reading her thoughts, he turned and smiled, patting the cushion beside him.

"Come over here, Callie Jo," he said.

She'd been up and down for the past hour. She was exhausted. She went to him, sinking down into the sofa, her head in the crook of his arm. The scent of her father was so familiar, Dial soap and cinnamon gum. She hadn't snuggled up with him in years. She missed it, the feeling of someone taking care of her.

"He'll call when he can, sweetheart. He's a man, our brains focus on one task at a time, and right now that task is this boy. When things calm down and he can stop worrying, he'll remember to check in with you."

"What if things don't calm down? What if he doesn't stop worrying?" she asked, not wanting to voice her worst fear.

What if Tate died?

Her father took a deep breath, his chest rising and falling under her cheek. "Well, then we'll deal with that if we have to. But let's pray we don't."

Callie's eyes squeezed shut, a tear dropping onto her father's sweatshirt. She couldn't imagine how Bennett would take the death of one of his players. It was too awful to even consider.

"I made some tea." Barbara walked out of the kitchen holding two steaming mugs. "Come on, sweetie; it'll make you feel better."

Callie sat up and took a mug, lifting it to her lips. It smelled rich. She took a little sip. It was delicious, a hint of Irish Cream mixed with half and half. She took another, the heat unfurling inside her, softening the tension in her shoulders. "What's in this?"

Her mother shrugged as she took her own sip. "Just a little something to calm your nerves."

Callie continued to drink, tuning out the sounds of her parents talking to each other. She knew they were worried. Tate crumpling right in front of her eyes . . . it was a sight she'd never forget. He'd looked completely lifeless. As awful as the sight had been, the thing that was breaking her heart was Bennett. Watching him run on to the field, then nearly carry Tate back before they'd both gone down . . . it was as if Callie could feel his fear. His pain. If she could just see him right now. Hold him. She squeezed her eyes closed and snuggled deeper against her father.

After a while Callie shifted on the couch, turning her head to glance at the television. She sat up. She'd fallen asleep and didn't even remember doing it. Her father patted her leg. "You okay?"

"How long was I asleep?" She scrambled up and found her phone.

No calls. No texts. Nothing.

"Maybe thirty minutes or so," her father responded.

It felt like hours. "I think I'm gonna go lie in my bed."

She stood up and so did her mother. "I pulled down your comforter, got it all ready for you," Barbara said. She followed Callie down the hallway.

Callie slid off her jeans and sank down onto the cool sheets. She sighed when her mother covered her up and then headed for the door.

"Mom," Callie whispered.

Her mother turned to her. "Yes?"

"Will you lie down with me?"

She couldn't see Barbara's face, it was too dark, but there was enough love in her voice for Callie to know she was smiling.

"I'd love nothing more," she said. Barbara slid under the covers on the other side of Callie and wrapped her arms around her. She closed her eyes and fell into a deep sleep.

Saturday at 8:00 A.M. Callie had had enough. She couldn't wait any longer, and she wanted to know what was going on. According to the school Facebook page, the doctors had put Tate into a medically induced coma. He was critical, had a severe concussion. There was some bleeding under his skull.

All Callie wanted was to hear from Bennett and she wasn't sure if she was more shocked or hurt that he hadn't been in touch by now.

CALLIE: How are you? Talk to me.

She went into the kitchen and started some coffee. She was grateful to her parents for staying all night, but she was relieved when they'd left a while ago. She wanted to feel sorry for herself in her own style. By crying alone. Something she hadn't done over a man in a long time. Something she swore she'd never do again. How had she let her control slip away? When?

Eric had been sweet enough to call this morning and tell her he and Emma would take care of the bakery today, so Callie didn't need to worry about coming in at all. She was sure that they were thinking that she'd want the time to be with Bennett. Taking care of him.

That's not at all what was happening. In fact, he still hadn't responded to her text.

CALLIE: Do you want me to go let Misha out?
BENNETT: She's fine. I came home late last night. On my way back to the hospital soon.

Callie's breath caught. He'd gone home last night? And not called, messaged, anything? Here she'd imagined him at the hospital, distracted, focused on Tate. But he'd been in a car alone, gotten in bed alone, and woken up this morning . . . alone. And never once needed her. Wanted her. Thought of her.

Didn't consider that she'd be worried about him. Or need *him*?

CALLIE: Wow. Thanks for letting me know. I've been really worried.

She knew she sounded pissed and that wasn't fair. But it also wasn't fair for him to shut her out all of a sudden.

BENNETT: We'll talk soon.

Was he serious? She pulled up his number and called. He answered on the third ring, even though she knew he'd just been holding his phone.

"Hey," he said, his tone short.

"What the hell, Bennett? Are we strangers?"

Her question was met with silence. She waited a moment before speaking again. She softened her voice. "Don't shut me out."

More silence. She wanted to know what he was thinking, feeling. If he was angry, sad, scared. She knew he had to be all three. "Bennett, talk to me. I'm scared for Tate. And you. You know this wasn't your fault, right?"

"Callie . . ." It was barely a whisper; she hoped she'd broken through. "I can't deal with this right now."

"I'm not supposed to be something you have to deal with. I want to be there for you."

"I need to do this on my own."

"Why? You don't *need* to; you're choosing to."

"Maybe I want to, okay?" He was practically yelling now and Callie was dumbstruck. She couldn't even speak. He blew out a breath; thank goodness he didn't yell again when he spoke. She wouldn't have been able to handle it. "I said I'd call you and I will."

"Don't bother." She hung up, angry and yet hating herself for treating him this way when she knew he was in pain. But so was she, damn it. The worst part was knowing the pain was only just getting started. She knew full well that Bennett Clark was going to break her heart.

Monday Callie showed up for team practice early, her heart set on seeing Bennett in the hall, the gym, anywhere. He never did call her over the weekend. Not Saturday night and not all day Sunday. Even after she hung up on him, it had taken all of her willpower not to call or text him again. Beg him to speak to her, let her come over.

She walked into the gym and set her stuff up on the front row of the bleachers, just like she did every other day. It was almost impossible to not think about the last time she'd been at practice, gone through this same routine. Back when she'd been happy. When it felt like something had changed in her life. For the first time she'd begun to consider that maybe life was better when you had someone you were willing to risk everything for. Put above yourself.

The problem was, it couldn't be one-sided, and if he didn't need her then clearly she'd been mistaken. She hadn't entirely given up on Bennett, but every day her heart cracked a little deeper. Too much more and it would be irreparable.

Footsteps sounded on the gym floor and Callie turned, hoping it was Bennett. It wasn't; instead a few of her girls were early, too. She waved and gave them a forced smile as they placed their backpacks against the wall.

She knew that Tate had remained in critical condition through the weekend; she only had to stay tuned into the local news to find out. *Preston High School football player Tate Grayson in critical condition after a sack at Friday's game* was at the top of every news hour since Friday at ten. Online social media had continued to buzz with discussion and updates; everyone was using the hashtag #tatenation. From family, friends, to strangers from all over the United States, people were posting on his Facebook wall and tweeting, the students had rallied over the weekend, churches had prayed, and rival schools had sent flowers to the hospital.

It was touching to see the community come together to support him, his father and sister, and one another as they feared for the worst but hoped for a recovery.

Because of the overwhelming changes that had taken

place in the past forty-eight hours, Callie didn't have anything planned for practice today. She was going to see how the girls were doing; maybe they needed to talk. She hoped they'd give her the slightest clue on how Bennett was doing. She was shocked when they all showed up five minutes later—all early—with an idea.

"We want to raise money for Tate's medical bills," Mindy said. "My parents were talking about how Tate's dad is single and these bills will be huge. He might need years of physical therapy. We just have to do something."

Callie nodded her head. "It's a good idea. We have the money from the Little Pantherettes Clinic, but it's not a huge amount. If you're all willing to add a few more fund-raisers to our schedule in the spring then I am."

The girls looked back and forth between one another. Callie waited.

Jessica spoke up. "Tate's dad needs the money for these hospital bills. They don't have much. We have to help if we can. We can give him the clinic money and do something else now to try and earn more."

Everyone nodded their heads, adding their agreement.

Callie stared at Jessica for a moment. She remembered their discussion the night of the bonfire. Jessica liked this boy. This had to be devastating for her. Callie could see the redness around her eyes, hear the unshed tears in her voice.

"Okay, I'm all for brainstorming. I've done a ton of fund-raisers in my time; let's see what we can do," Callie said. She sat down on the gym floor and the girls all scooted in close.

Within an hour they had an entire plan laid out, the

first part of which was a Tate Nation Day at the bakery, which they planned for that Wednesday. Callie planned to take some of the dance clinic money and use it to purchase all the extra ingredients she would need and then she'd have one full day to prep and bake with the team's help. Most of the girls agreed to be there Tuesday evening, but a few even planned to ask their parents to excuse them from school the next day so they could do more. Callie appreciated that; she couldn't do all the baking herself.

The entire day's profits would go to the Grayson family. The girls were also going to hit the pavement and start asking local retailers to give. It was worth a try, and Preston being as tight as it was, Callie had a feeling the effort would yield good results. She didn't know how much these medical bills would be or how much this would help, but the girls needed to feel like they were contributing. They would do what they could.

"I'm going to ask my mom . . ." Jessica spoke up and then hesitated. Everyone looked at her. "My mom is on the board for the dance competition at the Millard. I know they're giving the money to charity. Maybe they could give some of it to this."

It hurt to be reminded of the dance competition. Callie could only hope that Bennett still planned to participate, even if he wanted them to end things. But then again, how could she expect him to focus on something so ridiculous when one of his players lay comatose in a hospital bed, with everyone unsure whether he was going to live or die?

"Jess, I think it's up to you if you want to discuss this

with your mother. We can never earn *all* the money for Tate's medical bills; we can only do what we can do. Anything is better than nothing."

Jessica nodded. "I think I'm still gonna try. If that's okay."

"Of course," Callie said.

When they'd finally wrapped up their plans for the week, she dismissed the girls, suddenly feeling over-whelmingly exhausted. And sad. Wednesday night was the dress rehearsal for the dance competition. She supposed she'd show up and hope for the best.

Sixteen

Tuesday would go down as one of the most stressful of Callie's life, but she was grateful for the distraction. It had been an early morning, arriving at the bakery at four along with Emma and Eric, bless them. Callie's four senior captains had also shown up about eight—officially excused from class—and together they'd proceeded to bake nearly a thousand cookies of various flavors, three hundred cupcakes, and about two hundred muffins. Tomorrow morning they would bake six trays of cinnamon rolls. The dough was currently rising in three gigantic bowls in the refrigerator.

They were anticipating big crowds all day and hoping to sell out. Corinne Wilson had come to help, designing fliers, which had already gone up all over Preston, the surrounding towns, and even into Kansas City, according to a few girls who'd e-mailed their parents at work with instructions to forward the fliers on to their fellow employees.

Callie wouldn't be surprised if it worked. Locals loved to flock to Preston on the weekend; many people loved the little town and would be happy to come and show their support for a young man in need.

Word of their sale had spread fast and many people had already called and placed their orders, which they would pick up tomorrow. Several of the dance team mothers had come into the shop and decorated; the whole front of Callie's Confections was decked out in blue, yellow, and white streamers, pennants, and signs. Several classes had made giant get-well cards and sent them over for display. Callie intended to send the cards over to the hospital after the big sale.

Around seven o'clock, Callie wiped her brow with the back of her arm and glanced around the kitchen. She'd nearly depleted all her supplies in addition to what she'd bought the night before. She didn't regret it, at all. A few girls and their mothers were still out front cleaning up after their busy day of baking, decorating, and planning. The front, public space, of Callie's Confections had sort of become Tate Nation central station in a matter of twenty-four hours.

Eric peeked through the swinging door. "Barbara alert. I repeat, Her Hines just pulled in out front."

Callie laughed. "I got it. Thank you."

Callie threw her apron into a cotton hamper and went out front. Her mother walked in, a smile on her face and her hands balancing a giant cardboard box. "Hello, everyone. I need some help. Eric, I've got four more of these in my trunk."

"Yes, ma'am." Eric ran out front to do Barbara's bidding. As he usually did.

"Mom, what is all this?"

Barbara let the box slam to the floor with a loud thud.

"Dad and I called in a favor. Remember Jimmy Banks over at Tent's and T's? We've been sending him business for years. Told him we needed these immediately. Go ahead and look."

Confused and a little concerned, Callie bent down and opened the box. It was full of blue material. She pulled one out and tears sprang to her eyes. They were T-shirts; across the front was "#tatenation" in yellow; the back was a giant 12. Tate's jersey number.

"Oh, Mom." Callie stood and wrapped her arms around her mother, squeezing tight. She could barely hold in the tears.

"Well, don't cry, sweetie. I thought you could sell them. Make some more money."

"Thank you, Mom. These are perfect."

The girls circled around to ooh and ahh over the T-shirts. Barbara beamed, and Callie knew why. Her mother loved to help others. Take care of people. It wasn't a weakness or a lack of self-confidence. No, it was all strength. Callie could only hope she would one day be as amazing as her mother was.

By nine o'clock Callie felt like she could barely walk. Her legs ached, her feet were swollen, and her head felt too big for her neck. She couldn't believe what all they'd managed to accomplish in a little over one day. They'd finished the evening sorting T-shirts, packaging cookies and muffins for quick sale, all while the girls and even their moms had shared stories about Tate. There had been some crying but also laughing.

Preston was a small town; these moms had known Tate for a long time. Since elementary school, preschool even. Everyone was grieving for what happened and what might happen. They were all trying to remain optimistic, but it was difficult. The news kept spouting statistics about concussions and comas. None of it sounded good.

Callie locked up the bakery and got in her car, but instead of driving home she headed for the highway that led to Bennett's. She was done with waiting for him. It had never been her style to let someone decide her happiness; she figured why start now.

When she pulled up the porch light was on, but the inside was pitch-black. She parked and walked to the front door. When she rang the doorbell, Misha's yappy bark sounded from within the house.

Callie rang once more, waited and then finally decided he must not be home. She blew out a breath, got in her car, and headed back into town. She'd overheard someone talking about how Bennett hadn't been back to school since the football game and that worried her. Whether he wanted to admit it or not, he needed someone. If he didn't want it to be her, fine. But he couldn't keep dealing with this alone.

Callie drove through town and finally pulled into the drive of her duplex. There, sitting on her front step, was Bennett. Her heart leapt at the sight of him and then just as quickly sank. Even when the shine from her headlights hit him he didn't look up, his head resting in his hands.

She got out and shut the door, quietly making her way up to him. He was like a feral animal: one quick move might scare him off.

"Bennett," she said quietly.

He lifted his head slowly and met her eyes. His shone in the porch light, red and exhausted looking. He was in just sweats and a T-shirt despite the fact that it was cold outside. His shoes weren't even tied, and the sight of him so broken ripped her heart out. She knelt down and placed her hands on his face. "Talk to me."

"I'm okay," he said.

"You are definitely not okay."

She was shocked and hurt when he reached up and removed her hands from his face.

She stood up. "Will you at least come inside?"

He sighed and ran a hand through his hair, gripping it hard in his fist before releasing it. "I don't know yet." His words were harsh, nearly a groan.

Her first instinct was to say "the hell with him." He was being a jerk, pushing her away when she'd done nothing but want to help. But deep inside, something told her that this was not about her at all. He was here, and that was something. It was clear to her that Bennett was fighting an inner demon that she couldn't save him from. All she could give him was herself.

Callie reached out her hand and nudged him. He looked up and she widened her open palm. Reluctantly he grabbed it, and she helped him up. A small concession from him. Unlocking the door, she let them both in. She dropped her purse and bag by the sofa and then nodded at Bennett. "Sit down."

He did and she sighed in relief. The couch gave as she sat near him. "I've been worried about you. Will you tell me what you've been doing all these days?"

He leaned forward, elbows on his knees. "Mainly I've been at the hospital. I don't know why; nothing's changed. I just keep . . . waiting."

"Of course you do; everyone is."

His left leg started to bounce up and down. "My leg's fucked up."

"What? Did you get another cramp?"

"No, not today. But I didn't tell you, my leg is damaged. In my accident it was shattered. I have metal rods in my thigh and an artificial hip."

She was quiet for a moment, unsure of how best to respond to what he'd just said. She'd known about the accident. Known he'd been injured badly enough to rob him of a career in sports. But it had been eight years. She had no idea he still suffered.

"Why didn't you tell me?" Callie leaned down, trying to see his face. Why was he telling her this now? "We've been . . . dancing. A lot. You've been lifting me. What the hell, Bennett?"

His head dropped forward, a low groan emanating from his chest, and all she wanted to do was kiss the back of his neck where the hair was short and soft. And yet she needed to consider what he had just said. For all intents and purposes he had what some might consider a minor handicap and yet he'd attempted to win a fucking dance competition . . . for his players.

His players who meant everything to him.

Callie stood up and once again held her hand out to Bennett. She whispered, "Come on."

He looked up, so beaten, so vulnerable. So beautiful.

Seventeen

Bennett reluctantly allowed Callie to lead him to her bedroom. A bedside lamp was lit, casting a warm glow over the unmade bed. This was what he'd come for. To escape into her. How did she know what he wanted? *Needed*? The scent of her home, apples, vanilla, and Callie, had instantly relaxed his strung-out nerves.

His mind hadn't rested since Tate collapsed on the field Friday night. He played the events over and over in his mind. Jason had shown signs of weakness, costing them two pass plays. Bennett hadn't been able to tell if it was from a lack of playing for a few weeks or something more, but he'd ended up pulling Jason after the first quarter. The guy had flipped. Begged Bennett at halftime to put him back in.

Bennett had asked Tate how he felt about it, because he knew Tate was not only sick of getting sacked but also worried about his friend. But Tate had agreed to give Jason another chance, probably out of guilt for starting this fucking mess to begin with.

The long and short of it was that Jason shouldn't have

been out there. Tate should not have been relying on him. Jason's inability had made Tate doubt himself, and Bennett knew for a fact that Tate had been afraid that Jason might get hurt again. They all had been, and it had taken them all off their game. Literally. Bennett had made the call, let his own guilt take over and allow him to make a decision that he knew wasn't right.

And now Tate was in a coma, his brain swelling, while all they could do was pray that the swelling started to go down. Even then there was a very good chance he would end up in a vegetative state. Maybe forever.

Every night Bennett had woken up in a sweat, repeatedly reliving the sight of Tate's tackle. Sometimes it morphed into something else in Bennett's dreams, turning them into true night terrors. Tate falling on the field, Tate's head falling off, Bennett's own accident, the pain of losing himself, the depression, Tate dying. The nightmares were random and some horrific. Bennett couldn't do it anymore and his truck had driven itself to Callie's house. Now here he was, in her bedroom.

"Stop thinking," Callie whispered. She positioned him at the edge of her bed and he sat down, parting his legs and pulling her between them.

"Not yet," Callie said, guiding him back into a standing position.

He let her do as she please, watching intently as she unbuttoned his jeans and then pulled them down his legs. She removed his shoes one at a time and then guided his pants off before asking him to lie back on the bed. She could have asked him to do anything, he barely heard her commands, didn't process them. His body was on auto.

Her cool hands slid up his thigh, finding the scars there. He looked down, seeking her eyes, but she was focused on his body, her fingers massaging into his sore muscles. Oh god, he couldn't take her caring for him this way. It was too tender and sweet.

He reached out and stilled her hand with his own. "That's enough." He sat up slowly, a sharp pain shooting through his hip.

Suddenly he didn't want things to go slow; he needed to take control, strip her naked, and pound into her body until he could feel nothing else but his own release.

He pulled at her T-shirt and began to yank it over her head; she helped, dropping it on the floor. "Take off your bra." He was shocked at the anger in his own voice, but he couldn't bring himself to care or apologize. He wasn't sorry.

He was dying inside and right now this was the only thing that might save him.

His fingers went to her pants and he yanked them down, her panties with them, and immediately leaned forward to place his mouth to her navel. He wanted to taste her, smell her, and get lost in the softness of her skin.

"Bennett," she whispered, her hands tangling in his hair. He wished she'd pull, make it hurt. He palmed her backside and yanked her against him, his mouth rising up to suck her nipples into his mouth, one and then the other. The sound of her soft whimpers drove him insane and he bit down lightly, wanting to hear her cry out. Instead her hands tightened in his hair, pulling lightly at his scalp.

Yes.

He squeezed her breasts, he knew it was almost too hard, she should tell him to stop, but she didn't; she only pushed herself into his hands, silently pleading for more. He could feel her kicking her pants off of her body, and as soon as she went still he gripped her waist with both hands; turning her, he pushed her down to the bed. And still she didn't protest.

He stood up and slid his underwear down, never taking his eyes from her face. Her gaze wandered down to his erection and he took it in hand.

"How do you want me?" she asked, scooting back on the bed.

"Just like that." He put his right knee down, knowing full well that being on his knees while he fucked her would hurt like hell. He was going to do it anyway, because he wanted her underneath him. The other knee came next, a twinge of pain shooting through his thigh. He'd spent too much time sitting the past few days. In the hospital, in the truck outside her house, at the football field. Funny how it hurt if he stood and hurt if he sat too much. He couldn't win. He would never win. His games were over.

But he could have Callie tonight, and that would be the closest he would ever come to winning. Feeling whole.

He settled himself between her thighs and she reached for his face, her hands soft. He closed his eyes and leaned into her touch as he pushed into her. Nothing would ever feel this good again.

Callie let her eyes flutter shut; the sensation was so raw, so good she'd nearly lost her breath. The feel of Bennett's bare skin against hers, inside her, it was too much. A new experience, something she'd never done, and it was stupid. So damn stupid.

She didn't care. She'd do it again in a second, because right now it was the only thing that mattered. She could feel his pain—it was soul deep—and she felt desperate to reach him. It seemed the only thing that he wanted right now was release, and he set about it with a ferocious intensity, his eyes wide, low, rough grunts huffing from his lips with every thrust.

It was animalistic and indecent, the way he pushed her knees toward her chest as he pounded into her. She would love it if the circumstances were different, but although it felt like heaven, it was also breaking her heart.

He let out a strangled groan, almost as if he was in pain, dropping her legs and leaning his weight against her body. He stilled for a moment, deep breaths puffing from his lips and cooling her forehead.

Callie let her fingers slide over his behind and squeezed. She loved the way the muscles tensed and flexed in response. He was so solid and heavy, but she didn't want him to get up. He angled his torso and looked down at her.

"I'm sorry, I didn't mean to hurt you," he said. And though she knew he meant physically, she pretended he meant so much more.

He threaded his fingers between hers and lifted their linked hands above her head, pushing them down into the mattress as he began to move again inside her. This time his strokes were long and slow and Callie wasn't sure how long she could last, the sensations were so intense.

"You feel so good like this," he whispered. "So wet. Warm."

She wrapped her legs around him and locked her feet, never wanting him to stop. Or leave.

Bennett stretched their arms out, lengthening their torsos, using them for leverage as he continued his torturous assault on her body, over . . . and over . . . and over. He began to speed up, his forehead leaned onto her own, his lips hovering just out of kissing range. So close she could feel his breath and smell his skin.

Wanting to taste him, she lifted her head up and swiped her tongue against his bottom lip. That simple motion seemed to ignite a flame in him and his mouth crashed onto hers. Her body reacted, the tremors starting in her thighs, and then she was falling over the edge as their tongues tangled, teeth nipped, and his moans got lost in her mouth as he came along with her.

After that they lay quietly.

"I shouldn't have done that without protection. I'm sorry," Bennett said, breaking the silence they'd been lying in for the past five minutes.

Callie scooted up and rested on her elbow. "It's okay. I'm on the pill."

He seemed satisfied with her answer and went back to staring at the ceiling.

"Why didn't you just tell me about your leg?"

He shrugged. "Does it matter?"

"Well, yeah. I could have adjusted the routine."

"Yeah, that's just what I would have wanted. The gimp version of your dance routine."

"Bennett, that's not what I mean and you know it."

"I'm not an invalid; I'm just in pain." He stood up and

her breath caught at the sight of him naked and walking away from her. He was beautiful. He carefully leaned over, bending only his right leg, and picked up his underwear and pants. When he turned to face her she could see the faint scars running down his left thigh. She hadn't noticed them before, but she'd also not been looking for them.

So this was what brought a professional athlete to his knees. A debilitating injury. Did Bennett try physical therapy? Massage? Had he given up too soon, unsatisfied with his imperfection? She knew this wasn't the time to ask those questions.

"Are you leaving?" she asked, praying the answer wasn't what she knew it would be.

"Yes."

Callie closed her eyes. "Then why did you come?"

She opened her eyes to find him staring at her as he zipped his jeans. His jaw clenched tight and then he turned to find his shirt.

The pain in his face almost broke her. Why was he doing this? She couldn't understand it, as hard as she tried.

"Bennett, you're not responsible for protecting everyone."

"I don't want to talk about it. Okay?" He pulled his shirt over his head.

"Then tell me why you came here? Please tell me I mean more than a quick fuck."

"Stop it," he ground out. "I didn't come to fight; I'll tell you that."

"I don't want to fight either." Callie slid off the bed and grabbed her own T-shirt, shoving her arms through the holes. She was afraid he could disappear at any second. "I want to help you. Go to the hospital with you. Be there. I know this sucks."

"It does suck, but I don't need help." His voice rose, his arms shooting out to his sides. "I came tonight, we were together, but now I need to go."

Callie shook her head and ran a hand through her hair. "Bennett, don't you get it? I want to be together because you're running toward me, not away from something else. I want the ugly. I want the hard, the painful, the fear. Give it to me; let me share it with you. I'm a strong girl."

"I know that; don't you think I know that?"

"No, I don't think you do. I think you carry the weight of the world on your shoulders and you need help." He turned away, but she stepped beside him and took ahold of his chin and forced his face down to hers. "Shit happens, Bennett. Accidents occur, people get hurt. Sometimes badly. Sometimes they're never the same. It's not always someone's fault. You don't have to hurt alone."

"I don't want you hurting, too," he said. His voice was low and quiet, and she knew he was admitting to something real. He wanted to protect her. Protect himself.

"I'm already hurting, Bennett. It hurts to love someone and have him push you away out of fear. It hurts bad."

His eyes jerked up to hers and they stared for a long time. She couldn't believe what she'd just admitted. Wasn't even sure if he was in the right frame of mind to understand. But she'd said it out loud. She loved this man.

This wounded, impossible, and amazing man. All she wanted was for him to love her back. It appeared he might never choose to return her feelings. Whether they lived inside him or not, it might not matter. He had built walls between them and the bricks were made of his guilt, his shame, and his fears. Why couldn't he see that none of that had anything to do with the two of them?

He stepped away from her and suddenly she was certain what was about to come out of his mouth. She couldn't take it.

"Don't you dare say 'I'm sorry.' I'll hate you for it."

"You guys ready for this?" Callie called over her shoulder. Anne, Lindsey, Eric, Emma, Corinne, Jill Monser, and several other dance moms nodded their heads. They were all sporting #tatenation T-shirts and huge smiles on their faces. "Okay. Let's make some money."

The line outside of Callie's Confections Wednesday morning was down the sidewalk. Callie flipped the Open sign and unlocked the door. The first person in was Reggie himself.

"Hmm, mmm. It smells good in here. I got fifteen minutes till I need to be at school," Reggie said, heading straight for the counter.

And on it went, all morning, customers flowing in steadily. They were selling fresh goods at the counter, had a prepackaged station that took cash only for quick sales, and a T-shirt table. Eric had spent nearly the whole entire morning making coffee and restocking the buffet of creamer, stir sticks, and lids. It had been nuts there for a while between seven and nine.

Thankfully everyone had been incredibly patient and kind, expressing their love for the idea, their love for Tate and the school. The whole town of Preston and beyond was stricken that such a tragedy had happened in their community. By noon they'd nearly sold out and Callie headed back into the kitchen to bake more cookies and cupcakes. They were staying open until 7:00 in order to give everyone—even daytime workers and students—a chance to get in and purchase something.

After she pulled one batch of chocolate chip cookies from the oven Callie heard cheering from the front of the shop followed by the kitchen door bursting open. Anne carried an armload full of pizza boxes from the pizza shop down the street.

"Look what Pie Mia sent down for us. On the house."

Callie's eyes went wide. "Wow, that's so kind. And awesome. I think I could eat my weight in pizza right now."

They cleared some counter space and dug into the boxes. Callie groaned in delight when she found a chicken, goat cheese, and onion pizza. She motioned Lindsey and Anne over to help themselves.

"I think this is the best one I've ever eaten," Lindsey said.

"Everything tastes better when you truly deserve it. And we deserve this," Callie said before double-fisting her second slice.

The helpers ate and chatted, taking turns to work out front so everyone could get a break to eat. Callie opened her laptop. She'd been up till one in the morning finishing her blog post on s'mores cupcakes. She'd posted it at five this morning and was curious how it was doing. She clicked open the blog. The post wasn't there. A different post was at the top, with what appeared to be one of Tate's senior photos. He was so handsome, his happy face made Callie smile. And then she read, her eyes filling with tears.

Our Dearest Readers,

I'm sitting here in my warm kitchen, watching my beautiful daughter eat breakfast. I'm sure many of you are having a similar morning. However, here in our small community, another parent is hurting. His son, Tate, an extremely talented high school quarterback, was tackled Friday night and suffered a serious head injury. He's in a coma and we don't know what will happen. The only thing we can do is try and help. He's a single dad and I can relate very well to what that means. We can't ease his suffering, but we can help to ease his financial burden. I realize many of you aren't in a position to help—and that's okay—but if you can, any little bit would be so greatly appreciated. We've also set up a site page for well-wishes and encouragement for Tate and his family. Hug and kiss your loved ones today, and never take one second for granted.

Anne

There was also a video of some local news coverage about Tate and his accident. Probably so everyone would know that the request was legitimate and could see the details. Callie wiped the tears from her eyes and clicked on the fund-raising link. There was already $3,800.

"Oh, Anne." Callie sobbed, immediately walking

around the work counter to wrap her arms around her friend's shoulders. "Thank you."

Anne hugged her back, leaning her head on Callie's. "It's the least we could do. I know that this boy is important to Bennett, and I know Bennett is important to you, and you're important to me. That's how this works. Never mind that helping others is just the right thing to do."

Callie pulled back and sucked in her stuffy nose. The other ladies had circled around the laptop to read Anne's post as well.

By three that afternoon most of the day help had left, and the entire dance team was there as soon as school was out to pick up where the others had left off. Immediately Callie realized that the girls were all sporting little yellow and blue beaded bracelets. She lifted Jessica's arm and read the tiny metal piece in the center. It said: "#tatenation." It was precious and Callie was pretty sure she recognized the craftsmanship.

"Where did you get this?" Callie asked.

"Sweet Opal. Brooke, the owner, has spent the past three days making tons of them. Everyone at school has one, even teachers. She even has a guy version made out of leather. All the money is going to the Graysons' FundMe account."

Callie's shoulders dropped in shock. She was in awe over what everyone was doing to help. "Well, somebody needs to go buy me one!" she cried in mock annoyance.

The girls laughed and two of them volunteered to run down the street and do just that. She called after them, "Hey, wait. Here, take Brooke some of these cupcakes."

Callie loaded a box and sent the girls on their way

just as a Kansas City news crew walked in the front door. They were all shocked as the crew proceeded to film some coverage of people buying up baked goods, interviewing a couple of the girls and then asking Callie if she would do a quick interview for the six o'clock news.

She rushed to the bathroom to adjust her hair and check to make sure mascara rings didn't line her eyes. She was . . . passable. She didn't look like any beauty queen, but that didn't matter. Not at all. She went back out front and answered a few questions, explained why they wanted to help, and soon the news crew was gone. The entire thing had taken maybe thirty minutes.

By six they'd officially sold out entirely and decided to call it a day. She needed to be at the dress rehearsal in thirty minutes. "Girls, I'm so proud of you my heart could burst."

The girls all said their good-byes and within twenty minutes Callie sat alone in the bakery. She glanced at her phone. It was nearly 6:30. She had no idea if Bennett would show up tonight. She wanted to believe he would, but a deep part of her feared the worst.

Eighteen

He never came. Not for the rehearsal the night before, not for the cocktail hour this evening, and he wasn't there now, for dinner. Callie felt like she might suffocate, surrounded by the happy conversation and smiling faces of the people seated around her at the table. She still wasn't sure which emotion was more prevalent, anger or sadness. Or maybe they'd both meshed into an agony so acute she couldn't begin to process what she was feeling.

Was this the kind of suffering that Bennett was going through? No, his had to be worse, because right now—as much as her heart ached—she still longed for him here. Wished he would walk through the door. He clearly wanted nothing to do with her, anything, or anyone. So either his anguish had rendered him incapable of functioning, or he was the world's biggest, most selfish, asshole.

The truth was she hadn't been surprised. She'd texted him, told him she'd see him tonight. He'd never responded.

But even though the event had started, he could still make it.

If he wished.

Callie sucked in a deep breath and glanced around. The Millard looked lovely. She hadn't seen it since the remodel and she was impressed. She'd never be a member at the exclusive club—which was just fine by her—but she could see the appeal.

The main ballroom was decorated in shades of blue and gold. There were even blue uplights illuminating the walls. Callie wondered if that had been the plan all along in honor of the community or if it was a last-minute switch. Either way, it was beautiful. And fitting in light of recent events. The round tables had varying floral centerpieces, some tall, some short, all lit by the crystal chandeliers on the ceiling. The chairs were covered with white covers and gold bows and the clink of tableware and conversation filled the air.

She picked up her white wine and took a sip, trying desperately not to feel ridiculous with the seat beside her vacant.

"The chicken was delicious," Anne said from Callie's left side.

Callie pushed the food on her plate around with her fork. "Yes, it is."

"How do you know if you haven't tried it?"

Callie gave Anne a small smile. "Sorry." Callie cut a piece of chicken and took a bite. It was good, but she had no appetite.

Eventually the servers cleared their plates and Anne made her way to the center of the room once more to get the festivities going. Callie felt like she might be sick. She excused herself from the table and went out into the lobby.

A long mirror ran the length of the wall above an antique buffet. She glanced at herself. She'd put her hair up; tendrils escaped the edges, framing her face. The green bodice of her dress brought out the color of her eyes. The longer she stared at her own reflection the more hopeless she felt. Tears dropped from the corners of her lashes; she hadn't even felt them coming.

He wasn't coming.

She knew it deep inside. Had known it since last night when he'd no-showed. Known it when he didn't reply to her texts, didn't answer her call. And she knew it now when she looked into the mirror and saw the hurt in her expression. She hadn't felt this kind of ache . . . ever.

Callie couldn't go back into the ballroom. She pulled her phone out of her purse and texted Mike.

CALLIE: Please let Anne know I'm leaving. Tell her I'm okay, but I have to go.

She hit send and left the building.

Bennett touched his leg with his right hand and lifted his fingers. There was blood, but he couldn't see where it was coming from because the door was crushed in on him. He couldn't breathe. His left side was numb. He turned and looked into the passenger seat. Her head was bleeding, her eyes closed. *Oh god, no.*

There were lights, blinding lights coming in the window. The car had hit them on the driver's side. No, a truck; its lights were shining through the windshield. He was lodged between the door and the center console, completely unable to move.

"Ashley. Ashley, talk to me, babe. Can you hear me?"

She didn't respond for what seemed like forever and Bennett felt like he was going to pass out. "Ashley, can you hear me?"

She moaned. *Thank god.*

"Bennett," she whispered, and then began to cry before she'd even opened her eyes.

"Don't cry, Ash. Open your eyes; look at me."

"What happened?" she asked between quiet sobs. There was pain in her voice and he said a silent prayer that she wasn't damaged internally; she was delirious.

"We've been in an accident. Ashley, open your eyes; I need you to look at me."

Her head lolled to the side, her eyes fluttering open, tears rolling down her cheeks mixing with the blood from the cut on her forehead. He knew the minute her eyes focused and she realized what was happening. Her eyes went wild.

"Oh god, oh god, Bennett, you . . ." She began to scramble in her seat, grasping for the seat belt. "You're stuck. Oh god, your leg. What happened?"

"Shhh, it's okay." His head started to feel hazy. He still couldn't feel his leg at all. "Sit still, Ash. It's okay. Someone will help us."

"Don't die, Bennett. Please don't die. Oh god." She cried harder.

Someone knocked on the window. A fireman. Bennett could hear his muffled words, see him yelling outside the car. wasn't sure what the fireman said; his mind was going blank. This time the man pounded on the window, kept pounding, so hard, like he was trying to break it open. A dog began to bark.

Bennett gasped. His eyes flew open. His living room. He was on his couch. Dreaming again. Always reliving that night in his nightmares. It had been a while since he'd had one so vivid and real. Someone pounded on the door and Misha barked again.

He got up and walked to the front door, his hip throbbing. He pulled the door open and his heart sank in his chest. There stood the most painfully beautiful woman he'd ever seen. Her eyes shimmering with tears.

"Why didn't you come?" she whispered.

He couldn't respond; he was completely rooted to the ground, his pulse racing.

"Answer me, damn it. Why?"

He shook his head and then whispered, "I don't know. I couldn't."

"Bullshit." She reached forward and shoved him as hard as she could. He stumbled backwards slightly but caught himself.

"Callie . . ."

"No." She put out a hand, her lips going into a straight line. "Don't say my name. Don't make excuses. I don't want to hear them. I came here to tell you that you're pathetic."

Bennett's eyes went wide. A rush of anger surged through him. "You have no idea—"

"No, don't even start. We all deal with shit, Bennett. You're not special. You have a shitty leg. So what. You can't play football. You can't save all your players from injury. Poor you."

"Are you fucking kidding me right now?"

"The question is are you fucking kidding *me*? I spend all this time helping you get ready for tonight. Busting my ass, and then practically begging you to let me be there for you this week. I wanted to take care of you, Bennett. Be there for you to lean on, make sure you ate, take care of your dog. I wanted to *love* you."

Her voice broke on the last words. It was the second time she'd said the words and they gutted him just like they'd done the first time. She wasn't finished.

"But no, you're too wounded. Too stubborn, too fucking selfish to accept what I want to give you."

He had no words in response. Selfish? How could he be selfish? Everything he did was for everyone else. "I don't know what you want me to say. I could not handle dancing in front of those people. I figured you'd know that. How could I go out and act like nothing was wrong while one of my players lies in a hospital bed?"

Callie rolled her eyes. "Everyone there was thinking about him. The event had even become about him. But you didn't even know that because you made this all about *you*. So you can save it; it's too late now; I don't even know why I came here."

She turned and walked away, back to her car. He should stop her, say something. He didn't. Just watched as she pulled down the driveway and into the night.

Bennett shut the front door and then sat down on the couch, hating himself. Hating the situation. Had the event truly become about Tate? She was right; Bennett knew nothing, had completely shut down the past week. He hadn't taken calls, watched television. He'd barely checked his e-mail. Thankfully, Jensen had told him not to worry about this week; he owed the guy for that. But

Bennett realized that he'd completely lost it and seeing the pain in Callie's eyes would haunt him for the rest of his life.

He'd done that to her, and if he'd ever known a person who deserved to be happy, it was Callie Daniels. The woman who'd been there for him no matter what. Loved him.

Bennett squeezed his head with both hands. He had officially fucked up everything in his life.

Not quite two hours later he heard rocks popping on the driveway out front. He jerked out of his seat and ran to the front door to see her. He pulled it open in time to instead see Reggie getting out of his SUV. Disappointment pooled in Bennett's chest. He wanted her to come back.

"Man, what the hell is wrong with you?" Reg said by way of greeting. He stalked toward Bennett and pushed past him into the house.

Bennett sighed. "Sure, you can come in," Bennett said. He walked back inside and went to the kitchen to grab a bottle of water. He heard Reggie pacing in the living room.

Bennett went back out and sat down on the couch, sure that he was about to get his second lecture of the night. He deserved it.

"Have you lost your damn mind?" Reggie said. He didn't bother sitting; his hands were on his hips. He was wearing . . . suspenders? Obviously part of his costume.

"I wasn't fit for dancing," Bennett said.

"Did your partner know that?" Reggie bit off.

"Don't even start; she just left here a couple hours ago."

Reggie dropped his hands and sat down in a chair. "Man, what the hell? What is going on with you? I know what happened, but why? Why have you let it take you back? I wanna be there for you, Bennett, but you're making it really hard."

Bennett didn't answer, just dropped his head into his hands.

"It killed me seeing her, all dressed up, ready," Reggie said. "She never acted mad through dinner. When people asked why you weren't there she covered for you, man. Said that it was more important for you to be with the Graysons right now. But nah, your sorry ass was here sleeping on the couch and smelling like you haven't showered in days."

Bennett's head jerked up. "What do you want me to say?" he yelled.

Reggie shrugged. "I don't want you to say shit. I want you to *do* something. This girl has spent the entire week working her ass off for your player. You fell apart and she rose to the occasion. As far as I'm concerned, you don't deserve her."

"I already knew that, and if I didn't she just stood outside my front door and told me I fucking didn't."

Reggie shook his head and then stood. "Well, good. As long as she knows her value. A woman like that shouldn't have to put up with this shit." He headed for the door. "You better be at school tomorrow. I'm tired of doing this alone. Your team needs you. You're not the only one suffering, Bennett. How do you think Jason is doing lately? Have you even stopped to consider that? You need to get over yourself."

The front door slammed. Bennett fell back onto the couch, shoving his palms into his eyes. He wanted to yell, hit something, rage. He used his right foot to kick the coffee table as hard as he could across the room. "Fuuuuccccck."

He stood up, pain burning through his thigh. He was an asshole, a completely selfish dick, putting his pain above everyone else's because he had just stopped caring. It was exactly the same thing he'd done after his accident. Shut out the world, blamed everyone else, hated himself. It was easier than trying to deal with reality, pain, and devastation. He'd seen Jason at the hospital several times and hadn't taken the time to ask him if he was okay. That wasn't even like Bennett.

He sat back down again and picked up his phone. He opened the Facebook app and found the school's page. He was out of touch with what was going on, spending so much time at the hospital or sleeping. He'd never taken a sick day in all his years at Preston, but he'd been gone the past four days. What a fucking coward he must look like.

Every recent post was about Tate. His health status, messages from friends, and several links to ways to help raise money. There was a news video from yesterday. The frozen image looked familiar. Bennett watched it in pure disbelief.

Callie's bakery, his students—the dance team. He could barely breathe. And then there she was, so pretty, her hair such a damn wreck he almost laughed. She looked so tired but so beautiful it hurt to look at her. He turned up the volume on his phone so he could hear her speak.

"Right now Mr. Grayson needs to give Tate all of his attention, so we're doing what we can to help make this easier for him by doing our best to help cover his medical costs."

Bennett felt sick. The level of his selfishness hitting him hard. Misha jumped up on the couch beside him and rested her head on his thigh. He laid his hand on her soft back and stroked her fur.

With a deep sigh he opened his phone contacts and scrolled through the names to find one that he hadn't used in years.

He pushed the call button and put the device to his ear. It rang a few times and he considered hanging up.

"Bennett? What a surprise." Ashley's kind voice was so foreign and yet so familiar. When he didn't reply she spoke again. "Bennett. Is everything okay?"

"Yeah, Ashley. Hi." He cleared his throat and leaned back, squeezing his eyes shut.

"Hi." There were voices behind her. She must be out.

"I won't keep you," he said. "I just . . . I just had a question."

"Okay."

"How bad was I? How awful, after the accident?"

She was quiet for a moment, and he could tell she was moving to a quiet location. "What do you mean, Bennett? Are you drunk? You don't sound good."

He huffed out a laugh. He hadn't had a drink since that night, when they'd been nearly killed by a drunk driver. "I'm okay. Ashley, I've . . . met someone."

"Oh? Well, good. That's good, Bennett." She sounded

genuinely happy. He knew she was engaged. His mother updated him occasionally on Ashley's goings-on.

"I'm fucking this up, Ashley. I can't do that. I fucked us up, didn't I?"

She sighed. "Bennett, why are you asking me this?"

"Because I don't want to do it again."

She was quiet for a moment. "Is this about your player's accident? I'm so sorry about that."

"Did it go national?" he asked. Ashley was a sports newscaster in Texas. High school football injuries sometimes went national if they were bad enough.

"Yeah, it did. I've been trying to keep tabs on your local news. I almost called you myself. But wasn't sure . . ."

"Answer me, Ash. Why'd you leave?" He was long past missing Ashley, but he knew there was more to their story than the lies he told himself. He liked to blame her—she'd abandoned him, only wanted him because he was an athlete—but deep down, he knew that wasn't it. It was just easier to swallow.

"Bennett, you pushed me away. I couldn't do anything to make you happy again. I had to go for myself, because after a while I didn't even know who you were anymore."

Bennett's heart began to pound in his chest. He'd known. All along, deep down, he'd known. Ashley was a sweet girl. They'd loved each other; they'd planned to get married. But that accident had destroyed him. Stripped him of everything he believed made him who he was.

"We were given a second chance at life, Bennett,"

Ashley spoke quietly. "Whoever this woman is, you need to let her in. You deserve this."

The tightness in his Bennett's chest was crushing. It occurred to him that as much as he needed to hear what Ashley had to say, he wanted nothing more than to talk to one woman only. Callie. This past week he'd been in hell. How could he not have realized that his happiness was now wrapped up in her?

Yeah, he had been given a second chance at life, and he'd been alive for the past eight years. But he hadn't been *living*. Callie had brought him back fully, finally made him see what truly being happy looked and felt like. He couldn't lose her, no matter what it took he would have to make her forgive him. Before he let Ashley go he had one more question.

"Why did you abandon Misha?" Bennett looked down at the little dog who had perked up when he said her name, ears twitching. She was never far from him when he was home.

Ashley laughed quietly and then her voice softened. "Bennett, I didn't abandon Misha. I loved her, but I knew you needed her more than I did. You needed somebody; I didn't want you to suffer alone."

Nineteen

Friday morning Bennett was at school at 7:00. It felt good to dress normally, shower, get in the car with a mission. He had a lot to accomplish in a very short amount of time. The minute he'd gotten off the phone with Ashley the night before he'd called Reggie on his cell phone—the amazing friend that he was, he'd driven right back to Bennett's house and helped him make a plan.

With the help of Corinne, things were already falling into place. There was a game tonight, a Pep Assembly this afternoon, and the tone of the school was sad but focused. The students had come together through this tragedy and Bennett was heartbroken that he'd missed it all week. He should have been there, been the rock his students and his players needed. Instead he'd let the guilt and depression consume him, just like he'd done after his accident.

A knock sounded on his classroom door and Jason Starkey asked, "Coach Clark?"

"Jason, come in."

The kid tossed a wad of blue material at Bennett; he caught it with a flick of his wrist. "What's this?" He opened it up. It was a T-shirt, with "#tatenation" across the chest. A 12 on the back. Tate's number. "Oh man, this is amazing."

Jason shrugged. "Everyone was wearing them this week. Thought you should wear it today."

Bennett nodded. "I will. Thank you."

"How's he doing today? I haven't been up since Wednesday," Jason said.

"I called this morning. Found out that last night the swelling began to go down. Slowly, but it's something."

Jason nodded, swiping his fist under his nose. The sight of his player hurting made Bennett ache inside. This was what he should have been doing. After all the time he'd spent reminding his boys that life wasn't about football, that the team was the most important thing, he'd all but deserted them.

"Jason, I'm so sorry I bailed on you this week. I just . . . damn, I had trouble dealing with one of my guys being injured like this. I should have been checking up on you."

"You don't have to apologize, Coach. We all know how much you care about us. Everybody knew you were taking it real hard."

Bennett felt ashamed but also proud. He didn't deserve these guys; shit, he didn't deserve most of the things in his life right now. "You guys been practicing all week, right?" Bennett asked.

Jason nodded. "Yeah. The guys have been in the zone. Coach Wilson has been working with me, too. I think everybody wants to win it for Tate tonight."

"Good. I want that, too."

"Hey, Coach. Just a heads-up. According to Jessica, a lot of the girls are real annoyed with you today. About that dance thing."

Bennett nodded. "Yeah, I'm annoyed with myself. You have no idea how much. But I've got a plan, and since you're here, can you do me a favor?"

"Sure."

"Get all the guys together and the dance team, and be in this classroom during third hour. I'll make sure everyone's excused from their normal class."

Jason's eyes widened and he grinned. "Awesome. What are we gonna do?"

"Y'all are going to help me fix what I messed up."

Callie ran through the parking lot toward the school building. She was late. She'd never been late to a Pep Assembly. She could hear the band already playing as she yanked open the door and headed for the gymnasium.

The last of the students were just entering as Callie squeezed in and made her way to the spot on the floor she always sat. One of her dancers came rushing over and wrapped her arms around Callie, nearly knocking her back.

"Oh, thank god you're here. We were getting so worried." Mindy squealed before running back to the dance team.

That was weird. Callie had never missed a Pep Assembly, but even if she had, the team knew what to do. They certainly could have performed without her being there.

Callie glanced around the bleachers. It was a full house, not entirely unusual, but it was the most crowded she'd ever seen it here. She recognized many towns-people, customers and parents. It had to be in support of the football team after last Friday's game. This was a big deal, a sign that they meant to go on, and yet it was also for Tate. Nearly the entire student body—and even some of the adults—were sporting #tatenation T-shirts. She felt kind of bad for not wearing hers, but after two days of wear she figured it needed a wash. Instead she had put on a casual dress over leggings.

The students got to their feet when the customary football team entrance music started, and Callie stood also as her team got into kick formation.

Suddenly her palms began to sweat, her heart flutter. She had no idea if Bennett had decided to come today. She guessed not, considering last night he'd looked like death. After leaving his house, she'd gone home and cried herself to sleep. Woken up this morning still in her green dress. What a lovely reminder it had been of her shitty night.

But she was a strong girl—had said it herself—and she would move on from this. If her love wasn't enough for Bennett, than there was nothing else she could do. She wasn't going to throw herself at a man; she was too good for that. He didn't deserve her.

But that didn't mean she wasn't holding back tears at this very moment.

Callie watched as the cheerleader announced the football team and they ran in, earning earsplitting ap-plause. Callie grinned when she saw them. They all had their blue T-shirts on. Bennett would be so proud, she couldn't help thinking. In fact, the thought made her a little angry. He should be here. Should have been here all week. Last night she'd been devastated. Today she felt furious. She'd given so much of her time to him. It had been hard, stressful. And wonderful.

What had he done when things got tough? He'd ducked and covered, left her to fend for herself.

And then she heard his name. *Oh god.* Her heart began to race in anticipation of seeing him again. *Damn him.* Just like that her heart took over.

He walked in slowly, almost a swagger, and the minute he came through the kick line his eyes were on her. In fact, he didn't walk over to his team at all. He headed right for her. He was wearing . . . a tux. But instead of a dress shirt underneath, he sported a blue T-shirt like everyone else, "#tatenation" visible across his chest. Seeing him again made her own chest hurt. *What was going on?*

Callie glanced at the football players. They didn't seem concerned, they actually began to cheer and chant him on: "Coach Clark, Coach Clark, Coach Clark." The entire gymnasium joined in.

She swallowed, sinking lower onto her knees. What the hell was he about to do? A foot away from her, he knelt down, eye level with her. He leaned in close so she could hear him speak over the ruckus.

"Hi," he said. Callie couldn't respond. If she did, she might cry.

"I'm a complete asshole."

She stared at him, her brows knit. "I know."

He gave her a small smile. She didn't return it, even

though the sight of it made her want to wrap her arms around him.

"But I'm here," he said.

"For how long?" The crowd had begun to quiet down, obviously not sure what was supposed to happen next.

He spoke low. "For as long as you'll have me. Now come here." He stood straight and put his hand out to her.

Callie hesitated, looking up into his eyes. Finally, she put her fingers in his palm and let him help her to her feet. The crowd went wild as he led her to the middle of the gym. She glanced around, realizing that the football team, cheerleaders, and dance team had moved off to the side.

"What's happening?" she asked, leaning into his ear.

A cheerleader ran out and handed Bennett a microphone and he lifted it to his mouth. Callie's eyes scanned the bleachers and she gasped when she saw Anne, Eric, and Lindsey. Anne was crying and gave Callie a little wave. What the hell was happening?

"Preston High, I owe you an apology," Bennett said into the mic. He still had ahold of her hand, in front of everyone. He squeezed it. "I should have been here this week. Helping to raise money, feeling the loss of Tate's presence, supporting my team."

Bennett looked back at his boys and winked. Then he looked at Callie, and she felt herself began to tear up.

"What are you doing?" she whispered.

He gave her a little grin and then lifted her hand to his lips, kissing her knuckles. That caused another wave of cheers to pass through the crowd. He brought the mic back to his mouth.

"Coach Daniels, I owe you an apology also. But first, I think I owe you a dance."

Callie's jaw dropped open just as Bennett brought her hand to his face and pulled her against his body. Then she heard a familiar sound over the sound system.

Their music.

They stood there a moment, and she couldn't bring herself to do what he expected. It was too painful, the thought of just kneeling down in front of him, sliding her hand down his body in such a suggestive way. She couldn't do it. Not here, not now. Maybe not ever.

The music went on and she saw him swallow, his eyes wince a little when he realized the point in the song where she should have begun moving had passed.

Callie bit her lip, not wanting to cry. She was going to embarrass them both, but her feet were glued to the floor. She looked into his eyes, assuming she would see frustration. Anger. Instead he gave her the faintest smile, and the understanding she found there in his eyes was too much. He would accept it if she couldn't, or wouldn't, have him.

It hadn't worked. She wasn't going to dance. He had ruined everything, tossed her love back in her face. And damn it, she was strong. Too strong, too good, and too perfect for him. He couldn't blame her.

He'd have to fight harder.

Bennett lifted his hand to her face and palmed her cheek. Her eyes went wide for a moment and he slid his hand down her neck, her shoulder, her arm. Then finally slid his hand into hers, his other hand wrapping around her waist.

He began to count in his head; then he moved his foot into the first step, silently begging her to let him lead her.

Please, Callie. Follow me.

She did, her body melting against his as he pulled her into the waltz. His entire body sighed in relief as he led her around the floor, one step at a time, praying that he got it right. They hadn't started in the usual spot, so it had thrown him off a little. Callie stared into his eyes the whole time.

After a while he felt her give into the routine and they fell into sync. He dipped her, and she smiled at him when the audience cheered. He continued to count in his head through the entire dance, and when it was time for the lift his confidence was strong.

The screams were deafening as he held her in the air, and when she slid down his chest her eyes were glistening. They didn't go on after that. Callie threw her arms around him and shoved her face into his neck. Bennett squeezed his eyes shut and held her tight.

When the applause died down, Callie pulled back and looked into his eyes. "As soon as this is over, I'm coming over. Is that okay?" he asked.

"Yes," she said, running a hand down his cheek. "I've been waiting for you all week."

Callie glanced out the front window once more, hoping to see Bennett's truck pulling in the drive.

Not there yet.

She sighed and sat down on the couch, mindlessly fluffing a pillow. She'd been home for nearly twenty minutes, had been pacing the living room the entire time. Waiting.

The entire drive home her mind had been racing. One minute she was grinning like an idiot, the next she wanted to cry. She was confused. What Bennett had done was crazy and romantic. She'd fantasized about dancing with him—their dance—in front of an audience for weeks. She loved that he'd gone to all the trouble to get everyone involved, her friends there, the music just right. He'd even worn a tux. But she was still hurting over the events of the past few days. She needed answers from him.

She heard the engine of his truck and instantly stood up, listening for his knock, and when it came she took a deep breath before opening the door.

They stood there for a long moment, just staring at each other. He still had on that damn tux, his tatenation T-shirt peeking out beneath. Dark circles shadowed his eyes, but his smile was genuine. He was happy to see her, but he also looked unsure of himself.

Finally Bennett spoke. "Can I come in?"

She stepped out of the way and he walked past her, standing awkwardly in her living room. His familiar Bennett scent filled the space, sending her gumption shattering into a thousand pieces.

"Sit down," Callie said.

He did, and the sight of him there reminded her of the last time he'd come over. Broken and full of pain.

Callie walked around the arm chair and settled herself into it to face him. He eyed her, looking surprised. "How about you sit over here?"

She should have stayed right where she was, but damn if she didn't move over to the couch right next to him. He touched her leg and smiled. "Thank you."

Callie nervously fiddled with her hair as she spoke. "Today was . . . a surprise."

Bennett leaned forward and rested his elbows on his knees. He was nervous, she could tell. He turned his head to look at her. "Callie, I . . ."

The uncertainty in his voice pulled at her emotions. She reached out and took one of his hands into hers. "Bennett. You hurt me badly this week."

As if her words had broken a dam he sat up and turned to face her, grabbing both of her hands with his own. "I'm so sorry. I know those words seem . . . pathetic and meaningless compared to my behavior. But . . . I don't know how to explain it to you."

"Just . . . try," she said.

He hesitated for a moment, mindlessly running his fingers against her palms. Finally, he spoke. "Eight years ago I was on top of the world. I had the career of my dreams, I was making tons of money, shit, I was even in magazines. I was also engaged. I can honestly say now . . . that wasn't meant to be." He swallowed hard before he went on. "But at the time, things had seemed perfect. Then I was in this horrific accident. I lost everything, Callie. Everything that meant anything to me."

She wasn't sure how to respond to that so she said nothing. Just gripped his hands tightly in hers. He squeezed back.

"Things got really dark for me after that accident. I had myself convinced that everyone had abandoned me, but . . . the truth is, things were easier to deal with if I was alone. There's no pain when you isolate yourself. At least that's what I told myself."

"Did you push your fiancée away?" Callie asked.

Bennett nodded. "Yeah. I didn't see it at the time, but I'm gonna guess I was impossible to be around. If you can believe that." He looked up at her and smiled.

"I can believe that." She gave him a little wink. Their hands were still joined, his thumb running over and over her knuckles.

"I like things to happen the way they're supposed to happen. What I'm trying to say is, this past week I felt that darkness again. That loss of control. Helplessness. I don't handle that well, Callie."

"I wanted to handle it with you."

He nodded, staring down at the floor between them. "I know you did, and God, you don't know what it meant for me to hear that. It's just that . . . It's difficult for me to put my faith in someone else."

"You've been putting your faith in me for weeks. I know you didn't want to dance, thought you'd be terrible. But you did it. You trusted me then, why couldn't you trust me with this?"

"I was afraid."

"Afraid of what?"

He met her gaze. "Afraid of failing you. Afraid you'll see me at my weakest point and realize . . . I'm not the man you thought I was." Bennett's brow furrowed and he scooted closer, lifting a hand to cup her face. "You're way too good for me, and I know I don't deserve you, but I want you anyway. I *need* you."

Callie closed her eyes and leaned into him. "We'll deal with each struggle as they come our way. But we have to do it together. You can't push me away again."

"I know that, I just, please. Please, forgive me."

She lifted her head and smiled at him. "I already have."

Bennett responded with a kiss, his mouth opening her own. Callie wrapped her arms around him and leaned back on the sofa, needing to feel the weight of him, to know that he was real. Hers.

They kissed long and slow, hands searching and fondling, tongues sliding. After several moments Bennett angled his torso off her and looked down into Callie's eyes. "Does this mean you still love me?"

"What do you think?" she teased.

"You better. Because I love you. I think it's truly . . . the first time. The first time it's been this real. This strong. I love you so much, Callie."

Callie bit down on her bottom lip, urging tears not to fall. "I love you, Bennett."

Twenty

Callie squeezed Bennett's hand as they made their way down the sterile hallway. She wasn't a huge fan of hospitals, but she wouldn't miss this visit with Bennett.

The Panthers had won the game tonight and at half-time she'd been proud to announce that between the FundMe account Anne had set up, Sweet Opal's bracelets, the Midland Celebrity Dance-Off, and the dance team's fund-raisers, they would be presenting Tate Grayson Sr. a check for $38,000. Sadly, it probably wouldn't cover all or even most of Tate's medical bills, but everyone hoped that with the insurance money it would be a huge help for the family.

They'd made arrangements with the hospital to deliver it after visiting hours. Bennett stopped outside a patient room and turned to Callie, a giant fake check in his hand. The real check was in her purse. "Thank you. For everything."

She wrapped her fingers around his neck and reached up to place a kiss on his lips. "Don't thank me anymore. I didn't do this for you."

"I know, but I'm still grateful. I don't deserve you, Callie Daniels."

"I know." She grinned.

"Coach Clark?" A young girl peeked out the door. Tate's sister. She gave them a small smile. "Hurry and come in."

They stepped inside. Mr. Grayson stood when he saw them. "I thought I heard you out there. I'm so glad you're here." He nodded to the bed. "Look who's here, Tate."

Callie held back a gasp. The bed was slightly elevated, tubes and wires everywhere, beeping. But the most amazing sight was that Tate's eyes were open. Distant and a little expressionless, but open. His father had ahold of his son's hand.

"Tate?" Bennett said; his voice was a mixture of shock and pure joy. He sat on the opposite side of the bed and grabbed Tate's other hand, the sight nearly yanking Callie's heart out of her chest. The boy's eyes slid in Bennett's direction. "Hey, man. God, it's so good to see you. You feeling okay?"

He blinked slowly, and Bennett smiled. "Good. We miss you."

Callie glanced around the room. It was like a florist had exploded inside the space. Flowers, balloons, cards, posters, stuffed animals. It was insane . . . and wonderful.

"Everyone's asking about you. Can't wait for you to get back to school." Bennett's head jerked down to where his fingers joined with Tate's. Callie could see that Tate was lightly squeezing Bennett's fingers. "I know. You're ready to get back, too. You just have to do some more healing."

Tate's eyes slowly closed and then opened again. Bennett used his free hand to pull open his jacket and show off his T-shirt. "You'll never believe this. You have your own hashtag."

Callie covered her mouth, not wanting to kill the beautiful exchange by crying or, worse, giggling. She glanced over at Mr. Grayson, who had tears rolling down his cheeks. *That poor man.* She couldn't imagine what hell he was living through. His daughter put her arms around his neck.

Callie lifted the envelope with his name on it from her purse and laid it on the table behind his chair. She and Bennett had discussed it and decided that Grayson seemed the type of man who would rather find out about the money in private. She'd written him a short note, telling him that she and Bennett wanted to do whatever they could to help him and his family through this time.

They hadn't known for sure at the time that it would include Tate's recovery, but it appeared that might be the case. Thank goodness.

"They said it's like a miracle." Mr. Grayson finally spoke. "I don't care what they call it, as long as I have my son."

She and Bennett stayed a little while, telling Tate about the night's win, chatting with Tate's nurse. When they were finally walking through the parking garage, Bennett turned to Callie. "Maybe I should take a year off from coaching."

"Why would you do that?"

He shrugged. "I don't know. I've been so focused on it for so many years. Maybe it hasn't been healthy."

"Except now it won't be your only focus. You have me."

He took her face into his hands and tilted it up, his eyes serious. "Forever right?"

Callie smiled. "If that's what you want."

Bennett took her into his arms before placing a kiss on her forehead. "It is. If you're willing to put up with me."

"Bennett. I'm bitchy and a know-it-all. You'll have to deal with plenty of my shit."

His shoulders shook and he hugged her tight. "I'm sorry about last night. We should have won that dance competition."

Callie looked up at him and shrugged. "We should have, but it's okay. I'm happy because I did even better than that. I won you."

Epilogue

Three months later . . .

Callie stepped into the ballroom and took in the beauty of the rich decor. The Evan Award dinner was an elegant affair by anyone's standards. The tables were draped with cream-colored tablecloths and topped with beautiful candle centerpieces. A small band played in one corner and a bar was open in the other.

Callie took Bennett's hand and let him lead her to their assigned table.

"Here we are," he said, nodding to the table. "Mr. Bennett Clark and Mr. Bennett Clark's guest."

"Well, they must not know how important I am," Callie teased.

"No, they have no idea. Thank goodness I do." He helped her remove her jacket and draped it over the back of her chair before leaning into her ear. "You look so sexy tonight."

Callie smiled as Bennett placed a kiss on her shoulder. "Thank you."

Eventually they were joined at their table by three other couples, the men all coaches from around Missouri. One of them was also nominated for the Evan. All of them asked Bennett about Tate, each showing genuine concern and interest. Callie realized that what Bennett had gone through was all of those men's worst nightmare. A player injured beyond repair. Changed . . . forever.

Tate was recovering. He was home, going through physical therapy, talking, laughing. Doing quite well, actually. He had made a miraculous comeback.

But he would never play football again.

Bennett was still dealing with that truth. It wasn't easy and some days were better than others, but he and Callie were handling it together. He tried not to shut her out, and if it looked like he might . . . she pushed her way back in.

Callie squeezed Bennett's hand under the table as they spoke to the other couples.

They ate a delicious meal, drank champagne, and when it was finally time for the winner to be announced Callie squeezed Bennett's thigh.

He didn't win.

As soon as the other man's name was called she turned to Bennett. He gave her a wink and then started to clap for the man as he made his way to the podium.

She couldn't help it; she wanted to cry a little bit. He deserved this. Had gone through so much this year. The past eight years. But he didn't look sad. He grabbed her hand this time and lifted her knuckles to his lips. He hadn't won and he was soothing *her*. Was she that obvious?

They listened to the winner's acceptance speech. He was funny, genuinely surprised to have won, and very gracious. Callie clapped when he said "thank you" for the final time and left the stage.

A low hum of conversations struck up around her and Bennett as the servers began to bring dessert. He began to rise from the table. Callie looked up to find him holding his hand out.

"Dance with me," he said.

She placed her hand in his and stood. "I'd love to."

They walked to the small area cleared beside the band, and the man playing the bass nodded and smiled. Bennett turned and took her into his arms, her favorite place to be. He was wearing his tuxedo—with a shirt, vest, and tie this time—and he looked so sexy it should be illegal. She leaned her face into his chest and inhaled the scent of his cologne.

"Are you disappointed?" she asked quietly.

"No." He looked down at her.

"Not even a little?"

"Callie." He laughed. "Are *you* disappointed?"

"Of course not. I just know you like to win. And of course I like to win. But winning isn't everything." She shrugged.

"No, it isn't." He turned them gracefully, a slow waltz.

"Well, I still love you even though you aren't the winner of the Evan Award," she said.

Bennett chuckled and kissed her on the forehead and then looked into her eyes. "I love you, too."

She leaned her head on his chest and let him lead

her around the dance floor. After a few minutes she looked back up at him.

"You're a pretty good dancer, Coach Clark."

"I have a good teacher."

"You're damn right you do."

Read on for an excerpt from the next book by
Nicole Michaels

Draw Me Close

Coming in Winter 2016 from
St. Martin's Paperbacks

Derek Walsh shut the door to his truck quietly and exited the barn at the back of his friend Mike's property. He'd been using the space as his makeshift office while he worked on the house for the past couple of months. He didn't normally spend so much time on location. Shit, he didn't normally reno houses, especially not hundred-year-old farmhouses.

His normal work was commercial building design and contracting. Modern, sleek, highly functional. Expensive. The past eight years he'd worked his ass off. Long and hard hours, but they'd been worth it, and now his business was doing very well for itself. He'd established his name in the Kansas City metro area as one of the most sought after architects. He was proud, but exhausted, and this personal project for his best friend had come along at just the right time. A diversion of sorts. And the main reason for which was inside the old farmhouse at this very moment.

Lindsey Morales.

Derek stopped in the yard and glanced up at the

shadowy house, trying to imagine what she might be doing right now. He was nearly aching to see her face. Desperate. In fact, he was shocked that he'd managed to go this long without seeing her. It had been nearly five months since they'd last talked. That hadn't gone so well.

Derek watched as a snowflake fell, nearly glowing in the moonlight, before he continued his way around to the front door.

For Derek, Lindsey would always be *the one that got away*. No, he couldn't even say that. More like, *the one he pushed away*. But here he was, ready to surprise her, and he had a good idea of how she was going to react. It wasn't going to be pretty.

She was going to be pissed, but the question was, would she show it? Before the run-in last fall, he would have bet no. She would throw out nice words and fake smiles, anything but reveal her true feelings. But after the last time he'd tried to force her to speak with him in person, he wasn't sure. That day she'd caught sight of him and took off running, locking herself in Anne's bathroom. After she'd *yelled* at him.

He still smiled when he thought about it. Not because he wanted her to be angry, but because she'd shocked him. The Lindsey he'd known years ago didn't wear her heart on her sleeve. Apparently things had changed. God, he hoped so, because running meant there was still something there . . . some feeling. Even if it was hate, it was at least a strong emotion. He could work with that. For Lindsey, he'd do whatever he could to make things right. She wasn't going to get away from him again.

They had unfinished business and he was dying to

be in her presence. Look at her. Smell her. Touch her—although he knew that would probably never happen. Couldn't blame a guy for trying though.

Since joining the project as the interior designer, she'd avoided the job site while he'd been there, but he could always tell when she'd stopped by. The crew had gotten used to seeing little neon sticky notes all over the house with very brief, sometimes bossy, instructions. She used a lot of exclamation points. Things like *Don't paint this!!!!!!* or *Please move the electrical outlet over here!!!!* She had no trouble showing her emotions on a 2x2 piece of paper. Too bad he hadn't realized that eight years ago, he'd have bought her a stack of them.

Derek slowly opened the front door. Thank goodness it didn't creak anymore. He'd taken care of that himself. Stepping into the entryway, he gently closed the large door behind him before wiping his work boots against the makeshift entry rug.

And then he heard her. He grinned.

Lindsey was singing. It wasn't great singing, but he was pretty damn sure she wasn't trying to be great. This was a woman who thought she was alone, trying to impress no one. He recognized the song instantly and it surprised him a little bit. He stepped slowly down the long hallway that ran alongside the staircase and then glanced around the corner into the kitchen.

The first thing he saw was her long brunette hair. He couldn't help remembering what it felt like between his fingers—so silky and thick. It was a living thing, her hair. He loved it, the way it complemented the warmth of her skin and her sparkling hazel eyes. She was a beautiful woman. The most beautiful he'd ever had the pleasure of touching, which didn't say much for his ex-wife. Lisa was attractive, but no one had or ever would be Lindsey.

He bit down hard on his bottom lip—holding in a laugh—as she belted out another line, doing her best Steven Tyler impersonation. She was going to be really upset with him when she turned around.

He had no doubt that she'd chosen a holiday—and a Sunday night—to come out because she planned to be alone. When Mike had let it slip-on-purpose that he knew Lindsey was going to come by tonight, Derek had quickly processed three thoughts. One, Mike was a really good friend. Two, why the hell didn't a gorgeous woman like Lindsey have plans on Valentine's Day? Three, thank God, she didn't have plans on Valentine's Day. Now here he was, ready to back her into a corner, literally, if he got the chance.

He leaned against the door trim, arms folded across his chest as she continued to sing, humming a few notes as she took a measurement and then made a quick note on a giant spiral notebook. A block of neon sticky notes sat off to the side. The woman was like a walking office supply store. She made her way down the counter, and then stopped to write another note.

He took in her little setup. She'd brought herself an entire meal. Beer included. Huh. Was she drunk? No, she didn't seem to be drunk, just oblivious to the fact that she wasn't alone since she had headphones in.

"Your love is sweet mise—" She stopped immediately, her body going still. That's when he glanced up and realized she'd moved in front of a window over the sink. There was a reflection.

She'd seen him.

Her body jerked around, her hands ripping the earphones from her ears. "What are you doing here?" Her eyes were wide, panicked.

"Watching the show." He smiled. Couldn't help it. God, she was so damn cute he could hardly stand it. He pushed off from the door frame and stepped into the kitchen. The temporary island separated them and she looked like a caged feral animal for a long second, and then smooth as silk as she pulled a mask over her emotions. But she didn't run, yet. Small mercies.

She cleared her throat and set her pen down on the plywood. "How long have you been standing there?"

He shrugged. "Long enough to enjoy it."

"I'm working."

"And working hard, I see." He nodded toward her spread of food and drinks.

"I had to eat," she said. There was just a hint of defiance in her tone. "Did you need something? I have a lot to do."

He stepped around to the end of the island. Closer to her. She didn't move, but he could see the tension in her shoulders. She was wearing jeans and a baggy, long-sleeved Royals T-shirt. It hid her curves from him, but he had a good imagination. And a good memory.

He glanced down at the open cooler and then picked up one of her extra beer bottles. "You gonna share?"

"I hadn't planned on it."

"Of course you didn't but it would be the polite thing to do. Right?"

"I'm not really a polite person." She lifted her chin, trying to be tough. He knew better.

"Bullshit, Lindsey. You're *too* nice." He pulled a screwdriver out of his tool belt and used it to pry the top off the beer before taking a long drink. He swallowed hard with a wince. "Damn, that's some sweet shit."

"You can hardly complain since it wasn't for you. I happen to like it."

He took another drink and set it down on the island, the plywood wobbling, and then took another step toward her. He didn't miss how she backed slowly away, her eyes never leaving his. They were the most gorgeous color. Green fading into brown, like a mix of grass, honey, and chocolate. Her long lashes fluttered as he stared at her just a moment too long. She was uncomfortable. He knew that, but he needed this.

"I never thought I'd see you again," he said. Last summer he'd discovered their connection of mutual friends and had been shocked. And fucking ecstatic.

She looked down and immediately began fidgeting with her earphones which were connected to the phone in her pocket. "I *hoped* to never see you again."

That gutted him, but it wasn't a surprise. Especially after how she'd reacted last fall when he'd finally seen her for the first time face to face. He'd thought of her nearly every day for years after he'd broken things off eight years ago. As his son Tanner grew up, he'd become distracted and busy, but she'd never been far in the back of his mind. He'd dreamed of her.

"Surely you don't mean that," he said.

She looked up quickly. "Why wouldn't I? There is no reason for us to know each other anymore. It's just an unfortunate accident that our friends met and fell for each other."

"When Derek showed me that blog and I saw your face," he chuckled, remembering the moment, "I felt like I couldn't breathe."

Her eyes fluttered for a moment, but she quickly turned and walked around the island in the opposite direction. She picked up her beer but didn't drink, only squeezed it, almost as if it were an anchor to keep her hands from shaking. "Please don't say things like that."

"Linds."

"Don't call me Linds," she snapped. "That's what my friends call me. We are not friends."

Derek felt tension take hold of his jaw and he moved it around to unlock it before he responded. "We used to be more than friends."

"I barely remember that."

"You're a very bad liar." He cocked his head to the side.

"Well, you are a very good liar, and that I *do* remember. So forgive me if I don't wish to speak to you anymore or ever again."

Her eyes went cold and so did his body. She meant it. She was done with him. In no way, shape, or form did she want to use this opportunity, this second chance. He wasn't sure if he was ready to accept that yet, but one thing was certain, he needed to move slowly. It appeared that maybe tonight was not their night. So much for the holiday of love and romance, his girl wasn't feeling it quite yet.

Derek picked up the beer bottle and nodded to her. "All right then. I'll just leave you to your work. Happy Valentine's Day, Lindsey."

He turned and left, striding through the hallway.

Suddenly he was overcome with fury. She acted as if their breakup had happened a year ago. They'd been young, for God's sake. It was tempting to turn around and give her a serious piece of his mind, but he knew that definitely wouldn't have the desired effect.

He opened the door and strode across the yard while taking several pulls of that shitty fruity beer before throwing the nearly empty bottle into the giant dumpster behind the house.

Once in the barn he got into his truck and pulled out of the back end of the structure, down the drive— ignoring the lit-up kitchen window—and onto the main road. He sat there for a minute before pulling out, taking a deep breath. What the hell did he think was going to happen? He'd charm her into forgetting what he'd done? That was stupid thinking. Lindsey was a smart girl. She felt deeply—even if she didn't always show it. There was no way she was going to forgive him.

He'd hurt this woman, badly. He knew that. Shit, the whole thing had nearly killed him too. That whole time in his life was a complete clusterfuck. But he couldn't regret it because out of that mess he'd gotten his son. Tanner was everything to him and he'd done the only thing he could do at the time. Or at least he kept telling himself that.